FATED HEARTS

A LOVE AFTER ALL RETELLING

OF THE SCOTTISH PLAY

ALINA K. FIELD

Havenlock Press
PO Box 1891
La Mirada, CA 90637-1891

December 29, 2020

Cover Design by Melody Barber

With grateful thanks to William Shakespeare, the master at adapting history, myth and legend to meet the requirements of his audience.

About the Love After All Tragic Characters in Classic Literature project:

With complete artistic license, and an abundance of hubris, a group of Regency romance authors are retelling some of the great stories of literature, setting them in Georgian England, and giving these tragic heroes and heroines a happily-ever-after.

Fair is foul, and foul is fair.

—MACBETH, ACT 1, SCENE 1

CHAPTER ONE

London
Friday, 3 March, 1815

A crush was what they called these suffocating occasions, and the term was apt.

Major Finnley Macbeth, Scottish baron and late of his majesty's Highland Brigade, shifted his weight from the leg that still ached like the devil, and scanned the room for his quarry, an undersecretary in the Home Office who he'd met at the army's winter quarters in Frenada.

From his spot near a damask covered wall, he measured each breath, trying to calm his rising unease. The heavy scent of perfume mixed with fine beeswax and hothouse florals unsettled more than his stomach. The shimmering silks and waving plumes threatened to stir the disquieting visions plaguing him lately.

Fire, explosions, rain, the screams of men and horse.

He squeezed his hands into fists. These were not the hellish memories of the recent past, dammit, but rattling visions of some battle yet to come.

Or not. Foretelling the future was for Travellers and crones, wasn't it? Not battle-hardened men like himself.

He inhaled slowly, holding the breath for a count, and then eased the air out. Best keep his purpose in mind—he was here to track down Sir Thomas Abernathy, lately arrived in London, and rumored to be attending this rout.

His gaze swept the room, seeking the distinctive bald pate. In spite of his own forty-three years, his eyesight was still keen enough to make out a sniper or spot the dust of a fleeing stag. Keen enough as well to relish the deep décolletages and clinging, delicate, almost transparent skirts on display this night, a vision far more cheering than the one the Sight was showing him.

A more modestly clad woman stood alone halfway across the ballroom, her back turned to him, surveying the room as he was doing.

A memory stabbed him, laced with an old shame. He'd once known a lass with hair like this, so abundant, so near to black. The lady tonight had crowned all the loveliness with dark feathers, like a glorious cormorant. His hand itched to pull out those feathers and rake his hands through the tumble of hair, as he'd once done...

He caught a steadying breath. It couldn't be her. He'd simply been without a woman too long.

And these visions plaguing him of he knew not what? That foolishness grew from naught but fatigue, the wages of war, and the steady company of too much death. Napoleon had been defeated.

He must put the memories of battle and that more distant passion aside. The lovely lady with feathers atop her head was only a stranger wondering where her man had got to.

Yet he couldn't turn away. As he watched, she pivoted one way, and then the other, allowing a glimpse of dangling earbobs and a firm chin.

Drawn to her, he stepped out on his bad leg just as she turned.

Pain shot through his hip. The room threatened to fall away but he held onto the pain, let it shore him up whilst he swore a silent curse.

It *was* her.

Earlier that evening

As the lights of London came into view, Greer Douglas smoothed the silk skirt of her evening gown and glanced out the coach window again. "I wondered if we should be quite safe traveling so late at night." Chelsea seemed such a great distance from Mayfair, though at home in Scotland, she'd often journeyed farther back and forth on market day.

Her companion grunted. "I'd rather have stayed home and read the proposed Corn Law. Not to mention that it is Lent."

Greer would have chuckled, had she not been so nervous. Malcolm Comyn, Earl of Menteith, was a sober young man, but not a pious one. "We are in England now, Malcolm, two fish out of water and we must learn to swim. As long as we don't have to surrender my new earbobs to a highwayman."

"Aunt Fiona read the tea leaves and felt the coachman and groom shall be adequate protection." He patted her hand. "Do not ye worry, Cousin. I'm not wholly incapable of handling a dirk and a pistol. Though I had rather not."

"Ye had rather not mingle, either."

"So true. But Aunt Fiona insisted we must honor her friend by attending this affair, and so we are here."

Lady Fiona Carlin, who'd been widowed longer than Greer's thirty-eight years, had surprised them both at breakfast with this invitation to her friend's small gathering. The elderly lady did not herself feel up to attending. Nor would Lady Fiona allow Greer's daughter, Lucie, to attend until she had made her come-out.

When that would be, was anyone's guess. Poor Lucie. At the age of almost twenty, she was anxious to experience more of London, especially the social events of the *ton*.

Greer feared that her daughter's manners needed further refinement. Like her mother, Lucie was a country girl, unused to higher society. Life had smoothed out most of her own rough edges, but Lucie was often too direct, too outspoken. And her temper...

Greer pressed a hand to her chest and tried to breathe through the bad memories. Lucie's temper was an inherited gift from the father who had never met her.

"I suppose that honoring her friend is the least we can do to repay your aunt's hospitality," she said.

Two weeks after Malcolm's departure from Scotland, a letter had arrived for Greer from Lady Fiona inviting her and Lucie to join Malcolm as her guests for the London season. She'd even sent the means for hiring a chaise and post riders.

Greer had made up her mind to write back declining—Malcolm would not want his irksome relations crowding him in London. But as she read on, Lady Fiona mentioned the upcoming celebrations of the end of two decades of war, and the latest gossip.

And among the items of gossip she'd included the tidbit that Major Finnley Macbeth had arrived in London.

The time would come when they would speak—and just let her have a piece of him. But not tonight. Tonight, she wanted to see how the great world of London would welcome a woman like herself.

When their carriage jerked to its final stop in front of the brightly lit townhouse, Malcolm handed her out, and escorted her through the receiving line where their elderly hostess, Lady Estelle Walby, looked her over with a gleam in her eye that matched Lady Fiona's.

And then Malcolm abandoned her.

"I must step away to the gentleman's," he said, with his usual bluntness. "Where will I find ye?"

"Since I don't know a soul, I'll seek out Lady Estelle when she's free."

He shook his head. "Proceed to the middle of the room, and I'll find ye there shortly."

"Yes, my lord," she teased.

Wandering deeper into the room, she scanned the groupings of people. Not one familiar face. Not one. At home, in the Highlands, she'd know every soul at a local assembly.

Oh, but the gowns were far more magnificent here. The glow from the candelabra gleamed off exquisite jewels and sparkled in mirrors arranged to brighten the room. Large urns filled with roses and gladioli stood on pillars, and along one wall, chaperones kept eagle eyes on girls Lucie's age. Some of the young ladies looked as nervous as herself.

Across the room, she caught the curious gaze of three young bucks. One whispered to the others. She lifted her chin and turned fully around.

And for one desperate moment her heart stopped, and then started up again in a wild gallop.

A man stood watching her, a tall, broad chested man in a gold waistcoat and a fine dark coat, golden-eyed and handsome, with hair flaming in bright tones of red, hair pulled back into an old-fashioned queue, hair that used to fall to strong shoulders in wild tangled waves.

Finnley was here.

***

How had she not aged? was his first thought. Twenty years had slipped away, but her beauty hadn't. The most beautiful girl he'd ever seen. She was the same: her raven hair, her glorious bosom, her stubborn chin and the deep blue of her eyes.

Eyes that used to look at him as if he was one of the old gods. Before. Before she...

He caught his breath battling a surge of stinging emotion. What was the truth?

Desire for her flooded him. If he could but hold her again. If he could restore them to what they'd once—

A gentleman pushed through the crowd and joined her. Dark-haired and manly, 'twas Duncan.

Numbness settled over him. He ought to turn around and depart. By all that was holy, Duncan should have died of his wounds after their long-ago duel, but here he was, looking hale, with a braw strength that...

The man followed the line of Greer's sight, and his eyes met Finnley's.

This wasn't Duncan, but he was very much like him. Greer had found another.

Or had she? He was much younger, this buck, pushing himself up next to the lady. A couple passed into Finnley's line of vision.

He slid sideways, too quickly; his wounded leg seized, and he stumbled, catching himself on a footman who managed to juggle his tray of drinks and Finnley's weight.

"Damnation," he said, apologizing and thanking the servant. "Game leg," he muttered.

Face heating, he glanced back. It was too late for an orderly retreat. His ex-wife was advancing upon him, her young pup in tow.

At Finnley's stumble, Greer gave into instinct, and a mite of courage, and walked straight toward him, trusting that Malcolm would follow. Malcolm had been a mere bairn in those early days so long ago. He'd never met Finnley Macbeth, the man who'd almost made him lord of Menteith before his voice had changed.

Was Finnley already in his cups tonight? He'd been a young man much given to the whisky. And his face was aflame. Probably with anger.

No matter. As she drew closer, her resolve hardened. Now that she was in London, now that she'd found him, now that her feet were moving, she would ensure that Finnley Macbeth would meet and acknowledge his child. Not tonight, certainly, but soon. It would be done, at the point of a blade if need be. He would see that he'd never been cuckolded, that she'd never betrayed him, that Lucie was his. Not for her own sake, but for Lucie's.

As she neared him, he pulled himself up in his proud manner and dipped his head in a poor semblance of a bow, raising her ire. Pausing before him, she lifted her chin and gathered what dignity she could muster, hoping to belie the heat rising into her cheeks. In the past twenty years he'd grown into braw, mature manhood, and he still had the ability to stir her.

This close, she could see a scar tracing the side of his face, not fresh, but not terribly old either. Finnley with his hot temper and sense of his own power would be riddled with scars, wouldn't he?

She dipped in the slightest of curtsies and said "Sir."

"Madam."

The gruff voice was thick with emotion, triggering her own answering flood of moisture.

She swallowed it down. There'd be no weeping, at least not on her part.

"Greer." That was Malcolm, at her elbow, chiding her.

Finnley's hot gaze shifted, and his mouth firmed. He gave another head bob. "I am—"

"Macbeth," she said. "Finnley Macbeth, Baron of Calder."

Tension rippled from him. "Major Macbeth," he said, in the sort of tight voice he might have used before a fight.

She gritted her teeth. "And this gentleman is Malcolm Comyn, since last year, Earl of Menteith. Duncan's boy, all grown up."

Not a man to hide his emotions, was Finnley. Surprise chased the anger from his face only to be followed by something that looked like...shame? Could it be?

His shoulders dropped and he dipped his head again. "You'll know who I am then, Lord Menteith."

The two men exchanged a long look.

"'Tis perhaps not exactly a pleasure to make your acquaintance, sir," Finnley said, "Yet I'm glad of it anyway." He turned his golden eyes on her. "And glad to see ye looking so well Lady Menteith."

She gasped. "I am not—"

"Greer is not and has never been Lady Menteith," Malcolm said. "She's neither my wife, my stepmother, nor, may I add, in case ye're wondering, my mistress."

His forthright speech made her cheeks flame. Other eyes were turning their way.

"Put any such notion aside." Malcolm went on with his usual thoroughness. "We are kin, distant cousins. And she goes by the name Greer Douglas, Mrs. Greer Douglas, for to be called a Miss seems an injustice, Major Macbeth."

All the old hurts washed over her, the old shame rising. Spurning Macbeth's surname, she'd returned to her own name, but had adopted the missus, for the sake of her daughter.

Finnley's face drained of color, becoming as white as parchment, his abundant freckles in stark relief, only his scar blazing. For once, she wished Malcolm were not so direct. He'd left them both speechless and tongue-tied.

Before either of them could muster words, a man wedged his way through the crowd and stood beside Finnley. A hale and handsome enough man, he was, thickly dark-haired with a splash of distinctive white that streaked back from a peak at the top of his forehead.

She knew this man, another apparition from far in the past, one she'd rather not see. Giles Banquo, was another distant cousin to Malcolm and Finnley.

"Who have we here?" Banquo exclaimed. "Why, it's Gr—that is...I'm unsure what to call you. And is that Menteith, all grown up? And...Macbeth, is that you? I heard you were gravely wounded at Toulouse."

A flicker of emotion passed through Finnley, quickly shuttered. He greeted Banquo coldly, as did Malcolm. She dipped her head, unable to speak. Finnley had been gravely wounded? Lucie might not have had a chance to meet him.

In spite of the cold reception Banquo chattered on. He was said to have once been a good friend to Duncan. And yet he'd once been a good friend to Duncan's enemy, Finnley, too. In those days, he'd been another minor Scottish baron like Finnley, but he'd left Scotland not long after Finnley's departure. Any other news she'd received about him had been filtered and screened by her villainous aunt and cousins.

Her hands fisted in her new silk gloves. 'Twas another bad memory, one that she must not ever forget. She would never be that young, trusting, girl again.

She wouldn't trust others, nor could she entirely trust herself or her own instincts. Silky manners, sureness of belief, none of those could be relied on. In her youth, she'd not been able to see that. Nor had Macbeth.

They'd both been too young, too proud, too much in love. Until he'd stopped loving her and cast her away.

"I should be pleased to join you," Finnley said.

Join who? Drat, but while she was woolgathering in the last century, they'd made some arrangement or other.

"Why don't I come along, as well," Banquo said. "I've a new mount. Anxious to put him through his paces. I say, Macbeth, do you still have the gray you were riding at Madrid?"

While Finnley uttered a terse "no," Malcolm cast Banquo a stony gaze, then offered Greer his arm. "Come along, Cousin, our hostess is now free."

Finnley's eyes flashed with something that looked very much like longing.

Was that wishful thinking on her part? Foolish woman that she was. She swallowed her own answering surge of emotion and dipped her head, tongue-tied again.

Somehow, someday, somewhere—not tonight, and not here of course—she must dredge up her courage and confront the man.

Malcolm led her off, and as it turned out, he was not entirely unknown in this crowd. He'd secured a membership at White's, and several men greeted him. He introduced Greer to them and, in some cases, the wives who'd accompanied them.

'Twas curiosity that made her an object of interest and had them queueing up. The *ton* would be speculating whether she was more than a cousin to Malcolm. True it was as well, that though her personal scandal was twenty years in the past, divorce was uncommon enough for old muck to be dug up for a fresh flow of gossip. Finnley's presence here would ensure that it would be.

Was that why Lady Fiona had insisted they come? If so, she was in truth glad for it. She was ready to face the *ton*'s worst.

Malcolm's aunt had been surprisingly kind, welcoming Greer and Lucie, two strangers, and yet, as it turned out, distantly related to her by marriage. The lady's late husband had been kin to the Naughtons, the aunt and cousins who'd taken Greer in when her parents died. They'd never ever so much as mentioned Lady Fiona or her husband, unusual for her cousin, who'd been the sort to pursue any advantageous connection. The only reason the Naughtons had taken in a shameful divorcee had been the chance to dip into her dowry.

A man spoke, pulling her out of more woolgathering. She had better attend to the conversation, lest they think she was daft.

One of Malcolm's bachelor friends repeated an invitation for her to ride in the park in his phaeton.

Faith, and the man couldn't be much older than Malcolm's three-and twenty years, certainly no older than thirty. Far more appropriate for Lucie than for herself, not to mention that her life was so jumbled and uncertain now, she had no interest in being courted. Or was an invitation to ride not considered courting?

Goodness. She was as much a goose as any green girl.

She declined the invitation, pleading their residence so far out of town, and made a point of keeping her wits about her for the rest of the evening.

Finnley watched as Greer walked away on young Menteith's arm, his gaze moving to the gentle sway of her hips. Others noticed as well, and Menteith was stopped on the way by male acquaintances seeking to be introduced.

She was no longer his. She wasn't Menteith's either; the lad had made that clear. But she would soon be someone's.

Jealousy nagged at him again. It had been twenty years. Highlanders were not blind to a woman with such beauty and a home of her own. Had she had a man in that time?

Could he make her his again before someone else got to her? She was too fine-looking a woman to be cast to the side for long.

"Well, well," Banquo said quietly. "She's a fine piece. Quite a surprise, isn't it?"

"A fine piece?" he hissed. He tamped down a flare of anger and headed for the door.

"Menteith appearing here with Greer on his arm," Banquo said, dogging him. "A chip off the old block, isn't he?"

Banquo was baiting him. He longed to oblige with his fist, but instead he kept walking, setting his mind to the pain in his limb.

"You're leaving then?" Banquo asked. "Well I may as well leave with you. Safety in numbers, eh? There's whispers the folk will be rioting over these new laws coming."

He'd heard those rumors as well, but at present, his mind was elsewhere.

CHAPTER TWO

Outside, he took a long draught of the cold, damp air, and then turned on his companion. "Menteith made it clear that Greer is not his mistress. I'd thank ye to not spread that rumor about."

Banquo had planted himself in front of the gas lamp, his back to it, his shadowed face unreadable. "Why do you suppose he invited you to go riding in the morn? Seemed odd to me. Thought I'd best come along in case he meant to take you into the trees and skewer you."

He'd wager that the new Lord Menteith had his father's sense of pride and honor. "If he was to attempt that, he'd do so openly."

"You believe he's the forthright sort?"

"Aye. Ye do not?"

"Well, what's it about, then? Surprised me, he did."

Banquo had ignored his question. Macbeth gazed at his companion and then forced a laugh. "Ye'll likely nose about and know before me."

"What's that to mean?" Banquo asked.

"Hold man. Don't take offense. I only know that ye were always one to learn things first when we were boys."

He'd thought Banquo a friend once, twenty years earlier, warning Finnley of the rumor spreading about Duncan and Greer, and then trying to broker a peace between Duncan and Finnley. They were, as Banquo had reminded them, all cousins. Distant, it was true, but they'd all three descended down different lines, by different wives, from the same Thane of Menteith, hundreds of years earlier. They'd known each other as children, Duncan the eldest, Finnley younger, and Banquo the runt of the group running after them whether they wished his company or not.

"Weren't ye in Madrid nosing about for information, Banquo?"

"I told you then. I was there as an agent for one of the military suppliers."

"If ye say so."

"I heard later about Burgos. 'Twas lucky all went well with your court martial."

More baiting. "There was no court martial."

"Aye. I had an opportunity that winter after to chat with Wellesley—er, Wellington—myself, attesting to your character."

"Ye attested to my character? Had a chat with the commander in chief? About me?" Wellington was famously discriminating about social inferiors. He'd never base a disciplinary decision on the advice of one like Banquo, a man not even a lowly Scottish baron anymore, since he'd had to sell the family castle to placate his late father's creditors. The title had conveyed with the property.

The man wasn't just baiting, he was bluffing—flat out lying, and what the devil for?

"Aye. I was glad to have a wee part in restoring your reputation. Though...I don't like to bring it up, but I recently heard..."

Heart pounding, Finnley caught his breath. Banquo had actually appeared again at another difficult siege, San Sebastian. Trouble followed this man.

"Go ahead. Get the words out. What have ye heard?"

Still in the shadows, Banquo remained silent. Finnley wrestled his own face into a placid gaze and waited. And waited some more.

"Never mind," Banquo said. "Naught but a whisper of men in their cups at the club, and that other business was settled. As you said, not even a court martial."

Sensation swept through him, intuition rising, the fairies whispering. The evening chill seemed suddenly colder, seeping into his bones, setting his injured hip throbbing. Banquo spread stink like a tomcat marking his territory. He was kin, true, and when they were boys, Finnley had thought him to be a friend as well. But he'd had twenty years of lonely nights and hard fighting to contemplate the man who'd sighted and reported Greer's meeting with Duncan. He'd had twenty years of jealousy, and second-guessing, and regret gnawing at him, and, perhaps, this man to blame for it.

"You're awfully silent tonight, Macbeth. 'Twas quite a shock seeing her, wasn't it? Shall we stop somewhere, and you can pour out your heart? Menteith has been seen at White's, but you and I will do better at a good inn where we might get decent ale."

Macbeth forced another laugh. Aye, he was silent, and he'd be more so spending time with Banquo. Yet, he'd learn nothing going home alone to his cold rooms.

"I fear after the Peninsula, I've no heart left to pour out. But a pint or two in less genteel company sounds appealing. I know a place." He'd be on his guard with a man who expected confidences and shared none.

He stepped out, concealing his limp, steeling himself for what was to come. He'd long ago learned to measure his pints and mind his tongue and his temper. A wily adversary required a man to keep his wits on alert. And so it would be with this cousin, and "friend" Giles Banquo.

"Why?" Greer asked, pulling the carriage rug closer. They'd ridden along in companionable silence for the first few miles, but she couldn't contain herself any longer. "Why did ye ask Macbeth and Banquo to meet up for a ride in the morn?"

"Are ye quite warm enough?" Malcolm asked. He'd taken the seat beside her, there being more warmth in the arrangement, not for any amorous reasons. "There's another blanket under the rear-facing seat."

Her young cousin could be brash and direct enough to speak frankly in a houseful of gossips but wouldn't answer her question now? "I would like ye to tell me why, Malcolm."

"I didn't invite Banquo."

She glanced at his shadowed face and caught the grim set of his lips. He'd wanted to speak to Finnley alone. Not Banquo.

The silence stretched between them as they bumped along, stopping only to pay the toll.

Though the coach was finely made, wisps of cold air whipped in through the door seams. It must be bitterly cold up top, where the coachman and groom sat. Though it was not as cold as a Scottish winter, and hadn't she enjoyed many a head-clearing winter ride there? On one such excursion she'd encountered Malcolm's father Duncan in the wood that skirted her home and his, and thus had the last trouble started.

"Do ye know why I came to London, Cousin?" Malcolm's voice rasped with tension, jarring her back to the present and reminding her of her earlier question.

Perhaps now he was planning to answer her. "For business. So ye said."

"Aye. Business. Your mon's lawsuit so many years past brought me here."

"His lawsuit?" Shame washed over her. It had been her lawsuit as well, perhaps, in all justice, hers entirely, because her nagging and her badgering had brought it about; that and the legal claims drummed up by her cousin.

She let out a breath. Surely Finnley hadn't renewed the claim to Menteith? "'Twas settled long ago. We lost. Ye won."

His head swiveled and she sensed his gaze upon her.

She went on, determined to be merciless. "And your father almost lost his life at the end of it all." Oh, aye, that last smear against Duncan had been the crowning touch of that misguided venture. "'Twas a grievous mistake filing that suit, an unforgiveable one, as well as the slander that followed, and yet your da managed forgiveness. Can ye not also, Malcolm?"

"Ye mistake me, Greer. I hold no grudge, at least not against ye. And mayhap not against

Macbeth neither, though I'd speak with the man further and see what he's made of."

"Has he filed a new lawsuit?"

"No."

"Why then did the old one bring ye here? Why not let the past lie as it is?"

"Have ye done so, Greer?"

"So I have."

"Greer Macbeth, Lady of Calder?"

Anger spiked in her. "Why are ye prodding me, then, Malcolm Comyn, Earl of Menteith?"

"Have ye never wondered about the truth, Greer?"

A dull headache started. What truth was he talking about? The suit had been settled. The claim that Finnley was the rightful heir of Menteith had been denied by the court. Menteith was Duncan's and now Malcolm's. The other matter, the old smear that Duncan had cuckolded Finnley, surely that would not resurface now.

"I know the truth, Malcolm, as did Duncan. Lucie is Finnley's daughter. There was no affair between Duncan and me, not before the duel, nor after. I was never your father's lover or mistress."

"Not that truth, Greer. I'm speaking of the title."

"Ye were but a wee lad when all that happened. What truth is it ye wish to determine?"

He laughed, but it sounded false. "Naught but a simple one: who is the rightful Earl of Menteith, myself or Finnley Macbeth?"

"No," she said, quelling a sudden panic. "No, Malcolm. 'Tis settled. 'Tis not a sleeping dog—'tis a dead one." And must remain so, forever and ever. Too much had already been lost.

"So I'd thought, Greer. But some weeks ago, I received a curious letter from an anonymous sender in London, implying that there is evidence that would bring the dead dog, as ye called it, back to life. I thought, rather than send along someone to see to it, I'd instead come myself."

"Is it blackmail?"

He took a deep breath and exhaled. "Not so far."

"Was it from Macbeth?"

He shook his head. "I don't know."

Finnley was as direct as Malcolm. Finnley would have simply sought Malcolm out and flung whatever evidence he had in his face. "Was it something to do with my late cousin? He started all the trouble the first time."

"I don't see how. The letter was recent. Naughton is dead these few years."

Her cousins and aunt had died in a carriage accident. Malcolm had helped pull the bodies from the wreck.

"Might Naughton have had an accomplice?"

She felt the lift of his shoulder as he shrugged. "He had few friends at the end."

'Twas true. Her cousin had run through his family's money, and some of Greer's as well, and had died leaving outstanding debts.

"I'd not have ye displaced as Earl of Menteith. How may I help?"

"How would ye go about helping, Greer?"

"Is there a direction, a house number, for the letter's writer?"

"A print shop in the City. They could give me few details, and little description. 'Twas a gentleman coming in now and again to check for a reply, but not one with flaming red hair in a queue."

"He wouldn't..." Oh, why did she still automatically jump to defend him?

Probably because her own guilt was so heavy. It had all gone so wrong.

"How might I help," she mused. "I don't know London. I don't know anyone in London."

"You know Finnley Macbeth."

"Yes," she said. "And I must have a conversation with him. Tell me, Malcolm, what is it ye wish me to say to him?"

In the dark, she felt the comfort of his hand covering hers. "Rest now, Cousin, and let me ponder this. Your business must be addressed first, whereas mine might be more complicated."

She sat back and closed her eyes, all jumbled inside, but confident that Malcolm would arrange things. Somehow, this stalwart young man would bring her together with Finnley.

And what she would do then was the question to ponder.

Saturday, 4 March 1815

Finnley awoke to an off-tune humming that was as noisy and erratic as a bosky pipe player's melody. The window curtains had been drawn back admitting the dim gray of early morning, and Hyde stood at the washbasin, stropping the razor. The aromas of tea and fresh baking scented the air.

Hyde's humming ceased. "Awake then, are ye, Major?" he all but shouted, turning a broken-toothed grin his way.

A sturdy northerner of middling height and thick brown hair, Hyde was another veteran of the war. He'd suffered his own share of battle wounds, but, except for the loss of a good part of his hearing, he'd made a full recovery. He made for a ham-fisted batman, but Finnley had once saved his life, and his loyalty was unshakeable.

"Wake ye for a ride, ye said, Major."

"And if ye keep yelling mon, the landlady will put us both out."

Hyde laughed, and went to the fireside table where a teapot stood ready.

Finnley shoved back the covers. Water steamed in a kettle hanging from a jack. The fire below had taken the edge off the cold, and he stomped naked to the corner, pulled on a robe, and checked the time.

"Sent word to the stable." Hyde held his chair and presented a cup of tea and a plate of buttered rolls. "Fresh bread today." He winked. "Mrs. McCallum says for ye to come take tea anytime. Anytime, she says. Ought to consider that fine widow, Major, if ye don't mind me saying so."

His thoughts went to the dark-haired woman who had visited him in his dreams. There was no other for him.

"I do mind," he said, jovially enough to evoke a laugh. "I'll pay my rent in coin, thank ye very much."

"S'pose that's best." Hyde poured steaming water into the basin. "Your man last night made his way direct to a house near Covent Garden. A bawdy house, I'll warrant."

Banquo had mentioned the place, offering to bring Finnley along.

"That was fast. Good work, Hyde."

Hyde grunted. Never able to sleep much, he'd been hoisting a pint at the inn where Finnley had led Banquo the night before. Finnley had been hoping to find his servant there.

"Ye'll show me later," he said. 'Twas a pity Hyde couldn't read or write much.

"Aye," he said, and set about scraping the beard off his master.

Though the gray skies threatened rain, the day had dawned fair enough for a ride in the park. Finnley dressed quickly and limped around the corner to the mews where his horse was stabled, the beast eating better than he himself was.

And rightly so. The stout-hearted black gelding deserved it. He'd carried his last master through the fiercest of battles and safely home. The man wouldn't have sold him but he'd desperately needed the coin.

A groom gave him a leg up. On the back of a horse, the pain in his leg disappeared and he was a new man, one who could easily take on a young pup like Menteith if need be. He turned down the mews and onto the street.

He thought about Banquo's words hinting at a new rumor spreading at his club, the mention of Menteith's membership there, and the shiver of instinct that had gone through him. Who ought he to trust?

In battle, a man learned quickly who'd hold fast by his side and who would run. He'd not been a runner, that much he knew. But at Burgos, on a night as dark as hell, he'd been knocked flat by the impact of an ill-placed mine. He'd lost a chunk of that night and had awakened half a furlong away. But he felt in his bones that he hadn't run.

Banquo hailed him at the park gate and moved up alongside him. "Menteith's not here yet?"

"As ye see."

Menteith would come or he wouldn't. Thinking back on last evening, the young man had not looked at all pleased when Banquo invited himself along. "Fine mount ye have," Finnley said, changing the subject, and they talked about horses, advancing along the row, nodding to other riders, all of them strangers: gentlemen on their morning ride, or grooms exercising their masters' cattle.

When one of the grooms hailed him, he reined up.

The man, his fine livery impeccable, drew nearer and doffed his cap. "Major Macbeth?" he asked.

"Aye. I am Macbeth."

The man handed over a sealed note. "A message sir, from Lord Menteith." With another doff of his cap he rode away without offering to carry a reply.

CHAPTER THREE

"So. Menteith was too afraid to come," Banquo said. "How did his man know it was you...oh." He laughed. "No one has hair quite like yours. What does he say?"

Finnley turned his horse, moved off the path, and broke the seal.

Macbeth,

Unavoidable circumstances prevent me from riding with you this morning. Apologies for issuing the invitation and not appearing. But as Banquo invited himself along, you'll not be wanting for company.

My aunt, Lady Fiona Carlin, asked me to convey her invitation to dinner at six of the clock tonight at her home in Chelsea where I am staying. I'll add directions below. You will find her manor easily enough. She would write inviting you herself except that the hour is early, but wishes you to know that she will send a coach for you if you find the weather inconvenient.

Do come, Macbeth. I would speak with you after about a matter of interest to both of us.
  Menteith

"Well?" Banquo asked.

"He was detained by business."

The other man scoffed. "Business indeed. The man's a sniveling coward."

Was he? Instinct stirred in him again. Menteith had spoken forthrightly enough about his connection to Greer. He'd poked at the past as well, risking a fight with the man who'd nearly murdered his father. Oh, true, that fight with Duncan so many years ago had been a duel, but murder had been in Macbeth's heart.

Those were not the actions of a sniveling coward.

"How so, Banquo?"

"Isn't it obvious? He won't face you."

Well, and he knew that wasn't true, since he had the invitation right in his hand. Unless the lad planned to ambush him at his lady aunt's dinner table.

"Or did Menteith invite you to meet another time?"

"He did not." 'Twas Menteith's aunt inviting him to dinner, not Menteith. Lady Fiona Carlin was an unknown to him, leastways that he could remember. Mayhap there'd been Carlins among Greer's distant kin, but the name sounded too English.

"You know," Banquo said. "I've heard talk of a match between Menteith and Greer's daughter."

Greer's daughter and Menteith?

A chill slithered through Finnley, followed by a surge of longing. He'd known Greer had borne a lass. Try as he might to put the knowledge aside, it had gnawed at him for the last twenty years. What if she'd been telling the truth? What if the lass was truly his own daughter?

Perhaps Banquo sensed his regret, as wily as he was. His tone had been hushed, with an overlay of concern. Nevertheless, Finnley knew when a man was wheedling for a reaction, and he held his tongue.

"I know that Duncan and Greer denied everything," Banquo said. "But if they played you false, what Menteith is planning is incest."

Hot anger shot through him, with shame close on its heels, for 'twas the very same thought that had chilled him. And yet...why should the lass suffer such chatter? Nothing was her fault, or Menteith's for that matter.

Banquo laughed.

The man was too perceptive and took too much joy in the troubles of others. 'Twas a good thing he'd left his pistols and broadsword back in his rooms.

"Do you suppose the girl is here in London as well?" Banquo jabbed again.

He tethered his anger and forced a heavy sigh, shaking his head like a highland cow dislodging a swarm of persistent midgies.

"Banquo. 'Twould be a kindness to the lass if ye'd not spread those rumors. Not," he added, "that I mind hearing out your speculations. But I have naught to say, except that whatever the circumstances, there can't possibly be any blame laid on the lass."

Only on the lass's father.

He spurred his horse and galloped away, unable to run from the question clawing away at his conscience: And what if she's mine?

Not long after, a drizzle began to fall, and they turned their mounts to the gate. He declined an invitation to join Banquo for drinks that night and went back to his rooms. Hyde would need to brush out his regimentals and arrange for a hack. He wouldn't show up at dinner waterlogged from a ride in the rain, and he wouldn't impose on the lady's coachman either. He'd hire his own damn conveyance for the evening and leave when the time was ripe. Perhaps he'd have Hyde accompany him as well.

In any case, he'd go looking his best, because 'twas very likely that not only was Malcolm residing with Lady Fiona—Greer was there as well.

***

"Lady Fiona is back, Mother."

Greer sipped her cup of tea and watched her daughter, Lucie Macbeth hurry from the table where she'd been scribbling in her diary to the door where their hostess appeared.

"Come warm yourself near the fire, my lady," Lucie said. "And do tell my mother she must share everything about the party last night."

Greer smiled and pressed a finger to her forehead where the remains of the megrim that had plagued her still lingered. She'd only just dressed and come down to the parlor, knowing that their hostess liked to have tea at this hour.

"Mama stayed in her bed well past breakfast and the noon hour, all through this dreary day, and do look: it's almost full dark outside."

"I fear I slept late as well, young Lucie," Lady Fiona said cheerfully, laugh lines crinkling the corners of her eyes. A russet and black plaid wool gown covered her plump body in warmth, and her lacy white cap barely concealed a headful of white curls. "Darling girl, you are the only one here keeping country hours. But I'm sorry that I was closeted this afternoon with my man of business, instead of keeping you company. I know how tiresomely long a day can stretch. Which is why I'm so glad to have you and your mama here with me, and for as long as you wish to stay. My dear, Greer, are you ill? You are rubbing your head as if it's a magic lantern and you're summoning a genie."

Greer set her hand back in her lap and forced a smile. "I'm quite well now. I had a mere touch of the headache. I fear I'm not used to late hours."

Nor had she been able to sleep well. She'd lain awake until close to dawn, and, after finally dozing off, had awakened in late morning with the notion of seeking Malcolm out to ask about his morning ride. She'd sent a maid to inquire after him, and learned that he'd gone out very early, but in the carriage, and wasn't expected back until dinner. There was naught to do then but send the maid out again to tell Lucie her head was pounding, take a headache powder, and return to her bed.

"I'm sorry to have left ye alone this afternoon, Lucie. The party was a delight. As it happened, Malcolm had already made acquaintances in town, and so, I had the opportunity to meet some of his friends and their wives."

"And did you meet no one other than Malcolm's friends?" Lady Fiona smiled, her amber eyes, so like Lucie's and Finnley's, twinkling.

Her head buzzed and she reached for composure and an appropriate evasion. She wasn't yet up to discussing Finnley. "Well, indeed there must have been hundreds of people attending. Ye were very right about the gown, Lady Fiona. I ought to have chosen a brighter color."

"I told ye so, as well, Mama," Lucie said. "Red would have been lovely on ye. Ye're so lucky to be able to wear it. Oh, why was I cursed with this red hair?"

"And who says you may not wear red, Lucie?" Lady Fiona said. "Before these hairs of mine lost all their color, they were as bright as yours. And I certainly wore red when I felt like it."

"The dressmaker in Inverness always insisted the green was better for—"

"Hang the dressmaker," Lady Fiona said. "She no doubt had an abundance of the green to get rid of. And you'll be wary of that green cloth, as the dye often as not is set with arsenic."

"Scheele's Green," Greer said. "I've heard of this. Lucie, as a matron ye may wear whatever color gown ye choose providing your husband does not object overmuch. For now, we'll put ye in lighter colors, and ye may wear my red cloak when ye feel the need."

Color rose in her daughter's cheeks, a sign of her temper—so like her father's—rising.

Greer sent her a warning look. At almost twenty years of age, she was quite old enough to act the role of lady and go out in company. If only the girl might be welcomed somewhere besides Lady Fiona's drawing room and her near neighbors' parlors.

That bridge remained to be crossed. They'd arrived in Chelsea only days earlier. Aside from her and Malcolm's attendance at the previous night's party, they had yet to do more than rest from their journey, attend services at St. Luke's, visit a few of the local shops, and call on a few of the neighbors. Lady Fiona had promised them a visit to her London modiste, though Greer had equivocated on the date of it. Her own funds were perhaps not enough to answer their need for more fashionable attire, and whether Malcolm would bear the cost or vouch for her credit was ground she hadn't yet covered.

"Might we go somewhere tomorrow?" Lucie asked. "Might we borrow your carriage, Lady Fiona, and go into London?"

"Poor dear. What would you like to see? Perhaps the British Museum and the Rosetta Stone, and some of the other antiquities there?"

Lucie pressed her lips together.

She was so like Finnley. Completely transparent.

Lady Fiona sent Greer a wink. "Or perhaps something more dramatic. The Tower?"

"And the crown jewels," Lucie exclaimed.

The lady laughed. "You must have an escort. Shall we ask Malcolm if he is free? And perhaps the day after will be better, since it will be Monday and the shops will be open."

"Oh, yes. Has he returned?"

"He'll be along soon, I believe."

"Where on earth did he go to today?" Lucie asked. "He's always out and about."

"Lucie," Greer said. "I'm sure he had business to see to that is none of our business. And it was apparent last night that he has many acquaintances in town."

A footman appeared with a fresh pot of tea and a tray piled with cakes.

Lucie wrinkled her nose. "Perhaps he's arranging invitations for us."

"Perhaps," Lady Fiona said with another twinkling smile. "Now, do have some of these."

Greer availed herself of the fresh tea and light snacks, feeling better. The thought of an excursion had lifted Lucie's spirits, and hers as well. Even if for some reason they were unable to obtain entrance to tour the medieval Tower of London, perhaps they could visit St. Paul's, or one of the markets, or drive along Piccadilly. They chatted happily for the space of an hour until the mantel clock chimed the four o'clock hour.

"I must take myself off now," Lady Fiona said, "and begin dressing for dinner." She stood and straightened her skirts. "At my age, more time is needed. And we must all wear our finest tonight, as I know for a fact that Malcolm has invited a gentleman guest."

"Who is it?" Lucie asked.

"Lucie." Greer huffed, exasperated. "I'm sure we will find out soon enough."

"I'm sure of that as well," Lady Fiona said, and departed, laughing.

"My dear, ye must not be so curious and plain-spoken about it."

"Oh, Mama. Malcolm is so tiresome. He wasn't at all happy when we appeared in London. I do wonder if Lady Fiona invited us on purpose because she saw how dreadfully dull he is. I want to know who's coming. How will I know things if I don't ask?"

"Ye're too old to—"

"Yes, Mama. I'm too old to be plain-spoken. I'm too old to be making my come-out, as well. And I'm so old that ye mustn't expect me to be a simpering miss. It's just not in my very questionable blood."

Greer caught her breath and bit back a retort. She'd not hid the truth from her daughter. At home, there'd been no point to it. All knew the story.

In London, however, Lucie might have a better chance. Perhaps not with a nobleman of the *ton*, but there were other men who might ignore a worthy girl's mother's scandal. And despite the financial mismanagement of her cousin, with Duncan's help Greer had been able to arrange a small but respectable dowry for her girl.

"We will go out here in the local society. Lady Fiona has promised it, and ye must not embarrass her among her friends and neighbors by acting the hoyden. Ye will find a husband, my dear, if not here in London, then back home in Scotland."

"Mayhap, Mama. But whoever my husband might be, I'll choose a better man than the one who sired me."

The ache started again, and she pressed a finger to the space between her eyebrows. "Sure and ye have Finnley Macbeth's temper and tongue, daughter."

"So ye always tell me when ye're cross with me. If I ever see the man, I shall give him a piece of my mind."

She must be sure to arrange that future meeting when they were not in company.

"Remembering that he is your father," she said, rising, "and that along with the same blood, ye share the same temperament."

Lucie scoffed. "Meaning what, mother? Will he think to clout me?"

"No." Finnley wasn't a gentle man, but he'd always been a gentleman, more so than many of the Highland men of their acquaintance. He'd never laid a hand on his wife, or to her knowledge, any other woman.

And perhaps the army had thickened his skin and moderated his temper. Last night, he'd taken Malcolm's harsh words in stride. Yet one never knew what he might have said if they hadn't been in company. "I'm quite sure your father won't lash ye with anything more than his tongue."

When Finnley wielded his tongue and his temper, the wounds could be bitter, a flavor she tasted with her daughter more often than she wished. Lucie had sorely missed the influence of a loving father.

"Come," she said, "ye may wear my white gown with the red flowers upon it, and we'll put your hair up with a red ribbon."

"Your gown won't fit. My bosom is too small. And the flowers will simply make my freckles stand out, as if I were trying to match the gown to them."

"Or, I have the cream gown embroidered with purple flowers. We'll pin the bodice smaller, and powder your freckles."

She stood, and Greer linked arms with her.

"I hate when ye do this, Mama. Ye're humoring me."

"So I am. And I want ye to be happy, Lucie. Now come, let's dress as if this mystery man is a handsome young prince and not a stodgy banker old enough to be your granddad."

Lucie's answering laugh eased the pain in her head. Would that the girl was settled, and happy, and she herself could cease wringing her hands about where she'd gone wrong raising her.

"If I wanted that sort of man, Mama, I would set my cap at Malcolm. If this man is old, ye're welcome to him. But not if he's stodgy. I don't wish for a stodgy stepfather."

***

The hired carriage smelled of damp, and dust, and the many bodies transported within it. Fortunately, it managed to keep the drizzle outside.

'Twas a dreich night with all the bluidy rain. He'd paid dearly for the privilege of dry travel and a full night of service, yet so be it. His crimson coat, his black watch plaid kilt, and his bared knees were dry.

He would see Greer tonight. Anticipation rose in him, driving out most of the chill.

Hyde eyed him from the rear-facing seat. "Ought to have worn the trousers. Woulda kept ye warmer tonight, those trews would, sir."

Hyde was as mouthy as any Highlander. Truth to tell, they'd grown used to each other's ways, and in any case, he preferred an honest lackey to one sneaking about behind his back.

"Ye and the driver will find a warm fire and drink here."

He'd brought Hyde along to keep an eye on the hired coachman and make sure the man didn't run off and leave him stranded. Hyde was also a dab hand at nosing about, whilst keeping his master's interests to heart. Not that he'd asked it of the man tonight.

"Aye, well, in your full glory ye are, sir: sash, and sporran, and great shiny medals. Would that I could see the greeting ye'll be getting."

He laughed. His hostess was kin to Menteith, so he was hoping she might be a Scot. Not that he knew her, as far as he could remember. For the others, well it was true, he'd no idea who else the lady might have invited, and if a man had a medal, he might as well wear it. Menteith might back down then from skewering him, and Greer...

A medal wouldn't touch her heart, would it? He thought of the sight of her at the rout, her fine bosom, her blue eyes, her gleaming hair.

If the kilt and the medals had no effect, he'd find another way.

"Visiting a fellow Scotsman, be like a bit of home, sir?" Hyde prodded.

Home. He hadn't been home in twenty years.

"I'd like to see those bluidy high hills meself sometime, sir, since I've been forced into the plaid. What about ye sir? Are ye anxious to go there?"

It wasn't a topic he wanted to think about, much less discuss. "Tell me the story again, Hyde. How did ye wind up in a Scots' regiment?"

"Weel. As to that, sir, as I told ye afore, me shipmates and I found a smart little tavern in Inverness and next day woke up wearing skirts, er, kilts. Beg pardon."

Finnley laughed. After Walcheren decimated the ranks and enlistments flagged, the regiment had found other ways to replenish the Highlander ranks.

Hyde's story hadn't changed, and it always set the man on another conversational path.

"And then the next thing ye knew after that, ye were eating Portuguese codfish."

"Aye, though I ate plenty of good English cod back home in Yorkshire." He glanced out the window. "I thankee for allowing me inside your covered chariot, Major. Glad to be out of the wet tonight. May be that this rain will stop soon. How late do ye reckon to be tonight?"

"Hyde," he cautioned.

"Right, sir. Right, right. I'll just keep my good ear tuned to whether ye'll need me." He paused. "Saw that same fellow lurking on the street near the hackney stand."

Finnley sat up. "The man ye followed last night?"

"Aye. Not kitted out to the nines like yourself."

What the devil was Banquo up to? Mayhap Menteith had decided to invite him. But he doubted it.

The coach turned onto a lane and pulled up before a manor house, a goodly-sized dwelling of red brick, on a plot carved out from the market garden fields of Chelsea. 'Twas a far cry from the single-tower family castle he'd turned over to Greer for her use when they'd parted.

The windows blazed with light, and the moment they stopped, the front door opened with a splash of more. A liveried servant trotted out, while a groom sprinted around the corner from the back of the house.

Hyde exited, held the coach door for him, then climbed onto the back and ordered the driver to follow the groom.

When Finnley stepped onto the portico, Menteith appeared in the open doorway, scanning him up and down and blinking.

"Going into battle, Macbeth?" he asked.

The insolent pup. Menteith had donned the same well-tailored full evening dress he'd had on the night before.

He fixed the lad with a direct gaze. "A man never knows."

Menteith's lips quirked, and he shrugged.

He followed the younger man to a door off the hall and entered a drawing room. The blaze of candles dazzled him, but his eyes swept the well-appointed room and its occupants, his senses buzzing, his intuition stirring, like watching the enemy mass on the field.

He took in a breath, reminding himself this was Chelsea, not Spain, and surveyed the room.

An older white-haired lady rose from a sofa that shimmered in a silvery pink brocade, the padded back and arms nestled in carved ebony leaves and curling vines. The lady's eyes tugged at him, and a memory flashed, chilling him, and disappearing before he could grasp it.

Her sudden smile sparkled with kindness and good humor. She was round and soft and her warmth poured out and touched him, meeting the cold in his heart like a warm breeze hitting a block of ice.

He blinked and watched the light she emanated grow from her gentle demeanor, so oddly discordant with that wisp of memory creeping up his back.

His breath caught. Had it been her? Or had it been someone very like, someone who'd planted the witch's seed in his heart?

Greer moved into his vision, hands gripped tightly in front, face set in a frown. Red glistened around her, flickering to tones of pink.

Longing pumped through him. She could frown all she wished but she was still the loveliest woman he'd ever met, and now, surrounded by light...

His breath returned and he saw that 'twas naught but the gown that had lit up around her, a bright red that caressed skin as pale as that of a fairy tale queen. Her dark locks twisted in shiny curls, begging his hand to set them free, and a single stone hung from a chain at her neck, teasing her creamy breasts like a lover's caress.

Lightheaded, he shifted his weight, longing to touch her, knowing he couldn't, not here, not now, longing for something to lean on. Greer was here, and she was beautiful, and stirring, and...angry. Sparks flashed from that frown, like the first blast of enemy guns. What was he to do?

Skirts rustled and another vision came into view. His breath caught in a spasm. Dear God. Had he gone mad? What the devil had he walked into?

Framed in orange light, his sister Charmaine, come to life again, halted beside Greer. 'Twas her, sure enough, in heather-sprigged muslin, red curls pulled back, eyes flashing annoyance. He'd forgotten the ribbons she'd asked for. He'd come home empty handed.

Someone spoke... a man, the words indecipherable.

Air whooshed from his chest. This couldn't be real. Charmaine was long ago buried under the heather, her babe at rest with her.

The room spun. His feet tingled and black dots appeared, spotting Charmaine's face and Greer's, taking them both away again.

"Finnley." Greer's voice reached out from a distance, and then the whole room went dark.

CHAPTER FOUR

A stiletto of pain pierced all the way to his brain, and he swung out.

A hand clamped his wrist. The stench of ammonia filled him. "Come to, Macbeth," a man said.

"Does this happen often?" a woman asked. The voice, laced with kindness, was unfamiliar.

"'Appened once before, milady, at Vitoria. Just before a cannon blew up and knocked a wall down. 'E must've sensed it comin' 'cause he dropped like this, right on top of me, and me pushin' at him to get off so we could get to that wall. Saved us from bein' buried in bricks, he did, just in the nick."

Blasted Hyde was here shouting at everyone. His eyelids were heavy as lead, but he forced them open, trying to focus.

"It's him, isn't it, Mama?"

He sucked in a deep breath.

"That's right, sir," Hyde said. "Breathe in, Major."

His vision came into focus and he saw angels, fat cherubim circling above, looking down from the shadowed clouds. He opened his eyes wider.

A circle of faces surrounded the cherubim. Living faces. Hyde was there, and Menteith, and the old woman and Greer and...

He puffed out a breath. Not Charmaine. Charmaine was dead.

It's him, isn't it, Mama? That had been her speaking. She was Greer's daughter.

Remorse flooded him. Humiliation roiled and bubbled into hot shame. Greer was dark-haired, dark-eyed, and so had been Duncan.

This lass, this child of Greer's, this was his blood, his own daughter. Just as she'd sworn to him.

Damn it all to hell, why hadn't he listened?

He swallowed the aching pain. He and Greer had longed for a child. Why hadn't he believed her when she said the babe was his?

"Give me your hand," Menteith said. "Lucky I was near enough to catch ye before ye bashed that thick head of yours. We'll get ye onto the sofa. I'd not leave ye lying on my aunt's carpet all through dinner."

He squeezed his eyes closed a minute and silently cursed. He'd passed out onto the bluidy floor of this house.

He smoothed a gloved hand over the thick carpeting. Menteith's aunt. Who was she again?

Closing his eyes, he reached for the name. Dinner with Menteith. Invited by his aunt. This was her house. The old woman in the silvery pink light. A good witch.

"Take my hand, Finnley." Greer's gentle tone sent flames to his cheek. He opened his eyes, glad to see that the gentleness was only for show. The red glow was gone, yet she was just as unfriendly as she'd been every time he'd seen her since then.

He wanted no pity for this devilish weakness. Ignoring the offered assistance, he planted his hands and pushed himself up to sitting.

"Certain it is that you make a memorable entrance, Finnley Macbeth," the older lady said, smiling. "Hoist him up Malcolm and you there. Hyde was it?"

"Aye, milady," Hyde said cheerfully, sliding a hand under his shoulder while Menteith yanked on his other side.

He bit back an oath and allowed it, because, curse the chasseur who'd sliced him, he needed the help. Hyde straightened his coat and stepped back.

He leveled a gaze on the man. "I suppose they called ye in from your dinner?"

"Oh no, Major. Cook is still flitting about putting together food for her ladyship's table. Fretting about one thing burning and another getting cold. The staff will eat later."

He glanced at the ladies. Her ladyship still wore an unconcerned half-smile. Greer was still glowering. The young one's face had scrunched into a thin-lipped smirk.

"Thank ye, Hyde," he said. "That will be all."

While Hyde scurried off, her ladyship—what the devil was her name?—took his arm and led him to the sofa. "Pour us a whisky, Malcolm. You'll come and sit next to me, Finnley Macbeth."

"I don't wish to hold up your dinner, ma'am."

"Fiddlesticks. Cook frets over everything, even something so small as coddling an egg. 'Tis many an age since I've sat next to a braw man in a kilt, admiring his knees."

The girl snorted, and he plopped down harder than he'd meant to, making the sturdy piece creak. The thick cushions welcomed his backside and the hip that was beginning to ache like the devil.

"Ye've all got the better of me," he said. "I take it ye are Lord Menteith's aunt."

"Lady Fiona Carlin." Menteith handed him a whisky and passed one to the lady.

"*Sláinte.*" She touched her glass to his.

He tasted the brew. "It's verra fine," he said. "Thank ye, Lady Fiona, Menteith." He drained the glass and set it aside, pushing himself up from his seat. The others were still standing.

From here on out, he must make things right, whatever it might require.

"Greer," he said, taking a step toward her, his gaze sliding to the girl next to her. "Will ye not introduce me to my daughter?"

***

Heart hammering, Greer lay a hand on Lucie's arm, her mind racing to keep up with the changing, overwhelming emotions. She knew the look on her lass's face. She'd seen a flash of the same hot temper on Finnley's face, just moments before.

But...oh. Moisture flooded her throat. He'd seen that Lucie was his. He hadn't tried to pretend otherwise. That was one battle she'd not have to fight.

"I'm Lucie Macbeth." Their daughter's sharp chin shot up. There was no curtsy.

He took two steps closer, and she saw it then. The pronounced limp. That was indeed the reason he'd stumbled at Lady Estelle's rout. He'd been wounded, in body, and soul as well, if her heart guessed correctly.

And he did have fine knees under the regimental plaid. Fine knees and hardy, muscled legs still. She'd seen him in kilts...and naked...but she'd never seen him in uniform. He'd joined up after leaving her.

As he drew closer, Lucie's eyes widened. His hand shot out and took hers before she could snatch it out of his reach.

Lucie's gaze went to the large gloved hand clasping her own, then up again. "Ye saw me and fainted."

Greer let out a breath. Lucie was allowing the intimacy, but she'd adopted a mulish look.

A broad smile split his face. His teeth were still white, and the scant wrinkles crinkling his eyes and mouth only made him look more manly than ever he'd been as a young man.

"Mayhap it was your fault. I thought ye were Charmaine."

"Who?"

"My sister. Your aunt. Died in childbirth long before ye came along. Do ye remember Charmaine, Greer? She had the prettiest red hair and golden eyes."

"And the hottest temper," Greer said. "Perhaps hotter than her brother's. And I will tell ye, this red apple of yours didn't fall far from the tree."

"*Mother.*"

Lucie sent her a glare, and then looked back to her father, spluttering. He laughed out loud.

Greer's heart seized again. The bond was there, sprouting, as though the last twenty years hadn't occurred.

She'd expected rejection from him. Would she instead now lose her daughter to Finnley's charm? For he still had the ability to charm.

A footman appeared at the door, beckoning Lady Fiona, and she in turn signaled Malcolm.

"Are ye sturdy enough to go into dinner, Macbeth?" Malcolm asked. "Or are ye planning to swoon again?"

His grin widened. "If I do, just leave me on the floor and go about eating."

"Come, Lucie," Malcolm said. "Take my arm."

Lucie straightened. It was the slightest of movements, but one Greer knew well.

"No," Lucie said.

Greer cleared her throat.

"That is," Lucie said, "No thank ye, Cousin Malcolm. Finnley Macbeth will escort me in. Ye may take Mama and Lady Fiona."

Greer opened her mouth to scold, but Lady Fiona spoke first. "No. Macbeth will take both you and your mother in. If he faints again, he'll need the both of you to support him."

"I dare say ye have at least five or six stones on us, sir, so if ye faint, ye'll certainly find yourself on the floor."

"Lucie," Greer cautioned.

Finnley chuckled. "I'm not the fool I once was, Greer. I'll listen to sound reasoning like Lucie's. If I faint, let me slide down again to that verra soft carpet."

He drew Lucie to his side and extended his arm for Greer.

She set the tips of her fingers onto his crimson sleeve. The arm under the cloth was still muscled and hard, giving no evidence of whatever weakness had felled him. She must ask him about his injuries later, whenever the time might be that they could speak privately.

And if he wouldn't speak of it, she would ask his amiable servant.

***

The meal served was the best he'd had in months. Champit tatties, and juicy roast pork, fresh-caught fish, and peas so tender they melted in your mouth.

Mayhap the good meal would drive out the fairies plaguing him.

He set his mind to giving polite answers to the questions asked. The lass—his lass—wanted to know where he'd been, what battles he'd fought, and when he'd arrived in London. The rest looked on, the older lady amused, Menteith distracted, and Greer...Greer seemed to hold her breath each time their lass opened her mouth.

His daughter was a Macbeth all right. She was his, and he'd never walk away from her again. Nor would he ever leave Greer, unless she insisted upon it. And even then, he'd come back and try again.

"And what are your plans now, sir?" Lucie asked.

"Your father will want to mend from his wounds, I imagine," Greer said. "For ye were wounded, weren't ye, Finnley?"

"No worse than many."

"You limp," Lucie said.

He fought down a grimace. "So I do. Caught a French saber. Naught that won't heal in time."

Lucie opened her mouth again, and he cut in. "I'm here on half-pay, hoping to find a wee spot in the army or government."

"Doing what?" Lucie asked.

"Tied to a desk, if need be. I know a bit about what makes an army run, and the rest I can learn. There is always a tyrant somewhere challenging Britain."

Lucie looked from Lady Fiona to Menteith. "Might ye be able to help?"

Pulled from some deep thought, Menteith raised confused eyes. Lady Fiona smiled benignly at Lucie.

"Nay," Finnley said. "I've not come here tonight seeking patronage. I thank ye for the thought, Lucie, lass. We mustn't trouble her ladyship or Lord Menteith with my concerns."

"I see." The girl frowned. "I do beg your pardon, my lady, Malcolm. Sir."

"No pardon to be begged," Lady Fiona said. "I must be as straightforward as dear Lucie and say I do not know you well enough yet to extend my small bit of influence on your behalf."

The gleam in her eye, that half-smile, belied her words. It also made him wonder what she knew of him. The lady had much tucked away under that white head of hair.

Perhaps she'd heard the rumor about Burgos. That he'd left his men to founder and go wild. That he'd failed to go into the breach, and most of a whole squadron had died, the siege not just set back but lost.

"Malcolm," Greer said, "we didn't get a chance to speak to ye this afternoon. Lucie is anxious to see a bit of town—and so am I, to tell the truth. We wondered if ye would be available Monday to escort us."

She'd mercifully changed the subject, and he wondered if it had been done intentionally in his behalf. Perhaps her heart was thawing just a wee bit.

"We want to visit the Tower," Lucie said.

"Monday is not convenient. However, the day after..."

Finnley set down his fork. "I'm free Monday, Greer." In truth he was free every day until he'd found a position.

His gaze met hers, the blue eyes assessing him.

"Shall I ride out and meet ye here?"

"I should like that," she said.

At her ready agreement, his heart cheered.

"Lady Fiona, would Macbeth's escort serve?" Greer asked.

"Aye, it will. Now, shall we withdraw and leave the gentlemen to their drinks?"

He went around and held Lady Fiona's chair, while Menteith tended to Greer, and the ladies left.

Menteith moved closer and handed him a whisky. "Will this do, or would ye rather have port?"

"This will do. It reminds me of home. Is it your brew?"

"I do brew my own, but this is not mine. Lady Fiona has it sent down from some of her kin."

They drank in companionable silence for a few minutes, Menteith refilling their glasses, and then clearing his throat.

"I would speak with ye, Macbeth, about your claim on Menteith."

"I have no claim."

"Ye once thought ye did."

He pressed his lips together, holding back the bitterness. Greer's cousins and aunt had unearthed some bit of ancient genealogy, persuading him that he was the rightful earl of Menteith, not the lad's father, Duncan.

"'The courts ruled otherwise, and I've come to accept that verdict. 'Twas a claim concocted by Greer's scheming relatives. I ought to have seen it for what it was. No, sir, ye are the rightful heir and Earl of Menteith, and I pledge ye my sword whenever ye have need of it."

The lad speared him with a look. "And what if I possess a document that will prove otherwise?"

"Burn it."

Rising, Menteith paced the room as Finnley watched.

So like his father, was this lad, Malcolm Comyn. Might he be as true as his da was? Duncan had been a man of honor, and he, Finnley, had dishonored him with a vile lawsuit and then an even viler accusation that Duncan had cuckolded him. Duncan's charm had made the last charge plausible.

This son of Duncan had his father's dark good looks but none of his easy charm. This lad was all earnestness. Perhaps that came from the mother, a sickly lass, who'd miscarried nearly all her babes. Duncan had finally taken her off to Matlock Bath for several months rest, and returned with this healthy lad. Sadly, the boy's mother had died soon thereafter.

Banquo's whispered gossip about Menteith and Lucie came to him. He had no fog of jealousy clouding him now. They weren't brother and sister, yet from what he could see neither Menteith nor Lucie wanted a match, at least not with each other.

'Twas a reminder to be watchful of men telling tales.

"I meant what I said, Menteith." He got to his feet. "Now, let's join the ladies."

The dark eyes held him in place. "What will ye do if ye don't get a position?"

He'd spent twenty years chasing one enemy or another, whilst wrangling with his anger and guilt and regret in the quiet times. But with this war over, what was to be his purpose? He had plenty of strength and fight left in him, and for certain there would be other wars to fight. The muddled visions plaguing him may or may not be proof of that.

And he'd just learned the woman he'd loved—still loved—had been true to him, and had borne him a daughter, one who, so far, despite his neglect, had not spurned him. He would get to know Lucie, and he would find a way back into Greer's heart. That future had brightness, and color, and hope.

He made himself shrug. "I have some money put aside. Right now, God's truth, I'd like to have a few words with Lucie and Greer."

Menteith gave in wordlessly and led him through to the room where he'd so shamelessly swooned.

And there, seated in front of the fire, sat a soggy Giles Banquo, taking tea with his daughter.

The black dots started up again, pinpricks of certainty circling Banquo like a cloud of blow flies swarming a privy.

A hand touched his and his vision cleared. He'd removed his gloves at the table, and they were skin to skin. A jolt of desire shook him.

"Banquo only just appeared," Greer whispered. "I don't like this at all."

CHAPTER FIVE

The hot gaze he sent her melted her all the way to her toes, and where her hand touched his, the skin burned.

But his eyes had cleared from the threat of a swoon, and she kenned that he shared her nagging suspicions about Banquo. Suspicions of what, she couldn't form words to describe, but the slither down her back both last night at the rout and tonight when Banquo had appeared at the drawing room door could not be ignored. Her nerves had been twitching until Finnley walked in. Even Lady Fiona's omnipresent secretive smile had slipped as she poured tea for the newcomer.

"Banquo," Malcolm said, with a none too welcoming frown, "What brings ye here?"

"My horse stepped in a hole and acquired a limp. I thought I might ask for some kindly assistance."

Malcolm moved closer. "So far from your lodgings?"

"I was meeting an acquaintance at the Rose and Crown, since Macbeth refused my company tonight." He smiled at Lucie, leaning closer and patting her hand. "Though I can certainly see why he chose as he did."

Lucie pulled her hand away and Banquo chuckled.

Greer's breath eased. Hot-headed her daughter was, but not easily taken in. She could pick out a fool at twenty paces.

"Ye came here instead of the inn," Malcolm mused. "How odd."

"Not so odd. Lady Fiona and I met once in London many, many years ago, after I left Scotland. Though it's true, I'm not as well acquainted with the lady as all of you seem to be."

"Hmm," Malcolm said.

An awkward silence ensued.

Lady Fiona cleared her throat. "You are curious, Banquo? Malcolm is a great nephew of mine by marriage. And Greer and I are related through my husband and her cousins, so distant that we'd not met until she arrived in London. And of course, I've only made Major Macbeth's acquaintance this very night."

"That is so," Finnley said, "and grateful I am for your hospitality, my lady."

Banquo's eyes narrowed, his lips quirking with the hint of a smile. Or, perhaps a sneer.

"Be that as it may, Macbeth, do you not recall that you, our cousin, Duncan, and I once had a memorable encounter with Lady Fiona's aunt? I could not help but notice that Lady Fiona looks very much like her. Do you not think so?"

Finnley frowned and turned his gaze on Lady Fiona, and recognition dawned in his amber eyes. "I don't recall."

Finnley had lied. Greer had seen the moment the memory reared up in him. There would be a reason for his deception.

"My aunt believed she had the sight." Lady Fiona lifted her own teacup. "And I am here to tell you she wasn't always correct and, I fear not always in her right mind, may God rest her soul. Tell me Banquo, since the one time that we met, what have you been about? Did you ever take a wife?"

"Aye."

"And does she live?" Lucie asked.

"Why, Miss Macbeth." Banquo turned his full attention on Lucie. "Why are you asking?"

"My daughter is asking because ye were patting her hand in an overly familiar way." Finnley moved to stand behind Lucie. He set a hand on her shoulder and she covered it with her own.

Moisture flooded Greer's throat and threatened her eyes. She caught Malcolm watching her. He tipped his head as if to ask what the devil was going on.

She lifted her shoulder.

Banquo sat up in his chair and squinted at Lucie. "Your daughter, Macbeth?" He laughed. "Well, then, I suppose we were both wrong."

Greer's breath caught in a spasm of anger, and she could see the heat rising in Finnley's cheeks as well.

"Apologies," Banquo said, before either of them could speak. "And no, my wife is gone these ten years."

"Do you have bairns?" Lady Fiona continued.

"Two sons. They're at school. And they're not quite of a marriageable age yet, if you're wondering."

"I wasn't," Lucie said. "Were you, Father?"

Now Greer would cry if she didn't get hold of herself. She summoned her temper again and let herself feel the jealousy simmering in her.

Banquo had all but declared to the room that he'd though Lucie was Duncan's. To what end would he provoke a fight tonight with her?

Heavens. When Finnley divorced her, she'd spent most of the ensuing years in a fog of self-pity, one her cousins and aunt had encouraged. Her sense of victimhood had been a useful tool to her manipulative relatives.

Then they'd died, and she'd seen how her cousin had managed her money. All she'd had left was a portion of her settlement and use of the Macbeth family home, Finnley's grant to her when they parted. That had been occupied by tenants, the lease arranged by her cousin.

With no place for her and Lucie to live, she'd been at her wit's end. And then Duncan had stepped in offering help. He'd taken her and Lucie in for a time, while he saw to the removal of the tenants occupying her home, and taught her how to manage the lands. He'd augmented her income when needed, and helped her hire a competent factor.

"Ye've no need to offer Banquo a night's shelter," Finnley said. "He may ride in the carriage with me, and tether his limping horse."

They were leaving. What had she missed? Had Banquo been angling to spend the night?

Drat, but she would have to put off speaking with Finnley until Monday.

"What time on Monday shall we see ye then, Father?" Lucie asked. She stood next to Finnley, holding his hand.

He smiled fondly at her. "Shall I come for ye, then?"

"You have an outing planned?" Banquo asked. "It had best be early. I've heard tell of possible rioting over the Corn Laws."

Greer had read of the potential for violence in the newspaper Lady Fiona had delivered each day. Parliament was debating a tariff that would help landowners like herself, but greatly hurt the common man, who might not be able to afford the rise in prices for bread. 'Twas a dilemma that tore at her heart.

"With my father along for protection, we have little to fear. Isn't that right, Mother?"

Her eyes met Finnley's, and she blinked, clearing her vision. He was still a powerful man, and if he didn't keel over in a swoon, she knew in her heart he'd die for his daughter. And perhaps for herself as well.

Greer nodded. "Certainly. But I believe Banquo has the right of it. We'll make an early day of it and be out of danger before the gin takes hold of folk."

Finnley's eyes glowed bright in the candlelight, and he dipped his head. "Early it will be."

The butler appeared and let them know that Finnley's coach was waiting outside.

"Come along, Banquo," Finnley said.

Lady Fiona stood. "Malcolm, escort Banquo out. We'll give these three a moment to discuss their outing."

With an assessing look around the room, Malcolm stepped forward and led Banquo out behind Lady Fiona.

"Shall I bring my dirk Monday?" Lucie asked.

"Ye have one?" Finnley asked.

"Aye."

"And ye know how to use it, lass?"

"The sharp point goes in wherever one can find a soft spot."

He threw back his head and his laughter filled the room. The sound took Greer back three and twenty years, to the day they'd met at a village caelidh.

She shook herself. "Will we come for ye in Lady Fiona's carriage then?"

"Nay. I'll ride out Monday in the morn and join ye here. My mount can use the exercise, and I'd not have ye traveling alone into town with just the coachman and groom. Banquo is right about the mobs. When people are hungry, there's bound to be trouble." He squeezed Lucie's hand. "And ye're right that I'll look after ye. And your mother."

Malcolm appeared at the door and cleared his throat.

They would find a time to talk, but it wouldn't be tonight, nor would it be on Monday, not with Lucie along.

He took Lucie's hand and extended his arm to Greer. "Escort me, in case that I swoon again?"

Oh, that devilish charm. She set her fingers onto the scarlet sleeve again and reminded herself that she must keep her wits about her with this one, lest her heart be broken again.

***

"I take it you haven't tracked down your man, Abernathy, yet," Banquo said.

"He wasn't yet back in town." Or if he'd returned, his staff and servants weren't sharing the details. Abernathy was a busy man.

"Maybe I can help you."

In the dark, Finnley couldn't read Banquo's face. "I wouldn't want to trouble ye."

"No trouble at all. We are cousins, after all. And it would be the least I could do to repay your hospitality in freighting my wet self back to town."

Hyde had furrowed his brow over riding up with the coachman, but at least the rainfall had stopped.

Finnley grunted his reply.

"Join me tomorrow night—or perhaps Monday night would be better, at the same taproom?"

He hesitated to agree. He'd hoped to be invited to stay for dinner with the ladies and then perhaps... No, he'd best forget about time alone with Greer for a bit. They had too much ground to cover before he could proceed with his campaign to woo her, and a hard battle it might be.

"All right," he said.

Banquo chuckled. "Thinking of escorting the ladies back and staying for dinner, were you? Or...perhaps staying the night?"

Banquo was a wily one and perceptive. Skilled at punching a man where he was vulnerable—as in the way he'd reached for Lucie's hand. Skilled at punching a woman as well, the way he'd feigned surprise when Finnley claimed Lucie as his. And his fawning...

"I must ask ye, Banquo. Are ye planning to wed again?"

"Why...oh. Beg pardon if I was too familiar with young Lucie tonight. I suppose she's spoken for with young Menteith. Those rumors, well, we can put any ugliness aside. No doubt she's a Macbeth, and not a Comyn. Are you pleased?"

"Are ye daft? There's no wedding planned between those two."

"Ah."

"And, to be honest, ye're a bit long in the tooth for the lass."

"Younger than you, Macbeth."

As he'd been younger than Duncan. Banquo was likely not yet forty, and the twenty-year age difference between him and Lucie was not at all unusual in marriage, especially for a man seeking an heir. Though Banquo already claimed to have two sons—news to Finnley, as the subject had ne'er come up when their paths crossed on the Continent. In fact, he'd diligently avoided any discussion of family, including Banquo's subtle pokes about Greer's betrayal.

Which had been a lie, one likely birthed and brokered by Banquo. The man had best keep his hands away from Lucie or Finnley would have them wrenched off and fed to the dogs.

He reminded himself who he was dealing with, and summoned his breath and his brain, awaiting the next jab.

"What of you?" Banquo asked. "Are you planning to wed?"

Greer's lovely face came to mind. Hostile, aye, since they'd met at the rout, she'd looked unfriendly. How he'd love to kiss her frowns away. He shifted in his seat. "On a major's half-pay? Not likely."

"You could live very well on that in Scotland."

He had nowhere to go in Scotland. Though he still technically owned his family home, he'd ceded control of it to Greer in the divorce settlement, because too much of the money he'd promised for a dower had been thrown away on the feckless lawsuit. He'd not kick Greer out of her home. But he'd love to move in there with her, if she'd have him.

"What of ye, Banquo? Is Scotland calling you home?"

Banquo chuckled, but it was too dark to see the look on his face.

A shiver went through him. "Where have you been calling home for the last twenty years?"

"Norfolk. We lived with my wife's people there. My wife abided with them when I was away, which was most of the time."

Away doing what? Agent for a military supplier? That might be true, and might not. He longed to question the man more, but Banquo had finally fallen silent, and Finnley, exhausted, held his peace as the hired coach rocked on.

As they passed Green Park, the Sight stirred in him, not clear enough to discern any more than that Banquo was plotting and shouldn't be trusted.

He'd not learn more by staying away from the man. They traveled on in silence and parted ways at the livery stable, agreeing to meet on Monday night.

***

Greer was seated at her dressing table taking down her hair when she heard a tap at her bedchamber door.

'Twould be Lucie, no doubt, coming to plague her with questions about Finnley. She sighed and said "enter."

Lady Fiona stepped into the bedchamber, attired in a silk banyan gaudy enough to be a man's garment.

Greer rose. "Are ye well, Lady Fiona?"

"Shhh." The older lady held a finger to her lips and eased the door closed before approaching. "I'd not have that curious lass know I'm up and about. I wanted to speak to you alone."

"Oh." She sighed. Her daughter was incorrigible. "I'm sorry."

Lady Fiona chuckled softly. "Her curiosity will serve her well, as long as she knows when to employ it. May I sit?"

"Of course." Greer went to join her on the sofa in front of the fireplace.

"I hope it's not too late for a chat."

"No, of course not. I'd have expected our guests to stay later."

"Yes. Banquo's appearance put a damper on the evening, and it had nothing to do with his dampness." She smiled at the small joke. "It was odd for him to appear here. I'd only met him once at a party, years ago. What do you know of him?"

Thoughts of Banquo and what she did know of him brought up the pain in her past. Perhaps that was the root of her unease—not any present darkness, only the cloud of the past. "He's a cousin to Macbeth and Malcolm's father Duncan. He was the young lad following in their wake. He inherited when...'twas during the time of the lawsuit we'd filed against Duncan. Do ye know of it?"

"Aye. Malcolm has reminded me of it."

Greer sighed. "'Twas a mistake to have filed it. I was grateful that Duncan forgave me. In any case, Banquo inherited just before the judgment was rendered. His father had gone so deep into debt that... Well, while we were in the midst of our own troubles..."

The memory rushed her and she closed her eyes. It had been Banquo, she'd later learned, who'd seen her speaking with Duncan. He'd told Macbeth. Whether he'd also planted the notion of an affair, she couldn't be sure.

A soft hand touched hers, and she opened her eyes. Lady Fiona's face held only kindness.

"Well, soon after, Banquo sold everything to pay off the debt, sent his mother back to her people, and then he left Scotland. I didn't know he'd married, nor did I know his wife."

Divorce had been a kind of death, in her case, like a suicide. She'd plunged into her pain, into a pit of despair so deep, she could do naught but wallow in it, like a stupid sow.

"Did Macbeth ever tell you my auntie's prediction?"

"Prediction?" She shook her head. "I didn't know anything about your aunt or a prediction. Have ye heard what it is, Lady Fiona?"

"Not first hand. Nor even second hand." Lady Fiona rose and went to a side cabinet that housed bottles of spirits and glasses. "I see Malcolm left these behind when he changed bedchambers. May I?" she asked.

"Of course."

"Will you join me? I'll send up a fresh bottle of sherry tomorrow."

"Let me help ye." Greer stood and fetched the glasses.

When they had settled back onto the sofa, Lady Fiona poured for them.

"Now," she said, taking a sip. "I've teased you Greer, but I must do so a bit longer, in order to tell the whole story as it ought to be told. Tell me, what did you know of Duncan, Malcolm's father?"

An image of Duncan appeared in her mind. Tall, broad, and darkhaired, the lord of Menteith had turned heads among all the ladies. Not hers though. She'd never been drawn to him in a romantic way.

She had few memories of those early days. Duncan's lady, Malcolm's mother, had been already deceased when Macbeth introduced his young bride to his widowed cousin, the Earl of Menteith.

"He was kind to me and Lucie, after my aunt and cousins died. He'd not held a grudge, even though he had every right to do so. Before that, I saw him upon occasion at the kirk, or in the village, but he had nothing to do with my cousins and aunt. They weren't on friendly terms."

"And before?"

The amber liquid sloshed in Greer's shaking hand. "I did not have an affair with him. The man was ever honorable to me and to every other soul I saw him with."

Lady Fiona nodded. "And I believe you. It's the easiest thing in the world for a man—or a woman for that matter—to besmirch a woman's name."

"And a man's reputation, as well." Though the cost of the besmirching was usually higher for a woman.

"Yes. What happened, Greer? Why did the rumor start?"

She took a deep breath and set down the glass. "When the court ruled against Finnley, he was distraught and angry, for not only did Duncan win the claim, the court awarded Duncan damages, and we'd no idea how we were to pay them. So..." She squeezed her eyes shut. "Finnley doesn't know this, but I sent word to Duncan asking him to meet me. To see if I could persuade him to forgive the amount, or negotiate payments."

"And?"

"I told him what had happened. I told him that it had been all my fault, on account of my cousin's persuasions. That Finnley shouldn't suffer. I begged him, a man with far more income than my husband, to forgive the judgment. He agreed. And as we were shaking hands on the matter—and truly that was all that it was, a mere grasping of two hands—Banquo saw us."

Lady Fiona nodded.

"The whispering started soon after. And when I found I was with child... Ye know the rest." Her world that had been slipping crashed down upon her like the walls of Castle Macbeth. "I've been with no other man but my husband, Finnley." She swallowed sudden moisture. "My former husband."

Lady Fiona took Greer's hand in her own. "Malcolm confided Duncan's last words to me. They were a surprise to the lad, because his father had been barely coherent those last few days."

"Yes," Greer said. "I saw that when I went to help tend to him."

"At the last, he mustered his wits enough to share what he felt he must. Malcolm, when he heard this deathbed declaration, wasn't certain what to think."

"Ah," Greer said. "He's a sober one, is Malcolm, yet his da's death left him as close to distraught as I'd ever seen."

Lady Fiona's quizzical look begged more details.

"He stewed for a time after the death, then he tore through the library and the house, or so the servants told me," Greer said. "Not gossiping, ye understand. They were worried about him. He went off on business more than once, as well, even in the midst of the harvest."

Lady Fiona nodded. "One of those visits he paid to me. He'd written me a few months after his father's death. My aunt was dead of course, and I was the last in the family close to her age." She gazed off at the low fire warming the room. "I was, frankly, taken aback. You see, I'd never met Malcolm before. I'm not really an aunt to him, but to his mother, and then only by marriage. The Carlins were intertwined with many families, even your cousins, the Naughtons." She chuckled. "That is too much confusing information perhaps. Let me get to the point."

Greer nodded, encouragingly.

"Malcolm came to see me when I was in Edinburgh and relayed this deathbed tale told by Duncan: The three boys, Duncan, Macbeth, and Banquo, stumbled across my aunt one day while they were out roaming the heath. She kept a bothy near her cottage, and 'twas there that she worked with her herbs and her potions. I favored her in looks, and," Lady Fiona smiled, her eyes twinkling, "she wasn't a crone, not like one of your fairytale witches. 'Twas her preoccupation with more often than not ghastly potions, and perhaps the madness in her eyes, that stirred people to call her 'witch'. In the olden times she might have been burned." She paused, a faraway look in her eyes.

"How frightening for the three boys," Greer said, breaking the silence.

The older lady gave her an assessing look. "Malcolm being Malcolm, he'd written down everything Duncan told him, and we went over it together. I quite liked the lad from the very start. Well, from what we knew of my aunt and the three men, we tried to work out their ages. Duncan might have been seventeen, a man almost; Macbeth perhaps thirteen; and Banquo eight or nine years of age. 'Twould not have been so frightening for Duncan at his age. Macbeth though..." She leveled a gaze at Greer. "Finnley Macbeth has the Sight, does he not?"

The Sight? Greer disentangled her hands and stood, pacing to the bed and back.

"If he'd had the Sight, he would have known the child I was carrying was his. He would have known Duncan didn't cuckold him. He would have known there were no grounds to divorce me."

Lady Fiona let out a breath and looked away.

Greer waited, apprehension sending prickles along her spine.

"Perhaps the gift was not with him then, or wasn't as strong," Lady Fiona said. "Perhaps his time in battle... Death has stalked him for twenty years, has it not? And still he's alive and returned to you. That swoon tonight when he saw Lucie, that was almost repeated later when he laid eyes on Banquo sitting with her."

Returned to you, she'd said. Might that be so? Surely not.

"Might the swoon be merely the result of his injuries?"

Lady Fiona gazed into the fire again, and a slow certainty crept through Greer. Lady Fiona had the Sight as well. Perhaps like her aunt, and didn't it run in families?

If 'twas true about Finnley, she prayed Lucie might be spared the burden of knowing things better not known.

"I believe..." Lady Fiona pressed her lips together a moment. "When the lawsuit failed, Finnley was filled with doubt. He'd been told something by my aunt, and sensed that it might be true. And then your cousin Naughton found evidence, and Finnley was certain. When the court ruled against him, he turned away from his own inner guide. And so, with all he's been through in battle, the Sight has begun to tap harder upon his shoulder. And still, he's uncertain what's true and what's not."

Greer dropped onto the seat. "Tell me the rest, Lady Fiona."

CHAPTER SIX

"When the three boys came upon my aunt, there she was, stirring her kettle outside over a mighty fire. 'Double, double, toil and trouble, fire burn and cauldron bubble.' Aye, Duncan remembered the rhyme, as he was meant to, and Malcolm duly transcribed it. She was always one for a good fright, and three boys popping up from nowhere would be perfect victims, fearing they might be tossed into her bubbling cauldron. Except that Duncan had laughed, and that raised her ire. She demanded his name, and he told her he was Duncan Comyn. She knew who he was, what he was—the Earl of Menteith, for he already held the title. Then she caught sight of the others and demanded to know their names."

Lady Fiona took a sip of her sherry, a faraway look in her eyes.

"Macbeth held his tongue, but Banquo, all aquiver with fear, introduced both of them. Then 'All hail Macbeth, thou shalt be Earl of Menteith,' she said."

Greer's breath caught. Thou shalt be Earl of Menteith? She squeezed her eyes closed, her mind a jumble.

"You see? The lawsuit wasn't entirely your fault," Lady Fiona said gently. "The seed had been planted earlier, by my aunt."

She filled Greer's glass again and handed it to her. "There is more. She turned her gaze on Banquo and said 'Lesser than Macbeth, and greater. Thou shalt get earls, though thou be none.' Has Malcolm told you any of this?"

"No. That is, he said he's trying to determine who is the rightful Earl of Menteith. He received a letter from London and came to investigate. I offered to help him in any way I might."

"As have I. Monday when you are sightseeing, have a care in London. 'Tis true that the streets are dangerous right now, and if Finnley Macbeth senses a threat, don't seek to gainsay him, no matter how angry you might still be with him. Now, having shared this burden and this bottle of sherry, I find I am tired. I shall bid you a good night."

She saw Lady Fiona to the door and went back to her dressing table, working out more of the tangles in her hair, whilst trying to work out the tangled tale she'd just heard.

That Macbeth had believed the witch's prediction 'twas a revelation to her. It had not been all her fault, nor all the fault of her aunt and cousins, though they were greatly to blame in so many other ways.

Thou shalt be Earl of Menteith.

Did he still want to wrest the earldom away, this time from Duncan's heir? She wouldn't allow that. If that was his plan, she'd do all in her power to stop him. On Monday, she would listen and watch, and hope for a moment alone with him.

Wednesday, 8, March, 1815

As Greer had expected, there'd been no chance to speak with Finnley alone on their Monday outing, and no chance to see him the following day when a downpour kept everyone except Malcolm close to home.

Finnley had been charming, and affable, and quite generous with both her and Lucie. He'd purchased a guidebook for their sightseeing journey, and Lucie had played tour guide, reading aloud about the various sights. They'd been unable to visit the Tower, but Lady Fiona's coachman had humored them, driving through the Strand and the City. They'd stopped at St. Paul's and viewed the massive dome in awe, both inside and out, and passed Parliament, where here and there, men stood about outside, some seeking trouble and others preparing to guard against it. They'd driven down Piccadilly, stopping to look into shops, including a visit to Hatchard's where Finnley had bought Lucie a copy of Waverley, a new novel by a Scotsman.

They'd disembarked at Hyde Park for a chilly, but fortunately dry turn about the grounds, and then Finnley had taken them to a tea shop called Gunter's, before returning them to Chelsea. He'd declined Lady Fiona's invitation to dinner, having made other plans, and Lucie, unaccountably quiet, had gone off to her room after dinner with both the guidebook and her new novel.

Greer had turned in early herself two nights in a row, and thus, here she was, up at the crack of dawn before the cook had even started breakfast.

She found Malcolm in the hall, pulling on his gloves, dressed in a dark green frock coat, gray waistcoat, gray trousers, and shoes. Outside, the coach sat waiting.

The day before, he'd left early for town. In fact, she hadn't seen much of him since Sunday morning, when they'd all attended church together.

"Ye are up and about early again, Cousin," she said.

"As are ye. Lady Fiona said ye had no plans for the day, and that I may take the coach. Was she incorrect?"

"No," she said. "Today we'll be home to callers. Lady Fiona's friend Mrs. Tebworth has promised to bring her two daughters to call on Lucie. What a pity ye won't be here to meet them," she teased.

He winced. "How was your day touring?"

"Very nice."

"And Macbeth?"

"He was a congenial tour guide, though it was the blind leading the blind. Thank heavens for the guidebook and the coachman."

A footman appeared with his greatcoat, and he signaled the man to wait. "Step into the parlor a moment, Greer."

He ushered her into a room off the hall and a shiver went through her. The curtains were still closed, the fire in the grate still banked.

"Have ye learned something?" she asked.

"Lady Fiona said she spoke with ye about my father's last words."

"She did. I am so sorry, Malcolm. As I told ye, the earldom is—"

"Had ye ever heard that story before? From Macbeth, or perhaps from my father?"

"No. Never. Have ye mentioned the matter to Macbeth?"

"I didna remind him of Lady Fiona's aunt, no. But I did talk to him about his past lawsuit. His answer was the same as yours. He believes the matter is settled. However, today, I'm to meet with the man who wrote to me saying it isn't."

"And ye know it's a man?"

"A lady would not arrange a meeting at a public house, I think."

"Ye're going alone?"

"As agreed."

"Be careful, Cousin." A wild thought came to her. "Why not take Finnley Macbeth?"

"So he can knock me over the head?"

"I...I don't believe he would."

"Greer." He peered down at her, his dark eyes intense. "I was predisposed to distrust the man. But upon consideration, I don't think he would harm me. He says he doesn't want the title and I'm inclined to believe him, even if a witch did promise him the earldom."

"I see." Perhaps, like Duncan, Finnley had let go of the past.

"Do not worry so. As I told ye before, I'm capable of handling a pistol and sword, as well as my fists."

She nodded. "However, I never see ye as the sort to engage in a brawl."

His lip quirked. "I'm not the sort to seek battle, but sometimes it comes to me. My father always told me I ought to be more politic and less direct. Rather like ye chastising Lucie. Did she enjoy the time with her father?"

"Very much. He bought her a book by an anonymous Scotsman. She'll have been up all the last two nights reading it."

"Lucie? A bookworm?"

They both laughed and he opened the door and went through into the hall. "I must be off now. I shall see ye at dinner."

Brusque and abrasive Malcolm might be, but he'd shown he could wield some charm, distracting her. She went to the window and pulled the curtain open. As he boarded the carriage and drove off, the flicker of worry raged into full-fledged alarm. He might be heading into danger.

She wished, not for the first time since she'd come back to life, that she might jump on a mount and pursue her suspicions.

The voice of uncertainty roused and whispered: *remember what happened the last time ye took it upon yourself to take action?* She'd arranged that meeting with Duncan, and lost everything.

Almost everything. She still had her Lucie, who was now and most certainly, not just hers, but Finnley's as well.

***

Sir Thomas Abernathy kept Finnley waiting more than an hour.

Upon his arrival at the office near Whitehall, a clerk had offered him a seat on a hard, wooden chair. He'd waved off the man and stood, until the ache in his hip could no longer be borne. Then he'd taken the seat, and remained there, until limb and back had stiffened and the pain had resumed, putting him back on his feet. And he'd repeated that drill two times and again.

At least he'd managed to refrain from stumbling about.

He was strong, still in his prime, and ready for service, dammit. Trouble was coming, though at present he couldn't discern what it might be. The gray skies outside had carried into the atmosphere of the room, obscuring all his visions of upcoming trouble.

No. That wasn't entirely true. His instincts told him that Banquo, along with helping arrange this appointment had also whispered in Abernathy's ear.

"Major Macbeth," a voice called. "Do come through."

Abernathy stood in the doorway, his slight frame and premature baldness belying the craftiness and inner strength of the man.

He hauled himself up, holding his breath through a grinding pain, and steeling himself not to limp.

Inside the office, the visitor's chair in front of the desk looked no more comfortable than the one outside.

Abernathy seated himself. "Do sit down. Unless...I heard you were gravely wounded at Toulouse. Stand if you find it more comfortable."

He waved the invitation away and eased down onto the hard wood. "The wound is well-healed." Or at least the open wound had closed. The ligaments and muscles beneath were still knitting themselves back together.

Yet, he was alive, and he still had the leg, and it was mostly usable, especially when he was in the saddle.

"I am glad of it."

He and Sir Thomas had become acquainted one long winter in Frenada where they'd both been welcomed to the small congenial dinner parties hosted by Major Scovell and his wife. They chatted about mutual acquaintances until an aide tapped on the door and announced that the next appointment had arrived.

"Sir Thomas, I won't take more of your time. Did Banquo convey the reason for my visit?"

Abernathy tapped the desktop. "I was surprised to run into him. I'd only just arrived back in town. But yes, he mentioned you are seeking a position."

"Aye. Or, mayhap a command or posting. There's peace on the Continent, but there's always trouble about elsewhere in the world."

"Banquo said you have just reacquainted yourself with your daughter."

"I have actually just met her for the very first time."

"Would you be willing to go off and leave her?"

"Truth to tell, I'd rather be where I might easily see her or bring her to visit. Ireland perhaps, or somewhere here in England or the Low Countries. But she is of an age to marry, so it will only be a matter of time for her to go with a husband to a home of her own."

"Too true. We can't hold onto our offspring."

Did Abernathy have children? Finnley realized he didn't even know whether the man had a wife.

"Banquo also reminded me of some trouble on the Peninsula."

"Wellington himself exonerated me."

"Yes, I recall that. And I'm not reopening that particular wound. He hinted, however, at another supposed incident, at San Sebastian."

Finnley's fingers firmed around the chair arms. A long moment ensued while moisture dribbled between his shoulder blades and down his back, and he searched his mind for a whispered story or sidewise look, coming up empty. He'd blacked out but once at Vitoria—twice if one counted his swoon in Lady Fiona's parlor.

"I'm at a loss as to know what he's speaking of. Do ye know?"

Abernathy leaned forward and rested his weight on his elbows, rubbing his chin. "I do not. It was rather havey-cavey I thought, dropped sotte voce at the club when he could see we'd be interrupted by the man I'd arranged to meet there. He left before finishing the whisper." He frowned. "I only mention it because I thought you should know it was said. Is it true he's your cousin?"

"Quite distant, but yes."

"Is he your heir?"

The old memory shimmered up past Abernathy's shoulder in the gray light of the window.

Lesser than Macbeth, and greater. Thou shalt get earls, though thou be none.

He hadn't been able to look away, then or now. He saw her in the afternoon light, the witch sneering at the dark-haired young man who stood with his arms crossed laughing at her, while the young lad on his other side was shaking and wetting himself.

He blinked and the shadows mercifully disappeared.

"No. The barony will be my daughter's." If there were any legal challenges, he would address them. Though born after the divorce, Lucie had been legitimately conceived.

"I see." Abernathy sat back and steepled his fingers. "Wellington is in Vienna negotiating the peace. From time to time, we hear of a need to fill a position, or to refill one vacated by one of the men going there. I'll see what opens. When I put your name forward—and I shall try to do so—

perhaps more will bubble up on Banquo's rumor. Either way, I'll send word to you."

"Thank ye, Sir Thomas."

"You've been through a great deal. If you've a mind for a pleasure trip, now is a good time. Perhaps take your daughter on a holiday. If you do so, leave word on how I may reach you. Meanwhile, Macbeth, I've known you to have a hot temper. Have a care with your cousin." He smiled.

That smile was genuine, and it raised his spirits. He chuckled. "War has tempered that temper, Abernathy, but nevertheless, I shall keep your advice in mind. And I hope ye will keep me in mind should the Crown need a hardy Scotsman."

Both cheered by Abernathy's loyalty, and concerned by Banquo's whispers, he hired a hack and returned to his rooms near Piccadilly. Where the barony was concerned, Banquo wasn't Finnley's heir, but he was second in line to Menteith, should the lad not have a son. Someone had set that young man to worrying about the rightful holder of the title.

Might Banquo have set something in play? It was the only reasonable assumption.

Finding that Hyde was out and about and therefore no company, he changed from his regimentals into his third set of clothing, a plain brown frock coat and sober waistcoat, and made his way back to the Star and Garter in Westminster, on the chance that Banquo might appear there nosing about for news of the appointment with Abernathy. His hackney pulled to the side to make way for a contingent of the

Royal Horse Guards making their way to Parliament.

As the taproom filled with patrons, two solicitors' clerks squeezed in at his table and shared the news of the day with him while he ate his beefsteak and washed it down with ale. The parliamentary debates on the Corn Laws had been contentious, but fiercer still had been the voices on the streets around Parliament.

"It was said that Mr. Croker's carriage was set upon by ruffians," the younger of the two men said. "Pulled out of the carriage he was and bludgeoned."

"Aye," the other man said. "But then the miscreants set about fighting each other, and he was able to slip from their grasp and into the Lords' Coffeehouse and from there made his way into the Commons."

The ale in Finnley's pint glass shimmered and darkened. His skin prickled, and an ache made its way up to his head, bringing with it a new vision: a dark-haired woman pulled from a carriage, tossed about by a mob drunk with anger.

Greer.

He rubbed at his forehead, fighting the swoon that threatened.

Where had that image come from, and where was she tonight? Had she gone out? Should he ride out to Chelsea and check on her?

He forced himself back to the present, grounding himself in the conversation, agreeing that the trouble was bound to get worse. Then he settled his bill and made his way through the streets towards Piccadilly. Unable to find a hackney, he went afoot, grateful he'd had the presence of mind to change his attire. While his red coat might bring him help from the soldiers, it wouldn't endear him to the rough crowd sweeping along the streets westward.

Covent Garden was alive this night more so than usual. He passed by the house Banquo had pointed out to him, and wondered if the man was settled in with his favorite ladybird, avoiding the chaos outside.

Hip aching, he managed several hundred yards more and made the turn onto the street where his landlady's house stood quiet and dark. Like many of her neighbors, she'd been fashing about protecting her windows, settling on not boarding them up for now. Upstairs a curtain twitched in the window of his room. Hyde appeared, gesturing wildly.

He hastened his steps, stumbled, righted himself, and turned, just as a cudgel swooped out of nowhere.

Instinct gripped him. He knocked the weapon away, grabbed his attacker's arm, and twisted. With a crack and a yowl, the weapon fell. He had two stones in weight on the man, and he forced the attacker down.

But a flash at his side brought another blow, and this one knocked him squarely atop the first man, who squirmed about, and swung wildly. Finnley rolled away, shielding himself from the second man's kick. As he snatched the man's leg and brought him down, the first attacker jumped up again.

"'Ere now."

That was Hyde's voice, and one set of boots was diverted. But a third ruffian had joined in, and as Finnley got to his knees, the man attacked. Finnley ducked and dodged kick, after kick, after kick to his back, and his shoulders, and his head, some connecting, and one clipping his bad hip, sending him to the ground with a roar.

While Hyde grunted and swore, the clip-clopping of horses and squeaking of wheels grew louder, closer, and then boots pounded the pavement.

"Macbeth." The voice was Menteith's, and it was Finnley's last cogent thought.

CHAPTER SEVEN

Gregory, who had now found more breath cried, "Help an ye be men! Save Lady Emma and her brother, whom they are murdering in Brockenhurst thicket." This put all in motion. Lord Boteler hastily commanded a small party of his men to abide for the defence of the ladies, while he himself

"Lady Fiona."

Greer looked up from her embroidery. Lucie had paused, a finger on the page she was reading, a frown on her face at the interruption by Lady Fiona's butler who had called out his mistress's name in an uncharacteristically breathless manner.

And that lady was already on her feet hurrying to the door.

"Carry him up to a bedchamber." Malcolm's bellow resonated throughout the house. Greer poked her needle in and hurried out to the hall.

"I can walk."

Her heart squeezed and froze and heated, quaking inside her. Finnley hung between his own man and Lady Fiona's footman, fresh red blood staining the white cloth tied around his head.

"Aye, and ye may have to, Major, ye being a great big man, but if'n ye lean on me and her ladyship's footman here, 'twill be easier and 'twill ease the ladies' concerns about ye toppling down the stairs."

Hyde sported a swollen eye and bloody knuckles. Malcolm, too, had a bruise starting upon his jaw.

"Which bedchamber?" the butler asked Lady Fiona.

"Mine," Malcolm said.

"No." Heart pounding fiercely, Greer stepped in front of the men. "Bring him to mine. 'Tis larger than yours, Malcolm. I'll sleep in the maid's chamber when not tending to him. Send up hot water and linens and for a physician."

She beckoned Hyde and made her way up the stairs, leaving Lady Fiona to deal with Malcolm's muttering protests.

The bedchamber Lady Fiona assigned her was not a particularly feminine one. Upon her and Lucie's arrival in Chelsea, Malcolm had removed himself from it to a smaller room. Lucie's bedchamber was even smaller, and on the third floor near what must have once been a nursery and now served as a dormitory for Lady Fiona's small staff of maids.

It was madness perhaps, for her to give Finnley her bed, but who else in this household could tend to him? Not her cousin, her hostess, her daughter, nor any of Lady Fiona's servants. And not his ham-handed man, Hyde, who was himself injured.

She hurriedly pulled back the bedding, plumped the pillows, and fetched spare sheets from the adjoining maid's room, spreading them over the pillows to spare them the blood from Finnley's head wound.

With the two men's help, Finnley dragged himself through the door, grimly silent, clearly in pain. "Settle him on the bed and undress him."

"I don't need my clothes off—"

"Everything, Hyde," she said. "Let the surgeon check him everywhere."

"Greer," he said, grumbling over an added curse.

That he was too weak to protest more meant his injuries might be grave.

While the men stripped him down, she fetched a work smock she'd spotted in the clothespress, perhaps left by some visiting maid. Malcolm entered the bedchamber and sent her a glare.

"'Tis unseemly."

"With his injuries? What do ye think will happen? In any case, Finnley and I were once husband and wife. Were we English, we probably would be still." 'Twas said that divorce was easier in Scotland.

She spotted Lady Fiona in the hall. "Come Malcolm. I would speak with ye and Lady Fiona."

Malcolm followed, biting down on his lip, more like a petulant child than a man of three and twenty, putting her in mind of the young lad he'd once been, appearing in the neighborhood during school holidays.

Lucie came down the corridor, still clutching the copy of Waverley she'd been reading to them.

"What's happened, Mama?"

Greer heard the fear in her girl's voice, and she longed to take her into her arms and comfort her.

But Lucie had always been prickly, more likely to either squirm away from affection, or let the world know she was stoically enduring it.

"Your father has been injured." She touched Lady Fiona's arm. "Do ye object to the arrangement, ma'am?"

The lady's lips hinted at a smile and she shook her head. "'Tis the best course, I think. Our Malcolm wouldn't be much of a nurse. But what happened, Malcolm? Greer and Lucie want to know, and so do I."

"He was set upon outside his lodgings. That's all I can tell ye. There are crowds rioting in town, and it was all I could do to get out of the City. And then, I realized, I was near Piccadilly and Macbeth's lodgings, and I had a thought to invite him to come away from there. Perhaps I should have asked ye first, Aunt, this being your home, but I would have given up my bed if needed. Or I might have lodged him at the Rose and Crown. When I turned onto his street, I saw them. Three men were beating him outside his lodgings. Hyde reached him before I did."

"Were they rioters?" Greer asked.

"Mayhap." He rubbed his head. "Or...I don't know. His lodgings are out of the way, on a side street."

"How did ye know where he lodged?" Greer asked.

He leveled a long look at her. "I had made inquiries."

She remembered the business he'd been about that morning and she let out a long breath. "Did ye meet...the person ye had business with today?"

"No." He pursed his lips together "He didn't appear."

There was more—the long pause told her that. He was holding something back, perhaps because Lucie was studying him intently.

The butler appeared in the corridor and reported that he'd sent a man for the surgeon, and behind him, two footmen were bringing buckets of water. She stepped back and let them pass into the chamber.

Hyde appeared in the doorway, towel in hand. "All stripped down, ma'am," he said. "Shall we take a wet cloth to him?"

She looked at her hands. They were shaking like they'd done the night she'd first laid eyes on Finnley Macbeth. Two years married and twenty years divorced, and he still touched her like no other man ever had.

"No," she said. "I'll do that. Ye'll come with me and hold him down when he tries to act the fool."

"I'm coming as well." Malcolm glared at her.

She threw up her hands. "Fine."

"Me too," Lucie said.

"Lucie," Lady Fiona cautioned, "let your mother and the surgeon see to his wounds, and then you may pay him a visit if he is up to it."

"What if he dies?"

"He won't," Lady Fiona said with certainty. "These wounds won't kill him."

"Please, may I go to him," Lucie said.

"Lucie," Lady Fiona linked arms with her, and led her back to the stairs. "Your father won't want you to see him naked."

Lucie looked over her shoulder, her mouth agape. "But mother—"

"Is his wife," Lady Fiona said.

Is his wife. Not *was*.

Lady Fiona was right. She'd never stopped thinking of Finnley. Perhaps she'd never truly stopped loving him. She didn't want to lose him again.

How foolish was that?

Heart pounding, she sent the footmen away, and went to the bed.

Hyde had removed the head bandage and Finnley lay with a sheet pulled up under his armpits, his chest moving up and down in tight little breaths.

The lean warrior he'd once been had fleshed out in breadth and power. His arms, roped with muscles, bore their own tales of battles, and scars crisscrossed the freckles of his sculpted chest. Red welts mottled both arms and chest, and would soon turn to purple, but aside from a few small scratches and scrapes, the skin was not broken. She swallowed a surge of desire.

Her gaze traveled up and she gasped. His eyes were open and he was watching her.

"Hyde can do whatever it is ye have planned," he said.

"Ye see, Greer," Malcolm said.

Finnley's gaze looked past her shoulder.

"Malcolm," she said. "Ye may leave. Hyde, ye may leave as well."

Finnley let out a breath and winced. "Might as well both go," he spluttered. "Whate'er Greer has planned, I deserve. Fetch her my dirk, Hyde. She can make quick work of me."

Hyde's chuckle broke the tension. She reached for the towel he was holding and dipped it in the bucket. "This water is barely warm. Best put the others near the fire. Malcolm, if ye're insisting on hanging about, make yourself useful."

Finnley's attempt at a smile was more of a grimace, but it eased her heart. "Let's see then what we have here."

***

An hour later—or had it been longer?—the surgeon finished the poking and prodding that men like him relished, and finally departed. It had ever been so with Wellington's staff of sawbones, though considering the stream of injuries they'd treated, it was no wonder they were ham-handed.

While the drop of laudanum settled in, easing his aching self, Greer shooed Hyde and Malcolm out, then pulled a chair close to the bedside.

"Are ye hungry?" she asked.

For you.

The need came unbidden, a flaming desire within him.

He eased in a breath that twanged on the pain and reminded him who he was, what he had done, and what he deserved. And what he deserved wasn't Greer.

Though he was damned well going to go after her.

"Had a beefsteak at the Star earlier."

"That didn't answer my question."

"Surgeon said I wasn't to eat."

She sighed, went to the door, whispered to someone outside, and returned to the chair. "What happened, Finnley?"

He looked up at the rich blue of the canopy, like the rare clear sky of a Scottish summer's day. They'd made love on the heath on a day like that, she lying atop his plaid, he lying atop her. How had he been such a fool?

"Finnley, why did those men attack ye?"

He wrested himself back to the present.

"I don't know any more than what Malcolm and Hyde told ye. One minute I was walking along to my lodgings, and the next I was set upon by three thugs."

"I should like to lay hands on them."

Her fierceness cheered him. "Nay, ye mustn't fash about it."

"Ye're not angry?"

"More like than not, they were part of the mob. Ye may hate an enemy at the start, may even start a war over the hate, but the ones sent to fight, they fight to survive. Fight to end the fighting. This mob, they're hungry."

"Are ye sure that's all it is?"

Her brow was puckered, the look in her eyes thoughtful. Life had made her more wary.

"Did they follow your carriage from the inn where ye dined?" she asked.

"I had to walk. Hacks were all taken or staying away from the troubles I suppose."

"Or they might have thought ye'd be trouble." Her hand covered his.

"Aye." He closed his eyes and let the warmth of her touch seep through his being. "I was worried," he said. "I had a thought to come out and see that ye and Lucie were safe."

A breath escaped her and when he looked, he found her frowning down at him.

"Because of the Sight?"

He squeezed his lips together. He'd not share a vision that might frighten her. "Clearly not, since ye're tending to me and not the other way around. 'Twas only my imagination conflating the riots and…" He cleared his throat, and the effort pained him. "Thoughts of ye."

"Don't try to talk," she said. "He might have been wrong about your ribs."

"He wasn't. I've cracked one before."

She studied him, still holding his hand. Then she got to her feet and reached for the top of the sheet.

He gripped it against his chest. She'd only managed to mop as far as his waist before the surgeon arrived and rescued him.

"Let go, Finnley."

"I'm naked below, Greer, as ye demanded."

Still clutching the sheet and hovering over him, she chewed her luscious lower lip.

In spite of the ache in his head, in spite of the drop of laudanum they'd forced on him, in spite of their troubled past, his privy counsellor was stirring mightily. With a tug, he could bring her atop him.

"I know ye're naked. And ye're injured. And I want to have my own look. Let loose of the sheet."

"Nothing below has changed in the last twenty years."

"No?"

"'Cept more shriveled from lack of use," he teased.

Her lips quirked. "I'm to believe that?" She yanked hard, the movement so sudden he gave way. Her gaze went straight to the part of him that wanted more than a look, so much so, it twitched.

Greer huffed and flashed him a shocked look, her mouth softening, her eyes darkening to midnight blue.

He was lost. She was his. She must be his. There'd never be another woman for him, even the beastly parts of him knew that.

She tossed the covers to his feet and plopped down on the side of the bed, startling him. When he reached for her, she dodged the attempt, settling a finger into the gash on his hip.

Buried wrath flared in him and he squeezed his eyes tight on the memory. Not visions, but sights, smells, sounds seared into his brain. Men's screams, gunpowder blasting. He'd come through the gates of a burning castile and...pain, sudden and sleek.

Despite that, the Frenchman who'd butchered three men before dealing that blow had paid for his sins with his life.

"Leave it," he said, breathless.

"This is the cause of your limp?"

"Yes."

"It's beginning to bruise. Tonight, did they strike ye here?"

"Aye."

"So, they knew."

He closed his eyes, trying to remember. "'Twas a matter of chance. A random blow."

"The vile bas—" She puffed out a breath. "I'd know who they were."

He traced a finger along her jaw. "They were no one, *mo chridhe*, just part of the angry crowd striking out blindly. Ye'll not find them."

With a long, heated look, she rested her palm gently on the old wound.

Desire reared in him again. He covered her hand with his own. "Are we to be alone then, for the rest of the night?" he whispered.

A tap at the door gave him his answer. She pulled her hand away and fumbled with the sheet and counterpane, covering him up to his armpits again.

Lucie entered, followed by a footman carrying a laden tray.

"Just in time," Greer whispered.

Her nervous smile, so like the one she bestowed the very first day they met made his heart soar. She'd been as tempted as himself.

"Are ye able to sit up, Finnley?" she asked. "Come, I'll plump the pillows behind ye."

This was said loudly, in a voice of command. He'd best do as he was told.

He grunted his way up, while she fussed with the bedding. "Lucie, girl," he said, "throw me my shirt will ye, and stay turned away whilst I don it."

"There's no need." Lucie carried over a bowl and took the chair Greer had vacated. "I'm not some silly child. I've seen men without shirts before."

"Is that so? And how did that come about, may I ask?"

"'Twas nothing improper. On a hot day, men working the fields or chopping wood sometimes shed their shirts. Or, in the smithy with all the fires going, men go shirtless. Or when lads go for a dip in the burn, a girl might stand in the bushes and watch."

"Lucie," Greer cried.

"I take it ye never averted your gaze?" he teased.

The lass slid him a sly smile. "Of course not. I was curious. I'd heard whispers about..." Her cheeks colored prettily, and she lifted her shoulder in a defiant shrug. "Men padding their coats. I wanted to see what a man...er...a man's chest looks like. How else am I to know anything if I don't take advantage?"

"Ye're not supposed to know any of those things until ye're a married lady," Greer said.

Lucie scoffed. "I don't suppose ye have to pad your coats, sir?"

A laugh bubbled up, but Greer's motherly frown made him swallow it. "Mayhap a bit of padding would stop a blade."

Lucie frowned, considering. "Mayhap so. And I know, ye're teasing me. Will ye feed yourself, or would ye like me to hold the spoon for ye?"

He sniffed at the bowl. "What is it?"

She scrunched her nose. "Beef tea. The surgeon said it would build your blood back. But I've also brought ye biscuits and some cheese. And whisky."

"Wheest," he said, "I'm not a silly child either. Hand me the bowl and then go fetch me a glass of Lady Fiona's whisky."

She gave him a glowing smile, one that made her look far younger than her years, like the mischievous little girl she must have been, and perhaps still was. She seemed both wise, and innocent, his girl, and she surprised him by doing as she was told.

Sudden moisture pricked his eyes, and he blinked. What a handful of a chit she must have been for her mother. How had Greer managed it?

Had Lucie got up to aught else with those naked lads in the burn? Somehow, he didn't think so. His Lucie didn't seem the sort to be easily taken in, or to give herself away for nothing.

The mattress sank, and he found Greer perched next to him, her gaze soft.

"One for ye, as well, Mama," Lucie said, handing them each a glass.

He juggled his bowl and tipped back the glass.

"Mother," Lucie said. "I should like some time alone with Father."

Greer's chin came up. "He needs to rest."

"Please, Mama. I won't harm him. If he wishes, if I'm boring him too much, he may fall asleep whilst I'm talking and I promise to not be offended." She patted his hand and winked. "Ye need to rest as well, Mama. Ye can come back later."

His daughter wished time alone with him. The thought both stirred his heart and terrified him.

He'd abandoned her and her mother. He'd run away, leaving Highland society to name her a bastard. If she wanted to harm him, he deserved it.

As much as he wanted to claim Greer again, he must also make peace with this daughter of his blood. She must know she already had a home in his heart, had been firmly ensconced there since the moment he came back to his senses on Lady Fiona's drawing room floor and heard her whisper *It's him, isn't it, Mama?*

"'Tis a good idea, Greer, for ye to rest as well. I'm sure our Lucie here will have me yawning in no time, and both ye and I may have a good sleep."

Greer sent the girl a long look, nodded, said "Very well," and slipped out the door to the corridor.

Lucie watched her go and frowned. "Her dressing room is that door," she said, pointing. "She isn't going to rest. I wonder what she's about?"

CHAPTER EIGHT

"Perhaps your mother is hungry," Finnley said.

"We had an ample dinner." Lucie frowned, puzzling out a mystery of her own creation.

What must it have been like, raising this girl?

"When ye question her later," he said, "I'll thank ye to let me know what ye learn."

She turned the thoughtful expression on him, studying him a long time, and then she smiled.

Moisture constricted his throat and threatened to spill from his eyes, as if he were the silly child he claimed not to be. He rested the bowl in his lap, and reached for her hand.

"I am sorry, *mo chridhe*. I'm sorry I wasn't there for your growing up. Will ye tell me about it?"

She chewed her lower lip in an unladylike way, fetched the decanter of whisky and Greer's discarded glass, and filled both glasses again.

"*Sláinte*," she said, touching his glass.

He watched while she sipped. It was daintily done, and eased his worries she might be taking up excessive drink at her young age.

"We lived with Aunt Naughton and her son and daughter. And it was wretched, or would have been had I not had a friend in my long-time nursemaid."

He struggled to sit up. The whisky had cleared his head whilst dulling the pain in his body a bit more. The pains in his heart jabbed more fiercely, but he deserved those.

He handed her the empty bowl. "Will ye take this?" She carried it away, without comment or complaint.

'Twas chilled in the room, the fire dying down. Never mind. He deserved any discomfort that came his way, and in any case, 'twas warmer than any night spent chasing the French through the mountains of Spain.

But Lucie shouldn't have to put up with the cold. "Stir the fire, will ye, Lucie, and fetch a shawl for yourself."

Again, she did as she was told, surprisingly compliant. She carried over a shawl, and also a banyan someone had left for his use, draping it over his shoulders, so close he could smell the clean scent of her.

She was a comely girl, and with her fiery hair, she'd have the men panting for her. Perhaps already did.

With the exception of Malcolm, who'd been protective of Lucie, and not a bit interested in her the other way. How had that brotherly closeness come about?

"I'd know it all," he said. "Tell me."

He leaned back against the pillows and listened, shame and anger chasing each other around in his head and his heart as the story unfolded. They'd had a roof, and food, and clothing, and kin who demeaned and belittled the both of them, his Greer and Lucie.

"When the news came that my aunt and cousin's coach overturned and they'd all died..." Lucie's mouth firmed. "I didn't grieve, Father. I rejoiced. Mother scolded me, but not as harshly as usual. 'Twas...oh. Ye canna imagine. Men started sniffing around the both of us...tradesmen carrying Cousin Naughton's debts; gentry, both married men and bachelors, some hinting at marriage, others offering... Well, she didn't tell me all, but I found out. The debts, ye see, were stupendous. Oh yes, we were always comfortable, but much of it was on Mama's money and the rent from Castle Macbeth. Cousin Naughton had leased it, ye see."

She bit her lip, lost in thought. He waited.

"But very soon, Malcolm's father sent for us, and it was never like that with him. He wheeled himself around in a Bath chair, all shriveled and old, yet he was cheerful and kind. Malcolm has always been a grump, but that is his nature, I think. Lord Menteith settled us into a cottage on his estate, made it known to the world that we were under his protection. His factor helped Mama evict the tenants. The castle and farms are in good order now. Ye're coming home now are ye not?"

Finnley thought of his meeting with Abernathy that day. How could he traipse about the world when his Lucie wanted him to come home?

Would her mother feel as welcoming?

"The castle is your mother's to hold now. I gave her full use of it when we divorced."

She favored him with a long look. "Then ye must put your mind to winning it back."

He sat up, opening his arms. "Lucie, Lucie," he said. "*Mo chridhe.*"

She fell into his embrace, and allowed him to hold her, burying her face in his shoulder and shaking with what surely were silent sobs.

***

Greer slipped out through the door of the bedchamber, nodded to the footman who popped up from his chair, and made her way down the corridor.

She might not be gifted with the Sight, but she felt certain all the way to her bones that Finnley's battering had been no act of the mob. It had been a direct attack.

'Twas no mere woman's intuition either, at least not entirely. The back-and-forth between Finnley and Banquo, the mysterious threat received by Malcolm, and the prophecy recounted by Lady Fiona led to one logical conclusion.

She found Lady Fiona and Malcolm in the drawing room, heads bent together over a piece of foolscap spread out on the table between them.

The lady looked up first. "How is he?"

"In good spirits. Lucie is with him."

Malcolm stood. "Perhaps I should—"

"Leave them," Greer said. "They are rubbing along famously, and I would speak with ye, Malcolm."

As she drew closer, and took a seat, she had a better look at his face in the light. He looked pale, drawn. As if, besides the night's troubles, he'd just received news of a death. She glanced at the paper. It looked like a legal document of some sort, witnessed and sealed at the bottom. From this distance the writing was indecipherable. He folded the paper and stuffed it into his waistcoat.

"Are ye well, Malcolm?" The bruise on his jaw stood out in stark relief against his pale skin and a fresh white neck cloth. "Did the surgeon examine that injury?"

He grimaced and shook his head. "'Twas only a glancing blow. I didn't require medical care."

"He did examine Malcolm," Lady Fiona said, "as well as Macbeth's man. Shall I ring for some tea, my dear? Though I imagine most of the staff have gone off to their beds."

"No, I wouldn't disturb them."

"Well, you might have a long night. I've asked the butler to keep a man at the ready by the bedchamber door."

"He's still there, and awake."

"Good. Don't hesitate to call on him. He can rouse the kitchen boy to fetch anything you need."

"I'd not put any more burdens on your servants, ma'am. They've been very kind."

"Nonsense. Most of the time they have only one old woman to look after. What they are is very spoiled." She stood. "Now, I'm for bed."

Malcolm got to his feet again. The lady pressed a hand to his cheek, and dropped a kiss on the other one, making him blush.

"You're a good lad. All will be well in the end."

Her smile, when it came, seemed troubled.

"Good night, Lady Fiona," Malcolm said. "I am ever in your debt."

"Nonsense. Good night, Greer."

She left, her usual wobbling step a bit heavier.

Greer watched as Malcolm began to pace. "I will ask ye again, Malcolm: are ye well?"

He dipped his head. "I am. Shall I go now and relieve Lucie?"

"No. I think ye ought to retire as well, but I'd speak with ye first." She took in a deep breath. "I've been thinking."

He looked at her, his gaze shuttered, and said nothing.

"The letter ye received questioning your right to the title. Ye don't believe Finnley sent it—nor do I. He's not the sort of man to sneak around sending letters and making insinuations. On the other hand, from what Lady Fiona told me about the witch's prophecy, Banquo might believe his son will be Earl of Menteith. He might believe he himself ought to have the title first. If something were to happen to ye, or if your claim were invalidated..." She drew in a breath, a sudden thought coming to her. If legal means proved ineffective against Malcolm's hold on the title, the only other way to divest him would be his death. He might be in danger, as well.

She rose and went to him, determined to stay the course tonight and get answers. "If your claim to the title were invalidated, who would be next in line?"

She knew the answer of course, but she wanted to remind him.

He grimaced. "Macbeth."

"Might it have been something other than happenstance that Finnley was attacked? Might it have been purposeful?"

"It's a thought Lady Fiona and I have pondered." He rubbed his head. "But Macbeth and Banquo are on friendly terms. He's been seen with Banquo more than once, and the man organized an appointment for him with Sir Thomas Abernathy, a man from the Home Office. Ye remember Macbeth is seeking a position?

Banquo is helping him, not the action of a man trying to kill him."

He paced to the curtained window and back. "Banquo is oily, I'll grant ye, and I didn't like the way he was pawing at Lucie, but hiring thugs to murder his cousin all on the sly? I don't think he'd go that far."

"Hmm. What does Lady Fiona say?"

"About Banquo?" He looked away. "Nothing."

Greer recognized a dodge when she saw one. The lady had said something about Banquo, she was certain.

Malcolm might be more forthcoming on the morrow, after a chance to mull over whate'er was bothering him and a good night's sleep. The rest of her questions would bide until then.

And she would approach Lady Fiona tomorrow as well.

"Malcolm, ye've been a good friend to me and like a brother to Lucie. If there's ever aught that you need, ye must tell us. Call on us, and we will be there."

Irritation flashed across his face. For all that he was a man grown, he could sometimes be so much like a child—like her own child. She'd seen that prickly look often on Lucie's face, too, in response to an offer of kindness.

Dear God. Was she so old? She wasn't yet forty. And she didn't feel a day over twenty when Finnley looked at her.

Parts of her that had been dead for years stirred. She eased in a breath, trying to tamp down a building excitement. Best not let Malcolm sense what she was imagining with the man in her bed.

"I'll return to my nursing duties. As for yourself, ye've had a full day. Whatever the trouble is, it will look better in the morning." She hoped that was true.

He wished her a good night. Taking one of the candles for light, she made her way up the dark stairs.

Malcolm was too caught up in his own troubles to take her suspicions about Banquo to heart. What Lady Fiona thought was entirely a cipher. Perhaps neither distrusted Banquo as much as she herself did.

Perhaps they were right. What was one to think? If Finnley had the Sight, as Lady Fiona believed, and doubted himself, how could a woman relying on feminine intuition be certain?

She'd talk to her hostess and cousin again in the morn, and if they wouldn't help, there was naught for it but to seek out Banquo herself and learn what he was up to.

The corridor was quiet, the oil lamp burning low, and the footman, poor tired devil, had dropped off and didn't stir until she turned the latch and the door creaked.

When he shot to his feet, she put a finger to her lips and quietly entered. A candle gleamed on the far bedside table and the corner bedpost hangings obscured everything else. She closed the door and went to the foot of the bed.

Finnley lay back, a banyan covering his shoulders and wadded up under his back. Next to him, atop the counterpane, Lucie lay huddled in a shawl, her book sitting open upon her chest, her head nestled upon Finnley's shoulder.

Both were fast asleep...or...

Finnley's eyes shot open, his mouth grim, until he blinked and his lips relaxed into a smile.

Greer went to the side of the bed and touched Lucie's shoulder. "Lucie," she hissed.

"She was reading to me and we both fell out. The girl's all done in."

"And she sleeps like a rock."

"Leave her here," he said. "I'll find a blanket and head for that soft carpet in Lady Fiona's drawing room."

"Nay. Ye need to rest in a warm bed and recover." She set a palm to her daughter's head, watching her stir, her heart warming. In sleep, Lucie appeared ever the angel. Awake was a different matter. "'Tis unseemly for her to be falling asleep next to ye, ye know, as grown as she is."

"Ye sound like Malcolm now," he whispered. "Don't fret, Greer. I'd not lay a hand in any way on the lass." Eyes shining, he turned a fond gaze on the girl, blinking.

Greer's heart twisted and warmed with conflicting emotions. Could she trust Finnley to stay? Would he be a father to Lucie or run off to fight somewhere?

Did it matter? Lucie wasn't a child any longer, except in her mother's heart. She was a woman and ought to be thinking about marrying. If only they could find a worthy man.

It took much prodding and shaking to wake her, and when they did, she sat up, looking around, puzzled.

And unsurprisingly grumpy.

"Why did ye wake me? I was comfortable and warm." She tilted her head and grimaced. "Except for this crick in my neck."

"Off to bed with ye," Greer said. "Wish your father good night and take my candle. And no loitering about sending the footman on errands.

Let him sleep. The lad will have a full day of work ahead of him tomorrow."

Grumbling, Lucie closed her book and slipped into her shoes. "Good night, father," she said. "Would that ye had a bit of that padding we talked about on your shoulder."

He laughed. "I'll tell Hyde to see to it. Goodnight lass, and thank ye for reading to me. I'll hear more of that story another time."

"Tomorrow."

He nodded. "Mayhap. But if not tomorrow, then another time, be sure of it."

Lucie quirked a lip and would have gone on, but Greer shooed her out. She closed the door carefully and looked at the key set into the lock.

"Turn it." Finnley's voice came from the dark bed, gruff and dangerous. "And come here."

She pressed a hand to her breast and squeezed her eyes shut, trying desperately to contain a wild rush of feeling. *Remember*, her good sense cautioned, *remember he hurt ye, he left ye*.

She grasped for the memories, seeking the pricks that had wounded, and found only heat, all the sharp dagger points melted to shiny desire.

He is her husband, Lady Fiona had said. The bonds of their marriage had been fragile; the bonds of fate, the bonds of the heart, those were not so easily broken.

Hand shaking, she turned the key and crossed to the bed, hugging the fearful trembling inside her.

He stretched out his arm and opened his hand, and she set her palm to his.

***

Framed in the candlelight, there was no lovelier vision then this woman he'd loved all his grown life. Even when he'd hated her, he'd done so with a passion, and a sorrow, and a grief that could only have been born in and sustained by love. He'd been such a fool. He would make this right.

"*Mo chridhe*," he whispered. "Greer." His throat thickened, and he cleared it. "Lay with me tonight. We need do no more than sleep."

She raised an eyebrow and scoffed.

He laughed, glad she had lightened the mood.

"Go then. Change into your nightclothes and decide what ye wish. I am here behind a locked door and with a footman guarding it outside. I'm your captive, and ye may do with me as ye desire."

"And the key is on your side, and the young man an easy match for a warrior, even an injured one."

"Aye. Yet I'll be here. And I'm feeling much better." The next move must be hers. Except...

He tugged her close, captured her neck, and stole a quick kiss. Then he tossed away the banyan and threw back the covers, bare-arsed as the day he was born.

Greer froze to the spot, only her hands twisting together beneath her beautiful bosom.

Biting his lip against the soreness in his bruised body, he hoisted himself to the side of the bed and stood before her in all his glorious nakedness.

She blinked. Her mouth opened, and closed, and then opened again. "Ye'll rest and recover," she said. "Ye're not leaving. I'll hide your coats."

Lightheaded he might be, but the breathlessness in her voice roused that part of him that promised to carry on. If she would let him.

She needed to choose, and she needed a few moments of time for that. After all, it had been twenty years.

And truth to tell, he needed to piss. He might have told the old Greer that with honesty, and she would have laughed her earthy laugh, a lass who would let a man be a man. The new Greer, he couldn't be sure about.

He cradled her face in his palm, and she closed her eyes with a look that said she was savoring his touch.

"I need the privy," he said, "or the chamber pot will do. I didna wish to bother Lucie with it. Nor yourself, 'tis a fact."

She sighed, and then laughed the laugh that warmed him to the soles of his feet. Disentangling herself, she fetched the chamber pot, and then hastened out through the door that Lucie had pointed out earlier.

He must put his mind to winning *it* back, Lucie had said. But he knew what she'd meant. He must put his mind to winning back her mother.

He'd mulled over Lucie's advice, whilst the lass read to him from the novel he'd bought her. An engaging adventure, the story was, but not engaging enough. He'd been lost in the closeness of his girl, and the cadence of her voice, and the way she relished the tale, all of those exciting his heart more than the book itself. He'd closed his eyes wondering what it would have been like, him seated on the coverlet next to her in the nursery reading her stories at bed time, wondering how he could go about winning her mother's heart back and return home.

For the castle was no home without the beating heart of a loving woman. He'd learned that watching his father thrash about after his mother's death. Theirs had been a true love, damaged by the loss of one bairn after another, and finally, fatally marred by the loss of their only remaining daughter birthing a babe who would never have been conceived if they'd all been more vigilant, if Charmaine hadn't been so headstrong. Lucie had just as much stubbornness as his late sister. Now that he knew she was his, he must look after her.

He found the discarded banyan, struggled into it, and sat down at the table set up near the fire. The food Lucie had fetched for him lay on the tray next to the empty bowl. He picked up a hunk of cheese and chewed, remembering the way she'd wrinkled her nose over the beef tea.

Tears welled in his eyes, and he wiped at them, cursing his surge of unmanliness. What a damned foolish, blockheaded Scotsman he'd been. Even if Lucie hadn't been his blood, he ought to have been there when she was born. She'd have still claimed a place in his heart, from the very first moment she opened her toothless mouth to howl at him. And she'd have still been the child of the woman who'd owned him, body and soul since the moment they'd met.

He wanted Greer, he wanted her to be his, for the rest of his life, no matter how short or how sorry it might be.

He must go about it the right way, though. She must see him in all his nakedness, with all his wounds, and she must decide.

As the fire dimmed, and the moments ticked on, he waited. No noise came through the stout dressing room door.

She wasn't coming. Heart sinking, he pushed to his feet.

The latch rattled and a draft of cool lavender wafted his way, drawing him around. He gripped the back of the chair as time melted away and carried him back twenty years.

The dress—and, praise God—the corset, were gone. She stood in a lacy transparent shift, her dressing gown loose and untied, her feet bare, and her hair... her hair was unbound, rich tendrils reaching to tease the peaks of her breasts.

Blood pounded into his arms and his legs and his loins, screaming *Take her*.

He breathed, struggling for control. *Consequences, Macbeth*. 'Twas a discipline he'd pressed into his men, sometimes with the lash when nothing else would restore self-restraint. A woman, any woman deserved better than to be taken unwillingly. And Greer...Greer was much, much more than any woman.

"Greer," he said, searching for breath. "*Tha thu brèagha mo ghaol.*"

CHAPTER NINE

Tha thu brèagha mo ghaol.

Greer's hands tightened at her waist, her emotions a jumble. *You are beautiful, my love,* he'd said.

And but look at him, stretching the shoulders of the generously sized dressing gown, his hair in those wild flaming tangles of waves she remembered, falling all the way to his broad, muscled shoulders. In the light of the table lamp, she could see also his whiskers coming in, glistening like the hair on his muscled chest visible in the vee of the gaping banyan.

And his eyes...his eyes glowed a dark, compelling bronze. Heat leapt in her, unfurling long-repressed needs.

"*Mo ghaol,*" she said, her heart beating wildly, sudden shyness holding her back.

Finnley had ever been eager. Why didn't he come to her now?

Her gaze traveled over him, and she spotted his hands, gripping the chair back, the knuckles white and crisscrossed with scars. He loosened one hand and reached out to her.

"I am here," he said.

I am here. Simply that. He expected her to capitulate even more, and come to him.

Or...he was tempting her fiercely and letting her choose.

"For how long?"

He blinked. "How long do ye wish me to stay?"

The hand beckoning her was steady and strong, the pull of desire, his and her own, even stronger. She would have him tonight, him, the only man she'd ever made love to. The only man she'd ever loved.

"Ye must stay tonight, certainly," she said briskly, "and perhaps tomorrow night as well if the surgeon requires it."

The slow smile, the intense gaze, reached through her and squeezed her heart. "Greer," he said.

Heart pounding, she went to him and slipped under his arm. "Let me help ye back into bed."

In a flash, he scooped her up and juggled her, grunting. "*Mo ghaol*," he said, nuzzling her cheek. "Ye smell like springtime."

She smoothed a hand down his bristly cheek, unable to speak. He smelled of the lemony soap Lady Fiona kept for the washstand, and the faint manly musk that was his alone.

His breath rasped carrying her, and then her bottom touched the mattress, and her dressing gown disappeared, along with his banyan.

"Greer."

He knelt before her, his big hands cupping her shoulders, moving down her arms, touching, measuring, and inflaming, moving up again, bracketing her chest under her armpits and then sliding down, his thumbs tracing the sides of her breasts, gliding along her belly, down her hips, and along her legs all the way to her feet.

He cradled one foot and dropped a kiss on the top of it, and then repeated the move with the other.

Eyes squeezed shut, she held back the desire threatening to burst her apart.

She lifted his chin and brought her lips to his, touching, nibbling, and then angling her head for an open-mouthed kiss.

While his lips and tongue worked, his hands traced their way from her feet, up her legs again. Cold air touched her thighs and she broke away to look. He'd raised the lacy hem of her nightgown, his thumbs circling the insides of her thighs.

His gaze went to the dark hair of her center, and then he raised his eyes to meet hers.

He was naked, his skin glistening with heat, his shaft...

She sucked in a breath, scooted the nightgown from under her, and yanked it over her head.

"*Tha thu brèagha*, Greer," he said. "*Mo ghaol.*" He nibbled one breast. "*Mo chridhe,*" he said to the other one, like an incantation.

"Come," she said, preparing to swing her legs up.

"No." His hands framed her hips and stayed her. "Lie back, love." He set a palm to her shoulder and gently urged her.

"I want ye."

"And ye shall have me. In a moment." His gaze raked her, his fingers touching, caressing, persuading.

She sighed and surrendered.

***

Finnley steadied his breath and ogled the feast laid before him, moving his hands to grip the edge of the mattress.

He'd been years without a woman, and the few he'd had after Greer had never meant more than mutual release. Lovely, they'd been, but Greer... In the twenty years they'd been apart she'd grown into the lushness of full womanhood in her breasts, belly and hips. He wanted her again, and again, and again, like the night of their wedding. He might be that lusty young groom once more, so great was his desire.

First, he must see her satisfied.

He pressed his lips to the slight swell of her belly, where tiny wrinkles betrayed that her womb had nurtured his child.

Consequences, Macbeth.

Desire surged in him, and he steadied himself, counting to ten. He might plant a seed again. He wanted that. He wanted her. He would marry her again, no matter what.

She rustled herself up, bracing herself onto her elbows. "Are your wounds paining you?"

What a sight she was.

'Twas not the night's wounds paining him, but his balls aching for release. "'Tis only me mastering my hunger for ye." And he would suffer the wait.

"Ye don't need to...."

He lifted her legs over his shoulders.

"Oh..." She laughed, breathless.

His lips touched her there in her womanly center, tasting, touching, until her gasps turned to a soft keen of pleasure.

Then he gathered her into his arms and she backed onto the bed, pulled him over her, welcoming him.

"Greer," he breathed, entering her. "Greer."

She clasped him to her, raised her hips, and then they moved in the dance neither of them had forgotten.

He awoke and the lamp still gleamed brightly, the oil not burned down yet. Greer lifted her head, her eyes still burning a molten blue.

"Ye fainted again," she said.

He laughed. "Mayhap I've died and gone to heaven."

She wrinkled her nose. "We are both alive."

"Are we? Then why have I awakened with an angel in my arms?"

Laughing, she walked her fingers down his chest, and lower, raising that part of him from its collapse.

"Come here." He drew her close again.

Thursday, 9 March, 1815

Greer awoke to the feel of a hand stroking her back and opened her eyes to find bright light streaming into the room.

And someone was tapping at the door.

"Mother?" Lucie called. "Father? Are ye all right? The door is locked, and the dressing room door as well."

Greer sat up. Finnley grinned at her and pulled her down, smacking a kiss on her lips. "All is well, Lucie," he called. "Your mother is dressing."

"Oh, ye rascal," Greer murmured.

She rolled to the side, stood, and tucked the covers about him, conscious of his eyes moving over her. "None of that. I'll send Hyde to ye after I'm dressed."

She gathered her discarded nightclothes, rushed to the dressing room and hurriedly washed, dressed, and pinned up her hair. A bath would have been glorious, but a request for a tub and hot water would also have signaled to the whole household what she and Finnley had been up to. For now, she'd rather keep their intimacy private.

When she walked back through the connecting door to the bedchamber, Finnley lay back with his eyes closed. In the light of day, the bruises on his chest and face stood out in stark relief, and she felt a sudden wash of guilt.

He opened his eyes and smiled again.

"Ye look done in," she said. "Are your injuries—"

"Don't fash about these bruises. They're nothing, and I've no thoughts of pain when I think of last night," he said, sitting up. "Though I am hungry. I'll dress and come down and perhaps Lady Fiona will deign to offer me breakfast."

"Your breakfast will come to ye. Ye'll stay in this bed and heal." She didn't wait to hear his response.

Outside the chamber, the footman rose. 'Twas a different young man than the one who'd kept guard the night before. She felt her cheeks warm, hoping the doors had been thick enough to keep their coupling private.

She sent the footman off to fetch Hyde, and made her way to the breakfast room.

Lucie looked up from the news sheet she was perusing. "Ye locked the bedchamber door."

Greer glanced at the footman on duty. Yet a different one, and he was pretending not to have heard.

She went to the sideboard, filled a plate with toast, and sent the footman off for fresh eggs before returning to her seat.

"Your father didn't need ye or anyone else intruding on his slumber."

"Hmm." Lucie smiled and returned to the paper she held.

Greer's heart pounded, heat rising in her cheeks again. That smile had been a sly one, almost a smirk, and she was grateful her stubborn daughter—who apparently was not as ignorant of carnal matters as she'd thought—had dropped that line of questioning.

"Is Malcolm about?" Greer asked.

"Nay."

"Lady Fiona?"

"Her neither."

"I suppose it's too early for Lady Fiona." The lady wasn't usually an early riser, and she'd been up late speaking with Malcolm.

Greer bit into her toast.

"She's gone away for a day and a night." Lucie passed her a note. "Perhaps two nights. She told me to give ye this."

Greer unfolded the paper—clearly Lucie had read it already.

Lady Fiona wrote that she'd been required to visit a friend in Brighton on some emergent business. The butler and housekeeper had been informed, and Greer was to avail herself of everything the household had to offer. The surgeon would return later in the day to see to Macbeth's injuries. She'd fetched a post chaise from the inn, so Greer might make herself free with the carriage as well, but Lady Fiona cautioned her to be careful about venturing into town because of the unruly crowds.

"What is the news from town?" she asked Lucie.

"'Tis no wonder Father was beaten," Lucie said. "The military was called out in the evening to quell the rioting near Parliament. Then the mob moved to the homes of the men who proposed and supported the Corn Laws. At Mr. Robinson's— here's what is says exactly, Mama: 'they broke the windows in every floor, demolished the parlor shutters, and split the doors into pieces. Rushing into the house they then cut to pieces many valuable pictures, destroying some of the larger pieces of furniture, and threw the rest into the street.' Imagine? Only the arrival of the Guard prevented the rioters from lynching the Lord Chancellor."

The footman entered quietly, carrying a covered dish with the eggs, followed by the butler who delivered two letters.

"For me?" The only letter Greer had received since her arrival had been from her factor. She wasn't expecting to hear from him again until the end of the month, after Lady Day, when he'd have news of the quarterly accounts. A letter arriving sooner would bode ill.

Lucie rose, and tucked the newssheet under the letters. "Those will be invitations arranged by Lady Fiona. I do look forward to someday being able to attend something more exciting than tea with an elderly neighbor. Perhaps before I reach my majority."

The last was said with raised eyebrows.

"Your cousin has been making acquaintances at his clubs, and Lady Fiona has been writing to people she knows, quality people with good connections. And she is planning a Venetian breakfast party when the weather is better, after

Easter. Ye must be patient. Where are ye off to now?"

"To see Father."

"Let Hyde attend to his shave before bothering him."

Lucie pulled a face and flounced off.

Greer scanned the newssheet, set it aside, and picked up the letters. One was from Malcolm—she recognized his terse and very legible hand. The writing on the second letter was just as masculine, yet unfamiliar; certainly not her factor's.

Malcolm had sealed his letter. That was interesting, but then, he must have wanted to safeguard it from Lucie's prying eyes.

She snapped the seal and unfolded the missive.

Dear Cousin,

I have urgent business to attend to that may require my absence for several days or perhaps longer. As this business involves the matter we discussed earlier, you will appreciate me not sharing more detail in writing. I am grateful for your kind offers of assistance made last night, but it is a matter I must handle alone.

I do hope that Macbeth may be a suitable escort for you and Lucie, so that you may go about once the army has settled the turmoil in the city. I have written to two of my friends and asked them to facilitate his membership in my club. I've left a note for him with the details.

Please convey my apologies to Lucie. I know that I have promised to help arrange the sort of introductions that would help her appear in society. Lady Fiona assures me she will continue to make efforts in that regard. Perhaps Macbeth will be able to help as well.

I've also written to my man of business so that he may take care of any of your and Lucie's expenses. It is the least I might do for you.
As ever,
Menteith.

Malcolm was gone?

And, more amazingly, he was offering to take care of any of her expenses? Since Duncan died, she hadn't received a farthing from Malcolm, nor had she asked for any.

She looked at her plate of eggs, now going cold. The footman had made a special trip for them, and though Lady Fiona had assured her of her welcome, she felt a duty to be gracious to the lady's staff.

Plus, after the night's exertions she was hungry. She raised a forkful of egg, thinking. Where had Malcolm gone off to? It had something to do with the document he'd stuffed into his waistcoat the night before.

And Lady Fiona was gone as well? This was most strange, and likely not unrelated.

She remembered the second letter and opened it, scanning the flowery language of the note inviting her to a rout that night, her spirits rising.

Until she reached the signature. It was from Giles Banquo.

CHAPTER TEN

Finnley had just dropped back to sleep when the door opened and a train of servants bustled in. One man carried a covered tray. The next cleared and carried away the tray and dishes from the previous night. A third brought two buckets of steaming water, and the fourth, a housemaid, clutched a stack of folded linens.

Last of all came his man, Hyde, holding a slim black case, and ordering the others around like a majordomo.

Hyde's eye sported a purple bruise, but otherwise he looked hale and hearty. He'd also availed himself of fresh linens, wash water, and a razor.

When the door closed on the others, he dropped the black case on the washstand and carried the banyan over.

"Wheest," he said. "I could be very used to this."

Macbeth chuckled.

"Shall ye eat at the table, sir, or at a tray on the bed? Given the exertions of last night—"

"Watch yourself, man." Finnley pushed back the covers, stood, and slipped the banyan on.

"Shall we be moving our lodgings to this fine establishment, Major?"

"Ye'll be moving your lodgings far away from mine soon, Hyde, if ye keep on this topic."

Hyde grinned, and went to lift the covers off the dishes. The scent of eggs and onions, kippers and bacon, fresh rolls and butter, and strong coffee drew him.

"A fine cook, her ladyship employs. Keeps a good larder as well."

He grunted and tore into his food. He'd had too many days of poor rations to pass on a good meal. Somehow, he would have to repay Lady Fiona for her hospitality. Difficult for a man with no home and limited funds, but there must be some task the lady would need done.

Hyde went to the washstand and took out a razor, checking the blade on a newssheet. He poured out hot water and began lathering the shaving soap.

"The butler loaned me the razor. A fine one, it is."

"I hope ye sharpened it after ye used it."

"I did," he said cheerfully.

"Is that the newspaper?"

"Yesterday's. Today's is in the breakfast room. Though the butler read it first while he was pressing it."

Hyde wore the cagey look that meant he had something juicy to share.

"I take it ye were made welcome again below stairs."

"Aye."

"How is your eye?"

Hyde chuckled. "Naught wrong with it that a few days won't heal. Are ye well, Major?"

"Yes. Now would ye like to tell me today's news?"

Hyde's brow furrowed as he applied a hot towel. "Ye were lucky last night that his lordship came along with his carriage."

While he removed the towel, lathered his master's cheeks and shaved off his whiskers, Hyde reported the news the butler had shared with the staff.

"The Horse Guards were called out," Hyde said, draping him with another steaming towel. "Makes me want to grab my rifle. Been a while since we had a good fight. Last night didn't count."

Eyes closed, he let the heat seep in. For a man who'd been forced into fighting, Hyde had a soldier's heart. As did he. But this fight... People were hungry and likely to get hungrier when corn was scarce and the prices high. Which side deserved his sword?

He didn't have to ask himself that question. He'd sworn to serve the Crown, and so he would.

He pulled off the towel and wiped his face.

"This came for ye." Hyde handed him a letter.

Who the devil would write to him here? He cracked the seal.

The letter was from young Menteith. He'd been called away on business, but had arranged introductions with two friends from his club who offered to recommend him for membership in Malcolm's absence. The lad hoped he could make influential contacts that would help him find the position he sought as well as help Lucie find her way in society. He promised to stand any membership cost beyond Finnley's means.

Damn, but it was generous of the young man. Suspiciously so.

He rubbed his freshly shaved chin. Instinct told him it had to do with the lad's concern over rights to the title. For his own sake, he'd not take charity to join White's club; but for Lucie's...

And then there was the matter of these riots. He'd seen more hungry people in the Peninsula than he'd ever want to encounter again. As a mere Scottish baron, he had no place in the English Lords. But at White's, he might have a chance to drop some sense into the ears of men with more power.

Hyde stowed the razor and returned with a hairbrush.

"Give me that." Finnley grabbed the brush. "I can brush out my own damned tangles. Go get my clothes."

"I grant ye, there's barely a scratch on your head this morning and only a few bruises, yet ye're supposed to stay in bed. Yer wife—"

"Get my clothes now."

"Surgeon can't come until later."

"I don't need the surgeon."

"I suppose ye can wait for him down—"

"I'm returning to town."

"But your horse—"

"I'll hire a horse. Or mayhap a gig to take ye back with me. Unless Lady Fiona doesn't mind ye remaining here while I go back to the fighting."

Hyde frowned. "No, Major. Ye might stumble into trouble again. A gig it will be. I'll go see to the arrangements."

"First get my clothes." He'd dress himself and find Greer before returning to town.

Finnley's coats had been brushed, his trousers cleaned, his boots polished, and somehow Hyde had procured fresh linens—Malcolm's probably, another debt to repay. He dressed quickly and was about to leave when Lucie peeked in without knocking and then walked through the door.

She eyed him head to toe. "Should ye not be in bed, Father?"

"Lucie." He pulled her to him and kissed her cheek. Now that he'd found her, he could not get enough of her. "Walk downstairs with me. Can I still get a cup in the breakfast room?"

"I'd imagine so. Mother is still there."

Greer. He'd like nothing more than to carry her back to the bedchamber and lock the door again, but with Lucie and Lady Fiona underfoot and a houseful of bustling servants, that wouldn't happen.

They found the breakfast room deserted, except for a footman clearing away dishes. He informed them that Greer had moved to the drawing room. The newspaper still lay on the table, and Finnley retrieved it, scanning the headlines while Lucie ordered coffee sent to the drawing room.

They arrived there to find Greer seated at a small writing table, sharpening a quill. She looked up and then stood. "What are ye doing out of bed?"

"Father says he's feeling much better this morning," Lucie said.

"All due to your skillful nursing last night." He smiled at the color rising in her cheeks.

"Ye bacon-brained Scotsman. Those ribs are bruised. Ye ought to be resting and letting them heal."

"Hyde brought me the latest news of the riots." He pointed at the sofa. "May I?"

She waved a hand, and he seated himself.

He shook out the newspaper and scanned the lines.

"It's dreadful," Greer said.

"Aye." 'Twas as bad as Hyde had said, worse than he'd have expected. The havoc had escalated over the week. The troops had been needed.

"Will they riot again tonight?" Lucie asked.

The vision that had come upon him yesterday crept into his mind again: Greer taken by a mob, only this time, in the image, Lucie was present.

He took in a deep breath, praying that 'twas only his overactive imagination at work, fed by the memories of war rattling about in his brain. He riveted his gaze to the paper, but the words scrambled. Will they riot again tonight?

The stark rage of starving people wouldn't be settled in one night. Blood lust might take days of head-knocking and saber-rattling to contain.

But he wouldn't tell Lucie that—there had been too much interest in her tone. "The Life Guards are out in force. They'll quieten things down."

Lucie being the adventurous sort, might take herself off to town. Best let her think the excitement was over.

A servant came with a tray, and Lucie poured him a cup of the strong bracing coffee.

***

Greer returned to her seat at the writing desk and slipped the note from Banquo under a stack of stationery paper, while Lucie and Finnley discussed the riots and the proposed legislation, and the likely outcome of everything. There was an edge of excitement in both their voices.

"I hope that Malcolm is safe in town," Lucie said. "He's gone off again today."

"Aye. And he's done me a great boon, arranging for me to meet friends who might sponsor my membership in his club. I'm to meet two of them today."

"Ye're not to go anywhere, Father. The surgeon said so. Not until he's looked at your ribs again."

"In the Peninsula, if I'd stayed in my cot all day after such a minor skirmish, Boney would still be raising havoc there."

"Ye slept well then?" Lucie asked.

Greer turned away and busied herself with squaring up the sheets of paper.

"Aye," Finnley said, "best rest in years."

He did look much recovered this morning. Oh, but his battered and bruised appearance the night before, and the unprovoked attack—if he was planning to return to a city still in discord, his enemy might strike again.

She must speak with him.

"Lucie," she said, rising and coming over to take a seat on the sofa with Finnley, "Will ye go and get my knitting bag from my bedchamber?"

She stared at her daughter, daring her to object. Surprisingly, Lucie rose without a word.

At the door, she turned. "I suppose ye'll need a few minutes to talk sense into Father. I shall stop in my bedchamber as well and retrieve my book. If ye decide to be sensible, Father, I'll continue reading where I stopped last night." Then she left, closing the door with a sharp *snick*.

Finnley's soft chuckle raised her hackles.

"Spunk and bite," he said.

His hand came over hers, and she pulled away. "Ye canna go into town today," she said. "Ye must abide here a bit longer. I have a theory."

"A theory?"

"Aye. I'd meant to talk to ye about it last night before...before ye distracted me."

He grinned, reaching for her. She jumped up and took the chair across from him.

"Malcolm has received a threatening letter regarding his rights to the title."

His head shot up. So, that bit was news to him.

"From whom?"

"He doesn't know."

Finnley frowned into his cup and set it down on the tray. "He mentioned a document. 'What if I had a document,' he said. Does he have one?"

She thought of the paper he'd shoved into his waistcoat the night before. 'I don't know." Worry threaded its way along her nerves. "'Tis Malcolm's title. I'd not reopen an old wound and repeat what we—"

"No. Ye're right, and so I told him. He is Menteith, and in fact, I told him I pledged my sword to his service, Greer. I meant it."

She let out a long breath. "And what of the witch's prophecy?"

Color drained from Finnley's face, and his gaze flew to the far wall.

"Duncan told Malcolm about it on his deathbed. Then Malcolm told Lady Fiona. And she told me."

"The title is Malcolm's," he said. "Malcolm is Menteith."

His stony demeanor both tugged at her heart and poked at her anger. "Why did ye not tell me that the witch called ye the true Earl. That she said Banquo's son would rule. I thought... I thought 'twas all my fault, and the Naughtons' for goading ye into a lawsuit. All those years ago—why did ye not tell me?"

His mouth firmed into the same obstinate line she saw so often on Lucie's face, but when he looked at her, his eyes shone with emotion. "I am sorry, Greer." He braced a hand on the sofa arm and stood, steadying himself. "I'll go."

"No. No ye're not running off. What I wanted to say...if Malcolm isn't the true Earl of Menteith, then it'd be Finnley Macbeth acquiring the title. Ye're next in line, are ye not?"

"I'm not—"

"Let me finish. I know from that lawsuit ye're next in line, and if something should happen to ye, it would be Banquo—"

"Father," Lucie called from the door, "Hyde is here with horses for the both of ye."

Greer closed her eyes and huffed. "Will ye let me finish?

"Lucie, love, give us a few more moments," he called.

She heard the door close and felt his hands cover hers. "Banquo's a cunning fellow, and yet he did help me secure an appointment with a man in the government. And now Malcolm has arranged introductions which may help Lucie. I must go into town and call on these men. And though I've offered my services during the troubles in town, if the Crown doesn't need me, I'll return for ye, tonight, Greer, if ye'll have me, even if only to have dinner with ye and Lucie and Lady Fiona."

"Lady Fiona has gone away until tomorrow or the next day."

He frowned. That was another item of news to him.

"I see. Ye must stay close to home then, the both of ye. And ye mustn't worry, *mo chridhe*. After last night, I'll be on my guard."

"But Banquo—"

"Will never be a worry to ye, nor to Lucie. And we don't truly know what he's up to. Ye leave him to me."

His lips were soft on hers, and he held on to her, deepening the kiss, stirring the fresh memories of their night together. She slipped her hands around his neck, surrendering.

A loud gasp drove them apart. Greer peeked around Finnley. Lucie stood by the door with her arms crossed over her chest, her face flushed with color. Finnley chuckled.

Greer mumbled an oath, her thoughts so jumbled, she forgot why she wanted to scold him—for embarrassing her with Lucie certainly, but there'd been another more important reason as well.

He bade her farewell and walked to the door with only the slightest of limps.

Lucie accompanied him, closing the door behind her, and Greer plopped down in the chair. He was going to town, the stubborn man. And neither Malcolm nor Finnley would entertain her concerns about Banquo.

She thought of the invitation Banquo had sent. In spite of the city's unrest, Lady Camden was hosting a rout tonight, and Banquo had invited Greer to attend with him. She'd been sharpening her quill to write him a note declining the invitation. Banquo was of an age with her and a handsome enough man. Of middling height and a slimmer build than Finnley, yet he was another well-formed man who needed no padding to fill out his shoulders. 'Twould be uncomfortable attending with him, and might subject her to more talk, and quite frankly, after last night, it felt more than a little disloyal.

But perhaps she shouldn't fash about being disloyal to a man who'd divorced her and failed to acknowledge their child for twenty years, and who now would not listen to her concerns.

He would come for her, Banquo's note said.

That wouldn't go over well with Lucie, nor would she like to be confined in a carriage with the man. But she could meet him there. She could take Lady Fiona's carriage and one of the footmen. At the rout, she could draw Banquo aside and perhaps learn more about what he was up to.

She crossed to the writing desk and picked up the quill she'd sharpened. With Lady Fiona absent, she'd have one less person questioning her plan.

Putting off Lucie was another matter. She set her mind to dealing with her strong-willed daughter.

CHAPTER ELEVEN

Finnley's ribs ached like the devil as he plodded along the Chelsea road. As it turned out, Lady Fiona's head groom had loaned them two horses, lazy fellows, who apparently didn't get out much and didn't care to. Hyde'd had the devil of a time with his nag, who wanted to turn around and go back to his feed.

He'd have laughed, but his head ached worse than his ribs, and it had naught to do with the previous night's attack. 'Twas the memory awakened by Greer's mention of the witch, as well as the aching vision that nagged at him. The nearer they got to the city, the fiercer it stirred. Smoke still hung in the air from the previous night's arson, and here and there workmen were boarding up windows, and the very air crackled with a current that smelled like a coming battle.

What news had pulled Malcolm away from the women he was charged with protecting? And Lady Fiona—why had she left so suddenly?

The lady's brace of sturdy footmen and grooms would guard Greer and Lucie should he be needed in town. After he called on Malcolm's acquaintances, Lord Stockwith and Mr. Harling, he would stop by the Home Office, and perhaps Horse Guards as well, and offer his services again.

Still... he didn't know Lady Fiona's servants. 'Twould be better to have a stout man who he trusted in place there.

"Hyde," he said. "Ye'll pack what we need from our rooms and go directly back to Lady Fiona's."

"Not sure I can get this fellow to walk that far twice in one day."

"Take your own horse. We'll leave the both of them at the livery and pay a boy to take them back later or tomorrow."

"Not sure ye won't need a man at your back, Major."

They reached the park gates and passed by them, spotting a group of soldiers riding down Park Avenue. One man in a Captain's uniform turned his mount and approached them. "Major Macbeth," he called. "Is that you?"

The familiar voice made him pull up and wheel around. "Rudgwick? Damn, but I'm happy to see ye home safe. But it seems we've brought the troubles with us."

Captain Lord Rudgwick, a wealthy earl, was junior to him only in age and military rank. Whilst his father was still living, he'd defied family expectations and gone off to join the cavalry. He was known for his brash courage, his fine horses, and his magnificent moustache. Which was now missing.

"Ye've shaved," Finnley teased.

"Indeed." The other man grinned. "The ladies in my life demanded it. It is a pleasure to see you looking so well, Major. I suppose the next piece of news will be that the little Corsican has popped up in Kent."

Finnley laughed.

"What are you doing here?" Rudgwick asked. "And is that you as well, Hyde?"

"In the flesh, milord," Hyde said, saluting.

"Jolly good to see the both of you looking well. Except for that bruise you're sporting, Hyde." Rudgwick laughed heartily. "Have the Highlanders been called up for this week's party?"

"Hyde is here, more or less keeping me out of trouble. We ran into some revelers last night, unofficially. Go on to our rooms," he told Hyde. "I'll be along directly."

Finnley rode along beside Rudgwick, who recounted the previous night's events. Having marshaled troops at various locations, he had little to add to the details provided by the newspaper. "And what does bring you to London, Macbeth?" he finally asked.

"I thought to find some other way to serve. I'm on half-pay."

"I heard you were wounded at Toulouse."

"Aye."

Rudgwick pulled up. "I heard something else..." He frowned. "I'd want to know, Macbeth, if something was being said. There's a rumor that you waved the white feather, though the details were sketchy."

Finnley's fists tightened around the reins. "I thank ye for sharing that, though ye're not the first to let me know. I'd like to get to the bottom of this. Will ye tell me who ye heard it from?" He eyed Rudgwick a long moment, waiting.

"My cousin said he heard it whispered about at the club." He screwed up his face. "Yesterday morning."

"So recent?"

"Yes. I promised to thrash him if he spread it about."

"My thanks for that." He drew in a breath. "Ye haven't asked me if there's any truth to it."

Rudgwick shook his head. "I don't need to. I've seen you in battle. If you're feeling bored tonight, put on your colors and ride out with us."

Finnley wished him farewell, and they parted ways, agreeing to meet again when they were able.

He rode on to the mews, both heartened by Rudgwick's faith in him and disheartened by the possibility of needing to clear his name again.

Bones aching, he left the horse in good hands and walked the short distance to his rooms. While Hyde tended to his coats, he quaffed the ale sent up by his landlady, pondering this new rumor. Rudgwick's cousin had heard it at White's. Banquo had brought up White's, though he hadn't said whether he was a member.

Malcolm however was, and Banquo had mentioned that.

Banquo couldn't have known that Malcolm would offer to help Finnley gain a membership at the club. And Malcolm wouldn't have done so whilst smearing Finnley's name with other members. Perhaps Banquo was scheming, trying to set Finnley and Malcolm at odds.

When Hyde brought over his freshly brushed coat, he sent him back for his regimentals.

He'd been presenting himself around London as Major Macbeth, Scottish baron and gentleman, though a heathen one from the north. He might as well don his uniform again, and if the crowd wanted to assault him, or if Banquo wanted to send thugs to see to him, they'd know they were up against a man who'd been in fiercer battles than this.

His gut told him Greer had been right about Banquo, and the thought made his heart swell more than ever. They were joined again, he and her, at the heart, in the blood of their daughter, and in this new bond, an uncanny sense of who not to trust.

Yet he didn't want her to fash about Banquo. He'd have Hyde seek out the man's lodgings, then he'd send his trusted man to protect Greer.

He wanted her safe. He wanted a future with her, and their daughter. They'd been of one mind about the claim he'd filed twenty odd years ago against Duncan, with the witch's words spurring him. Losing that lawsuit had shattered their belief in themselves and in each other.

Let the past be the past. It was heartening to know he and Greer were of like minds again, this time agreeing that Malcolm Comyn was the true Earl of Menteith.

The true earl. A red fog crept over him again. The lad had been sorely troubled, going off by himself in pursuit of the truth. He hoped Malcolm Comyn was not in danger.

He rubbed his jaw. His head was a spider's web of visions and gossamer threads.

"'Ere it is, Major." Hyde popped back into the room and helped him into the gray pantaloons he wore for marches and battles, and his scarlet coat, then went out again, returning with his broadsword and his pistols. "Sword is polished and pistols are all cleaned and ready. S'pose ye'll want those as well."

"Take one of the pistols with ye."

Hyde grimaced and thanked him. Hyde preferred his Baker rifle with its bayonet fixed, pistols being the weapons of gentlemen. The fact that he'd stayed silent on the subject meant he smelled battle coming as well and knew he couldn't tramp around London bearing a long gun, not if he wanted to borrow trouble with the Watch. He'd traded his red coat for a plain one weeks ago.

"Gather what clothing ye think I need and go back to Lady Fiona's in Chelsea before the trouble starts. First though, I want ye to snoop around and see if ye can find Banquo's lodgings. Somewhere near Covent Garden, he said."

"Will there be a particular message for your ladies when I go there?" Hyde asked.

"Tell them I'll join them as soon as I'm able."

"And if it 'appens you're delayed and the ladies start to worrying and sending me off to look for ye, where should I start?"

Annoyance bubbled up in him, but the vision of Greer being pulled from a carriage reared up again. Lucie was there too, yet he couldn't see her.

Bile rose in him, and he swallowed it back. With so much unrest in a city the size of London, a woman—or for that matter a man—might end up in the river, with no one ever the wiser. If Greer or more likely Lucie were to go off looking for him...

"I'm visiting Lord Stockwith and Mr. Harling." They might decide to not be home to him, if a rumor about him was percolating at White's, but he'd take his chances, perhaps ask them if they'd heard aught of it. "And then, I'll pay a call on Abernathy at the Home Office. If I'm not needed tonight, I'll stop at the Star and Garter for a meal. Ye know the place—off of North Street."

"I may as well stop there on my way and let ye know what I've found."

Hyde wanted to be in the fight, if there was to be one. "Fine, but if I'm not there, don't linger waiting for me. Get ye to Chelsea, and take care of the ladies. If I'm needed in town, I may not return until the wee hours."

Hyde listened, frowning, and finally grunted. "Happens the lady's footmen are a stout enough bunch that—"

"No. I'm depending on ye Hyde. Watch over them for me."

Hyde grumbled, nodded, and went about packing a bag.

As it turned out, Lord Stockwith and Mr. Harling had not been at home. At each of their residences, he was told they were out, but at Harling's, a footman rushed out after him and asked if he was there in advance of the troops. He'd confided that his master was, in fact, speaking in Parliament that day on the Corn Law, and the household was more than a little concerned they'd suffer the same looting as the Robinsons. Inside, they were making preparations for the mob.

He'd seen that sort of frantic haste in the cities and towns of Spain, and it rattled him. With a greater sense of foreboding, he turned his horse and made his way through the gathering crowds to Abernathy's office.

At the inconspicuous building Finnley was surprised to see a large number of horses tethered and attendants milling about.

He was even more surprised to be ushered into Abernathy's office immediately.

"You've saved me the trouble of sending a messenger after you," Abernathy said, closing the door. "Do sit. We've had disturbing reports out of Elba."

Less than a year earlier, the deposed Napoleon Bonaparte had chosen exile to the island in the peace treaty negotiated at his defeat. Given the man's character, it wasn't surprising there'd be trouble from him.

"Do you know Colonel Campbell?"

"The man assigned to keep watch on Bonaparte?"

"Yes. The official liaison of the Allies to the Imperial court on Elba." Abernathy grimaced. "Unofficially, we've had reports from many visitors. The emperor is getting restless, and his new constituents, the taxpayers of Elba, are growing disturbed by the burden of supporting a lavish imperial court. All of this I tell you in confidence."

"Of course. Understood."

"It's prudent to consider the possibility that the emperor might attempt to escape. A charismatic leader such as Bonaparte left behind many disappointed followers who might be happy to rise again. And we're hearing rumblings amongst his Polish adherents. His Polish mistress paid him a call a few months ago, and some of the hussars have joined him on Elba. He'll need to be moved. Sooner, rather than later, I fear. We're considering another location not quite as convenient to his old empire. Have you heard of the Island of St. Helena?"

England owned many islands throughout the world. "I don't recall it."

"It's our second oldest colony after Bermuda and quite a bit farther south, midway between South America and Africa."

A sinking feeling came over him. St. Helena was a far distance from the Scottish Highlands and Greer. If the island was primitive, she might not wish to join him. Nor would Lucie be likely to find a good husband there.

"I'm not asking you to go there," Abernathy said.

Finnley laughed. "That obvious, am I?" He shook his head. "I'm grateful to be able to serve, and ready to do so."

"As I see. Have you checked in with the Guard?"

"I've run into Rudgwick."

"I heard you encountered some of the rioters last night."

Abernathy was a man who made it his business to know things. "Yes. On the street in front of my lodgings. Lord Menteith came along before they bashed me too badly."

"What did the ruffians look like?"

He frowned, trying to remember. "The one I had the best grip on should have a very sore head. Burley fellow, with a crooked nose and...broken teeth. Bushy eyebrows and close-cropped hair. The other two were slighter. Good rough brawlers, all of them, with no gentlemanly posturing. Might have been soldiers once or sailors."

"Was it random?"

He'd surprised himself, dredging up that clear picture of one of his attackers. He glanced at the polished mahogany of the desk, his memory focusing more.

There'd been no other rioters on the street where he lodged. He'd seen no damage to windows or properties there. The worst of the rioting had been focused on the more prosperous squares.

Greer was right.

"Perhaps not."

Abernathy raised an eyebrow.

"In the past few days, I've not only spent time with my daughter," he said. "I've also become reacquainted with her mother, the wife I divorced before the girl was born. It's her belief that this was no random attack, but a purposeful one. Menteith, ye see, is another cousin of mine. Greer and my daughter are staying with his aunt, Lady Fiona Carlin, in Chelsea."

Abernathy leaned forward, supremely at ease and attentive, as if he didn't have a roomful of visitors waiting.

Finnley cleared his throat and went on doggedly. "Twenty years ago, I sued Menteith's father over an ancient claim to the title. I lost the suit. And then, I almost killed the man in a duel. It was damned foolish, and I've always regretted my actions. Now, someone else is threatening Menteith's claim to the title. Not me—as I've told the lad, the title is his to pass on to his heirs. I'll make no further claim on it."

Abernathy waited, silent as a statue. He was a fine interrogator.

What was it he wanted to know?

"Menteith is young, unmarried and has no heirs, not even cadet branches of the Comyn line. This we know from that folly twenty years past. If he should be displaced or die, I'm next in line. If I were to be killed, the title would go to our cousin, Giles Banquo. My wife's theory is that Banquo is suspect in all of this."

"Does she have a reason to feud with Banquo?"

Abernathy was a sly one, probably knowing the answer. It had been a young Banquo who'd spotted Greer with Duncan. The rumor had grown from that incident. Yet he himself had caused her far more pain by taking the rumor to heart.

"No more so than to feud with me."

"Is her quarrel with you still an active one?"

"No," he said, batting away a doubt.

Doubt was what had killed their marriage the first time. Her acceptance of him the night before had not been an act of vengeance. Certain it was though, he had twenty years of hurt to make up for.

"What does Menteith think?"

"We've not had much chance to talk after last night, and he's gone off today on business."

"This business?"

"Likely. But to where, I don't yet know."

"Have you confronted Banquo?"

"I've no proof of anything. Until I do, I've no wish to chase another duel."

He nodded. "A wise choice."

They talked further about the current situation on the streets of London and when the city might be at peace again.

"If you join Rudgwick, good luck tonight," Abernathy said. "I'll have a desk for you very soon. There's time for you to make a visit to your home in Scotland first, if you wish. Come back on Monday and we'll sort out the details."

It was dark when he left Abernathy's offices, gratified that he'd accomplished yet another goal and pondering whether Greer might let him visit the Macbeth family home.

At the Star and Garter, he found the taproom buzzing with news of the debates and the riots. As if he'd been stalking his master, Hyde arrived immediately after him carrying Finnley's cape, having decided the weather was turning and he'd need it that night. They ordered ale and meat pies, and ate quickly while Hyde reported that he'd had no success finding Banquo. Then they both left, and Finnley made his way up through Whitehall.

***

'Twas the footman Paul who appeared to hand Lucie and her maid down from Lady Fiona's open gig.

Well, and Sue wasn't really her personal abigail, but a housemaid sent along because Mama had taken to her bed with a headache.

A headache. Lucie had not been fooled by the lie. Her mother had been up all night with her father engaging in carnal relations. The thought made her skin crawl, and she'd been closing her eyes at intervals all day to shut out the image of them kissing.

"Shall I carry your package, miss?" Handsome and golden-haired, Paul's lips quivered on the edge of a grin most of the time. 'Twas likely unseemly for a London servant, but she didn't mind. At home their people were on friendlier terms, so she smiled back at him and handed over the package with her new evening gloves, slippers, and another novel she'd bought without permission. Mother had said she would need the gloves and slippers eventually. The book was a treat for herself, and she'd spent more than an hour at the bookshop perusing titles while Sue flirted with the young assistant behind the counter. Then, Lady Fiona's widowed friend, Mrs. Tebworth and her two daughters had appeared. Lucie had been so bold as to send the bookseller's boy off with a note telling Mama she was joining the ladies for dinner, and she and the two girls had spent the evening discussing novels, while Sue flirted below stairs with one of Mrs. Tebworth's footmen. It had been, overall, a pleasant evening all around.

She climbed down from the gig. Lady Fiona's house was quiet and dark. Mother would have had dinner in her bedchamber.

Unless Father had returned. He must have done so, thus there'd been not a peep out of Mother about Mrs. Tebworth's spontaneous invitation.

Drat but she would have liked more time with Father before he went off with Mother to...

She squeezed her eyes shut a moment. When she opened them, her vision was filled with the sight of a man riding up the short drive on a horse.

"Should we get you in to warm up, miss?" Sue asked.

In the porch light, Sue's cheeks were as red as a late summer apple. It had been a fine afternoon when they'd left the house, but it was cold now and starting to rain.

"Ye're chilled," Lucie said. "Go along inside. This is like a wet summer's day at home in the Highlands." And she wanted to see who this visitor was.

Not Banquo she hoped. He'd grabbed for her hand the other night, but 'twas Mama he'd ogled. Father had been too busy ogling her himself to notice. And Malcolm? He'd been wandering around in his own thick head when he wasn't pretending to be Lucie's older brother.

Ach, but 'twas true Malcolm had noticed the old lecher choking her hand. Banquo's white streak of hair made him look ever so much like a crafty warlock. She didn't need Malcolm to tell her the man was not to be trusted.

She hadn't needed to be rescued by Malcolm, either, or even by her father, though his presence at her side had been rather touching. She could rescue herself from the likes of Banquo. Just let it be him arriving now, and she would...

Oh. This wasn't Banquo. The jolly manservant who looked after her father was here, nodding to her and steering his horse toward the stable.

"Hold up," she called, waving to him. What the deuce was the man's name? She ought to have paid more attention. "Ye there, Freddy," she called to the groom who'd driven her to the shops, "pull up, and take this man's horse. Ye there..." She pointed again at the new arrival, "come this way with me."

The groom jumped into motion—well-ordered were Lady Fiona's grooms, she'd give them that— and Father's manservant came over and saluted.

Saluted. She caught the glimmer of amusement in his eyes, and decided to ignore it. "What is your name?" she asked. "I've forgotten."

"Hyde, miss."

"Hyde. Yes. Like the park. Are ye kin to that Hyde?"

"Not as I know miss."

"Come along then." She led him in through the front door.

The butler greeted them with a frosty look. Sue and Paul had not gone through to the servants' stairs yet and she caught the look of shocked amusement they both exchanged.

"My mother will wish to hear the news, Hyde. Or...has my father already arrived?"

"He's still in town, miss."

"Has my mother come down yet?" she asked the butler.

His eyebrows twitched a fraction in a look hinting confusion. "She's gone out, miss."

CHAPTER TWELVE

Gone out?

She drew herself up, lifted an eyebrow and stared at the man, the way she'd seen Malcolm do when he was being particularly stiff-necked. Sue and Paul stood like statues, filling their ears. What Hyde was doing, she couldn't be sure because she'd turned away from him.

She cleared her throat.

The butler cleared his as well. "Mrs. Douglas didn't say where she was going."

That remark came with the tiniest hint of distaste. Mother was, after all, a fallen woman, given that her husband had cast her off and she was using the surname she'd been born with.

"She told no one?"

"I'm not aware, miss."

"And what of Lord Menteith? Has he returned?"

The man blinked. "We were told he would be gone several days."

Malcolm was to be gone several days? How had she missed that news?

Anger spiked in her, heating her cheeks. No one had told her anything, and her mother had in fact faked a headache to sneak out of the house without her, which meant wherever she was going, she knew Lucie would have objected. Or...she would have insisted on coming along.

For as long as Lucie could remember, Mother had been the proper and amiable sort, not the sort to break rules. The reappearance of Father had unleashed a side of her that Lucie had never seen.

"Well, then, as it appears to be only me, would ye be so kind as to have a fire made in the drawing room and have the kitchen send up a tea tray?" She turned toward Hyde and gave the tiniest of winks, hoping that he was more perceptive than he appeared. "Hyde, upon consideration, I may have been hasty in keeping ye from your mount. He seemed to be favoring one foreleg. I think ye ought to go see to him and then come and report the news and anything else you might have learned. I shall await ye in the drawing room. 'Tis the same room where ye attended to my father the night he fainted."

"I know it well, miss."

He went off following the housemaid and the footman, and she retired to the frigid drawing room, circling its gloomy darkness.

Mother had gone out...how peculiar. Two notes had arrived for Mother that morning, and Lucie had forgotten all about them until now.

She fumbled her way to the mantel, found the tinderbox, and went around lighting candles and the Argand lamp on the writing desk.

The door creaked and Paul entered. "I'm to make the fire," he said by way of explanation.

She thanked him and sat down at the tidy desk, opening drawers.

"Your mother was dressed for the evening when she went out," Paul said, his tone casual. "She looked very fine."

She glanced back. His attention was focused on his task.

It was a cheeky thing for a footman to say, though she supposed that Mother, though old, was still beautiful enough to catch the eye of a young man like Paul.

"A social event, then."

"Very like."

Finding only blank paper and ink in the desk and drawers, she stood. "Paul, I've left something upstairs. If Hyde returns here before me, have him wait. Or, perhaps, he can go back to the kitchen and have some dinner until I return." She snatched up a candle and fled.

The hall, stairs, and upstairs corridor were deserted, as was her mother's bedchamber. Candle in hand, she methodically searched drawers, cabinets, tables, and bedding, coming up with nothing. Tucked under a china shepherd on the mantel, was a note. She held it up to the light, reading.

I have urgent business to attend to that may require my absence for several days or perhaps longer.

This was from Malcolm, and Mother hadn't bothered to mention anything at all about his absence.

As this business involves the matter we discussed earlier, you will appreciate me not sharing more details in writing.

What business was he talking about? And why did no one ever tell Lucie anything?

Please convey my apologies to Lucie. I know that I have promised, with my aunt's assistance, to help arrange the sort of invitations that would let her appear in society.

And when would that come about?

I've also written to my man of business so that he may take care of any of your and Lucie's expenses. It is the least I can do for you.

Well. She huffed. No wonder Mother had set her free to shop without worrying about cost. Had she known Malcolm was paying their bills she would have bought a new bonnet and more books.

She tucked the note back under the shepherd and looked around. Two letters had arrived this morning. Where was the other one?

Mother was sharing this room with Father. Mayhap, she didn't wish for him to see the other note. And if that was the case, where would she have stowed it to keep him from coming across it by chance?

She went along into the adjoining dressing room, lighting more candles. The maid who'd helped her dress would have put Mother's gowns in order. What place would be safe from a maid's prying eyes?

She searched the jewelry case, the reticules and pockets, and furniture drawers. Nothing. She blew out the candles and made her way back to the drawing room, thinking.

Mother must have taken the second note with her. She'd gone out dressed for the evening, Paul had said. So, 'twas likely the note had been an invitation, one Mother didn't want Lucie to know about. She'd taken it with her to know the direction or to prove she'd been invited. Perhaps one of Lady Fiona's friends in the local community had invited Mother for an evening event. She wouldn't have taken Lady Fiona's carriage into London, not with the rioting going on. Mother wasn't the adventurous sort. She wouldn't risk her hostess's property being damaged or her servants injured.

Would she?

When she returned, she found the drawing room was much warmer, and a tray with a teapot and covered dishes sat on the table near the fireplace. Hyde stood nearby, and Sue rose from her seat in a dark corner.

The butler...housekeeper...someone had decided she needed chaperoning in the presence of Hyde. Or the maid was their assigned eavesdropper.

"Sue," she said, "ye may leave. Hyde will not harm me."

"But, miss—"

"Thank ye, Sue. That will be all."

The girl bobbed a curtsy and left the door ajar.

"Close that door, Hyde."

While he quietly followed her order, she lifted the cover from the dish to find a plate of biscuits and cakes.

"Where has my mother gone off to?"

He frowned. "A party at Lady Camden's. Arlington Street."

"In town?"

"Yes, miss. The coachman didn't want to go out. Only gave in when she threatened to hire a carriage from the inn."

"Was she alone?"

"Two grooms rode along."

"And no other escort?"

"She sent a boy off in the morning with a note for Banquo."

"Banquo?" Lucie plopped down in her chair.

"So he said, miss. Then he carried a note back from him to her."

Unease tingled along Lucie's every nerve. Mother was on her way to meet Banquo? What the devil was Mother up to? Surely she wouldn't play Father false, not after last night...and this morning.

She looked at the blaze in the fireplace. The flames had died down to a quiet heat that couldn't dispel the sudden chills rippling through her. "Does my father know about this?"

"No, miss." Hyde frowned. "Lessen he's learned about it since then." He paused, took in a breath, and leveled a gaze at her. "Spent the afternoon trying to find Banquo and his lodgings for your da. Now at least, I know where the man is staying."

She thought of the way Banquo had ogled her mother, and the way he'd taken her own hand. Something was amiss with him and Father knew it.

Mother, whatever she was up to, might be in danger.

Hyde's weathered face reflected concern. Smaller than Father, but sturdy, he'd gained Father's trust, so he wasn't an utter dolt, and he must have some character behind whatever measure of cunning the fates had bestowed on him. Mayhap he would help her.

"Have you eaten, Hyde?"

"Aye, miss."

"Well, ye must fortify yourself more. Pull up that chair and sit down." She slid the plate of food toward him, then crossed to the sideboard where she knew Lady Fiona kept a bottle of sherry. "Sherry or tea?" she asked.

"Miss, I couldn't. Cook will give me a warm up below stairs."

"Ye won't have time for that if ye help me. Sit, and I'll tell ye my plan."

***

Mayhap he should have reconsidered wearing his regimentals. The restless streets teamed with angry men and even a few women, and there were others, gawps standing about, eager to see what excitement might occur. All in all, 'twas another night ripe for trouble.

Here and there, troops patrolled, and at one or two houses, whole groups of soldiers stood guard against a repeat of the previous nights' looting. Despite the crowds, the threatening unrest, and the escalating rainstorm, escutcheoned carriages rolled through the streets and squares, carrying their wealthy occupants to the few social events that hadn't been canceled.

He moved his mount to the side several times, letting them pass, fighting the vision that continued to plague him: Greer, pulled from a carriage like the ones tunneling through the milling crowds, and Lucie, dear Lucie, in danger somewhere. His nerves were aflame, the air around him snapping as if a whole host of witches and fairies were flaying him.

"What ho, Macbeth." Rudgwick appeared in the lamplight astride the biggest beast he'd ever encountered. "Seen a ghost, Major?"

He couldn't explain his visions to Rudgwick, or any man. He'd be carted off to Bedlam.

"Puts me in mind of Badajoz," he said, and it wasn't a lie. The freezing rain that March had made battle a misery.

"Ride along with me," Rudgwick said. "I'm off to check on this fellow's shoe while the crowd is still only grumbling."

***

Riding boots and crop in hand, Lucie slipped through the quiet corridors, down the stairs, through the hall and the breakfast room, and into the conservatory. The terrace doors with their glass inserts had been locked both inside and out. The gap in them let in a terrible draft and the lock was a flimsy one—Lady Fiona's butler ought to have seen to them. She slipped one of her sgian dubhs from the sheath in her pocket and slid the blade through the gap, jiggling until the latch gave.

Cold rain lashed her face. Shivering, she stood under the overhang, wishing she'd thought to acquire a man's greatcoat. She clumsily shoved her feet, and more carefully her sheathed daggers, into the boots before making her way down the drive.

"Miss," Hyde hissed.

His voice came from the shadows where he stood holding the reins of two blowing horses. He'd done as instructed and hired a mount for her at the nearby Rose and Crown, while she'd hurriedly changed into her trews and coats. Mother hated it when she wore trousers and rode astride. She'd packed them into her trunk at the last minute, never expecting the chance to don them.

"Don't like this, miss," Hyde grumbled. "Ye'll catch your death in this rain and the Major will have my..." He swallowed the last word on another grumble.

"Help me up."

He hesitated only a moment before handing her into her saddle and going to his own mount.

"We have to catch up with my mother," she said. "Are ye sure about the time?" The stablemaster had said Mother had just left before Lucie's own return home. And it had taken her no more than twenty minutes to implement her plan.

"Aye."

"We ought to be able to move faster than her. And I imagine the coachman is taking his time, not wishing to go there at all. And the rain will slow them down."

"'Twould be better we get the both of ye home safe before the Major skins me alive."

"Come along, then," Lucie said. She put a heel to her horse and nothing happened.

She glared at him. "What sort of nag have ye found for me?"

"Not many choices on a night like this," he said.

His horse stepped out. Lucie muttered an oath and with a sharp poke of the crop she'd hoped not to have to use, her mount followed.

***

Greer's head ached with the jolting and jarring, the stopping and starting along the road. After she'd donned her gown, her gloves, and her plumed headpiece, it had taken a great deal of time and all of her determination to force her will upon Lady Fiona's servants. She hoped the lady would not send her packing upon her return, but it had been a close thing to leave the house before Lucie returned. Mrs. Tebworth's dinner invitation had been a godsend.

She'd left a note for Lucie in the bookmarked page of Waverley, expecting that Lucy would go straight to her chamber to read for a while before bed.

In any case, Greer didn't have to answer to Lucie to go out to a social event. And even if Finnley returned to the house, which by the time she'd left had seemed very unlikely, she didn't have to answer to him either.

She'd halfway hoped he would arrive at Lady Fiona's and convince her to stay. Or, perhaps, attend the rout with her. Yes, that would have been better.

But she'd come this far, and she would see this through. After all, besides her plan to probe Banquo, she had a responsibility to meet members of the *ton* for Lucie's sake.

This wasn't the same circumstance as her meeting Duncan in the woods. She wasn't alone. She had a coachman and grooms and there would be a houseful of guests at Lady Camden's. And surely, after three days of rioting and the presence of soldiers, the crowds would have settled. Lady Camden must think so to be continuing on with her party.

When they slowed again and stopped, she called up to the coachman. One of the grooms popped down and opened the door. Rain dripped from the brim of his hat, and guilt stabbed at her.

"Toll gate, ma'am," he said. "Be a bit of a wait."

Perhaps she oughtn't to have come, yet she wouldn't turn back. She peered out the window, debating when she should take the evening slippers from the box on the seat next to her, deciding what she would say to Banquo and wondering whether she would be welcomed if he decided not to appear. This was a card party and rout, Banquo had said. She wouldn't play cards—the stakes at these events were likely too high for her meager purse, and should she lose, Malcolm would not like paying off gambling debts. She would look for an opportunity to speak with Banquo and then she would leave.

And what would she say to him? As the minutes drew on, her impatience grew. She would ask him directly if he was threatening Malcolm. She would ask him what he knew about Finnley's assailants. She would ask him about the witch's prophecy.

The coach lurched and stopped, lurched and stopped, lurched and stopped. After an interminable time, they moved on and as they passed Green Park her heart began to race.

Had she made a grave error? Ruffians lined the street, many of them jeering, some banging the doors of each passing carriage. Including her own.

The coachman wheeled the coach onto another street only to be pursued. Men shouted and cursed. One tugged at the door. A whip lashed from above, knocking away the would-be assailant, but up he bounced and attacked again, this time with others. Soon her coach was surrounded.

Panic stole her breath. She dropped to her knees between the benches, arms stretched, gripping both door handles, too breathless to shout. One of the windows smashed and she ducked, losing her grip.

A door slapped open. The smell of the streets rushed at her—unwashed bodies, and gin, and foul breath. Hands reached for her, tugging.

Still clad in her sturdy half-boots, she kicked out, catching a chin, screaming, punching, holding her own for a moment. All around was shouting, men's oaths, a turmoil above and around where the coachman and grooms fought with the mob.

The melee grew louder with shouts of "the Guard," and the clattering of horses. Still a man tugged at her leg while she fought. She kicked out again, aimed at his groin, missing, the blow glancing against his hip. With a bellow, he pulled back a fist. She reared back and delivered a solid kick, this time catching him in the throat.

CHAPTER THIRTEEN

Instead of the stables at Horse Guards, Rudgwick led Finnley to a mews in Knightsbridge behind a terrace of newly constructed grand homes, where he traded the gelding for another mount, a smaller, but just as magnificent mare, and quickly remounted.

"What think you of this girl?" he asked, patting the blond mane.

"One can't fault the quality of your horses," Finnley said. "How is she with crowds?"

"Fiercer than any stallion, but with a sweet mouth for the man she allows to ride her. I'll be sending her down to the country soon and see what I can get off her."

They rode back to town, passing the crowds at the toll gate, most of them heading the other way. In the distance, groups of men surged toward the squares of Mayfair. The shouting and angry voices grew louder as they approached. Carriages veered through the crowd, dodging the walkers. It was damn foolish for anyone to be out paying social calls this night.

"Where are your men?" Finnley called.

"They'll be coming up from St. James. Never fear."

Rudgwick put him in mind of Wellington, a cool head in battle if ever there was one. He'd be a general if he survived long enough. Finnley spurred his horse and followed him.

As they neared the end of the park, a familiar horse and rider appeared in a splash of light from the street lamp. The man had pulled aside and was having words with a scrawny man on a horse, signaling to them the need to turn back, the scrawny man shaking his head.

"Hyde," he shouted.

Hyde wheeled around. Relief flooded his scarred face, and in that instance, the other rider moved forward, swerving this way and that, expertly weaving through the mob, with sharp snaps of the crop for men approaching too closely. The horse looked to be a plodder, but well-tempered for this sort of crush.

When Hyde noticed the other rider's advance, he bellowed, the words unintelligible, and followed the man onto a side street.

Finnley spurred his horse and went after them.

The sight before him sent his blood pounding. A carriage stood, swarmed by rioters, the driver and two livery-clad servants lashing out with whips and clubs. A door flopped around on its hinges, silk-clad legs in feminine boots jutting out, and a man yanking on them. The lady launched a sharp kick, and the man roared, releasing one foot, drawing his arm back.

Finnley spurred his horse. Hyde's nimble companion had whipped and kicked his way near. As the villain delivered his punch, the crop cracked down on his arm. What happened next, he couldn't see, but the villain fell back, clutching his throat, and collapsing, losing his hat.

Damnation. It was the same burley fellow—crooked nose, close-cropped hair—who'd thrashed him the night before.

Two other ruffians shoved the big man aside and reached into the carriage. Hyde's companion battled on at a rioter tugging his leg, whilst Hyde attempted to wedge his mount in between.

Finnley forced his way through to the carriage just as the two attackers hauled out the woman.

Greer. His heart all but pounded out of his chest. His nightmare had come to life.

"Let her go." He drew his sword and smacked the flat of the blade on the nearest man's head.

The bastard raised his face in a shocked look and wobbled.

Recognition punched more air from him. This man was one of his attackers as well.

The third villain yanked Greer in front as a shield.

Finnley shouted again, the words swallowed by the noise of the screaming hordes.

Hyde abandoned his mount and clubbed the man. Greer squirmed from his grip, while Hyde fought on and the nimble man lashed about with his crop.

Above the shoving swarm of rioters, he saw Rudgwick waving toward a group of approaching troops.

Finnley reached for Greer's arm and hauled her onto his horse, the drum of hoofbeats growing louder. The great angry throng moved north, away from the coach and the soldiers.

He jostled her around, steadying her, holding her close while she trembled, gulped air, and snatched at the ends of her shawl, the plumes on her headpiece tickling his nose. He spotted the burley assailant Greer had kicked stumbling off.

"Hold that man," Finnley shouted.

Hyde lunged for him, and missed. The other rider who'd accompanied Hyde brought his horse around forcing the villain back toward Hyde.

Rudgwick shouted orders and soldiers grabbed the man, as well as the man Hyde had thumped.

"Do you know these men?" Rudgwick asked.

"Besides attacking my lady, they attacked me last night." He looked around. "The third got away." He ought to have used the sharp edge of his broadsword on the bastard.

"Madam," Rudgwick said, "are you injured?"

Finnley pulled her closer, filling his senses with her scent, willing her trembling to stop.

"Dear God, Greer," he whispered.

"I'm shaken," she said, surprisingly calm. "Not injured."

"Ye'll stay right here," Hyde shouted, drawing their attention. His normally affable servant had hold of his erstwhile companion's bridle and was staring fiercely up at the lean young man.

Greer gasped. "Lucie," she whispered.

"Damn and blast it," Hyde said, leading the horse their way. "This once, ye'll do as ye're told." He stopped in front of Finnley and Greer. "I did my best to stop her, Major."

Lightheaded, he clutched Greer close, steadying himself. 'Twas his vision of Greer, of Lucie somewhere nearby and in danger, come to life.

"Dear God," he breathed.

"No, Finnley," Greer shouted. "Hyde, lend a hand, quickly. Lucie, don't ye dare run off."

***

Finnley was fainting again.

Greer hiked her skirts higher and wiggled around to sit astride the great beast of a horse, while the other great beast seated behind her threatened to collapse and knock both of them to the ground.

The handsome cavalry officer sidled closer, thrusting a flask at them. "Drink, Major." Finnley's hand moved to take it, and she breathed a sigh of relief that he still retained consciousness. Hyde had appeared, ready to steady Finnley should he begin to teeter. Even Lucie had edged closer.

Dressed in men's trousers and coats with her hair shoved under a tight cap, she might easily be confused for a man in the dark. In the light of day—or in a lighted room—no one would be mistaken. If she wanted to ruin her chance at a season, she was a fair way to doing it with this escapade. Not to mention, she might have been injured or killed.

Greer bit back a scold. Lady Fiona's coachman and grooms, all of them bloodied, might be too stunned to realize that the young man on horseback was really a girl. This virile young officer and the soldiers dealing with the two villains wouldn't be fooled for long.

Finnley's arms came around her again, tightening. "Drink, my love." He passed her the flask and she tipped her head back, bumping his chin. The fine brandy burned her throat, warming and steadying her.

The rain had paused, and she was still dry, but Finnley's glove was wet and Lucie's trousers plastered her legs. While she herself had ridden in comfort, the others, including Lady Fiona's servants, had been drenched.

The officer raised an eyebrow. "Do you, er, know each other?"

"Greer is my wife," Finnley said, and the words heated her more. He was claiming her, and she ought to correct him. But he was right. She was his, and always would be.

Her breath caught. Perhaps she would only be his until he discovered her mission that night.

"Greer, this is Captain Lord Rudgwick. We served together in the Peninsula. And this young fellow," he pointed at Lucie, who had moved even closer while Hyde went off to find his horse, "is my daughter, Lucie."

Rudgwick blinked, and his lips quivered while he forced his face into a frown. "I see."

"Of course, ye don't," Finnley said. "I must beg off from my offer to ride with ye tonight and take these two back to Chelsea."

"You've taken a house there, Major?"

"No," Greer said. "Lucie and I are guests of Lady Fiona Carlin."

"For now," Lucie said. "Until she returns to find her coachman and grooms wounded and her carriage damaged."

"Lucie." She'd misjudged this night entirely and unfortunately, Lucie was right.

Rudgwick leaned closer, his gaze riveted on Lucie. "You are injured, miss," he said, pointing to his cheek.

Blood ran from a scratch somewhere on her face.

"Ye're bleeding," Greer said. "Good heavens, what were ye thinking?"

"I was thinking to rescue ye, Mother." Lucie swiped at her cheek and examined her glove. "Not the rain, then. But I am fine, do not worry, Mother, Father, my lord."

"Chelsea is far," the young Captain said, and she heard amusement in his voice. "I've a better idea, Major. Will you follow me?"

She felt the movement of Finnley's head as he nodded.

"I wonder if we might commandeer your carriage, my lady, to convey the prisoners?"

What would Lady Fiona say to that?

But of course, she must cooperate. She would somehow find the means to repair the coach and its furnishings. As well as pay any compensation for injuries to the servants and to the horses, who must have been frantic about the crowds.

She mustered her voice. "Yes, certainly," she said.

A drop of rain plopped on her nose, and the skies began to open again. Finnley swept a fold of his cape around her, holding her close.

The captain moved his mount next to Lucie's, unhooking his cape. He swung the dark covering off and settled it over Lucie's shoulder's, all the while, studying her shocked face closely.

"Wait one moment," he said, smiling, "while I talk to my men. I'll have one of them see to your carriage and servants after they deliver the prisoners."

Hyde came to join them. His neckcloth was bloodied. The full foolishness of her actions—and Lucie's—swamped her.

"Are ye injured, Hyde?"

"A scrape here or there, ma'am."

"I thank ye both—all of ye—for coming to my rescue."

Finnley's arm tightened around her. "What were ye thinking, Greer, coming out on a night like tonight, all alone?"

I wasn't alone. I had a coachman and two grooms. She bit back the protest, remembering her purpose.

Her breath caught. The last time she'd taken matters into her own hands, Finnley had divorced her.

Never mind. He couldn't do that now. He might call her his wife, but she wasn't, was she?

"Finnley," she turned. "Someone must look for Banquo."

"Banquo?"

"Yes. 'Twas the reason I came out tonight. To..." Not to meet him. She couldn't phrase it that way else his anger would cloud his thinking when they most needed clear-headedness. There'd be another foolish duel, and this time one of them might be killed. "I'd learned he was attending Lady Camden's rout, and I wanted to confront him."

His eyes glinted, his mouth firmed, and he leveled a long look at her. But before he could vent what he was feeling, the carriage with its prisoners began to pull away.

"Hold there," Finnley called, beckoning Rudgwick. "Lucie, ye'll take your mother up with ye." He dismounted and plucked her down, setting her on her feet, none too gently. "What is Lady Camden's direction?"

"She's on Arlington Street."

"Where is Arlington Street, Rudgwick?" he asked.

"Why...we're on Arlington Street," the Captain said. "If you're looking for Lady Camden's, that is her residence down there, the one flooded with light."

Finnley nudged her closer to Lucie's horse, the heat of his gaze searing her.

"We will talk later," he said.

His tone sent a chill through her. All the ghosts put to rest the previous night were rising again.

"Be angry if ye will." Her voice shook with her own fury. "Ye refused to listen this morning. Ye discounted my worries. And so, when the chance arose to confront Banquo, I decided to take it. Because ye wouldn't hear, ye wouldn't listen."

"Greer," he said in a low growl through gritted teeth. "I did listen, and I did heed. Yes. Ye most likely have the right of it. Those two men under guard now? They were two of the three who attacked me last night. 'Twas nothing random about this attack on ye tonight. The third one got away, and if he's Banquo's man, he'll be heading off to his master to report." His lips firmed. "Ye might have been hurt...and Lucie..." He glanced up at Lucie, who Greer prayed hadn't heard him over the din of the retreating rioters. A wave of pain crossed his face. "Perhaps later, Greer, ye'll tell me how ye knew to expect Banquo's attendance at the rout."

Her heart pounded. She straightened her spine and tried to ignore his distrust. For when had Finnley ever trusted her?

"If they targeted the both of us," she said, "he is certainly behind this."

Biting his lip, he boosted her up, settling her sidewise behind Lucie. "Wait," he said, and unbuttoned his rain cape.

"Don't think to give me that," Greer said. "If ye're planning to be out all night in this weather, ye must keep it. As it is, I'm the only one of us not already soaked. The captain has said it's a short ride to shelter, but if need be, Lucie will let me share the Captain's cape."

"I'll do so now," Lucie said, shuffling the garment around and covering both of them.

He reached up and grasped both their hands. "No foolishness, either of ye. Stay close to Rudgwick and do what he says." His mouth hardened. "I'll have your promises."

She could hear Lucie's stuttering breath.

"Lucie," he said.

"I promise, Father."

"And Greer?"

She clenched her jaw, swallowing the urge to lash out at him. He was treating her like a disobedient child—like her child; she, who'd lived twenty years as a single woman—not a spinster, not a widow, but something altogether disrespected and foolish and fallen in their world, a divorced woman. All the anger and betrayal and abandonment came flooding back and she gritted her teeth unable to swallow it all.

"Greer," he said, and it came out like a growl.

"A promise, Macbeth? Very well. There'll be no more nights of foolishness, for either of us." She tapped her own boot to the side of the horse and they sidled away from his shocked glare and stopped, waiting for Rudgwick to join them.

***

Finnley watched them, his heart pounding with anger and need. She hadn't meant the foolishness this night. She'd meant their reunion the night before.

Damn it all, what had she been thinking? She'd been caught once with Duncan, and now she'd arranged to meet Banquo?

He grasped the reins of his horse and the beast jerked away.

"Steady," he said, stroking the animal's shoulder, fighting for control. Confronting Banquo was his duty, not hers. He was a man. He didn't need her to risk herself to help him, and risk Lucie's reputation in the process.

Lucie. His foolish, headstrong girl. What was he to do about her?

"I'll look after them," Rudgwick said.

"I thank ye." He mounted his horse. "Hyde, ye'll come with me."

Rudgwick moved up closer. "What are your plans, Major?" he asked quietly.

"I'm going to interrupt Lady Camden's rout. If Banquo is there, I'll bring him along to join these other prisoners. Where are ye taking them?"

"My men will escort them to Whitehall. If I'm not back before you leave Lady Camden's, ask after them at Horse Guards. We'll have a surgeon tend to the servants' injuries and then send them home. As soon as I see the ladies safely settled, I'll join you." He saluted and grinned. "Damned deep waters with you, Major. So glad we're getting better acquainted."

"Where are ye taking my wife and daughter?"

He laughed. "On the other side of that mews we visited tonight is my townhouse. It's a bachelor establishment, except when my mother and sister are in town. No ladybirds about, if you're wondering. My housekeeper will see to them, and my sister will have left some gowns behind for your daughter to choose from. Probably not the first stare of fashion, but they'll do. Have no fear. As I mentioned before, I've seen you in battle and I've no wish for a fight over either lady's honor. I'll be a perfect gentleman." He wheeled his horse, signaled, and the coachman pulled away, accompanied by outriders.

"Ladies, if you please," Rudgwick said in a courtly voice, "ride alongside me."

Finnley watched them ride off, relieved to see another guardsman fall into line behind them. There would be time to think about Greer's actions, taking it upon herself to confront Banquo. Had it been foolishness, or betrayal?

And Lucie? Dear God, had she been born a boy, she'd have made a valiant dragoon. She was stubborn, headstrong, and so damned brave. He would never find her a husband.

The rain began falling again. He clamped his bonnet down more firmly, plucked out a kerchief and mopped at his face, then handed the square of linen to Hyde. "Ye're bleeding."

Hyde dabbed at his face and looked at the cloth, and then at Finnley.

"The young lady wouldn't listen," Hyde said, urging his horse into step beside Finnley's. "I did try, Major."

Lucie was just like his sister. And himself, dammit. "I believe ye."

"And finally, I thought 'twould be better to go along and keep her out of trouble." He shook his head. "Fetched the worst horse in the stable for her, and afore I knew it she had the nag well in hand."

Pride welled in him, despite knowing he ought to dish out a punishment for his willful daughter.

Punish her? Did he have any right? They'd only just met.

"Wanted to rescue her mother," Hyde said.

Finnley didn't know whether to laugh or weep. His emotions were more jumbled than was good for the moment. He might well be going into a fight, and he needed to think straight.

"Where are we going, sir?"

"To a society party."
Hyde's soft chuckle eased his nerves.

CHAPTER FOURTEEN

The rain pelted them in great drops that turned Captain Lord Rudgwick's coat a deeper shade of blue. Lucie knew that because they passed the occasional carriage with its lamps brightly lit and she couldn't help but watch to see whether he'd glance her way again.

Seated behind her, Mother was mercifully silent. Unfortunately, so was Captain Lord Rudgwick, and she had rather hear more from him.

Lord of what, she wondered, trying to recall her long ago lessons in noble ranks from her pompous great-aunt.

Father was a mere Scottish baron, lower than an English baron even, but he was a major. This Lord Rudgwick was a mere captain, but father had treated him more like an equal. So perhaps in the world of nobledom he ranked higher than Father.

Oh, of course he ranked higher. All English nobles ranked higher than the Scots.

She smiled. Being a lesser-than could sometimes be freeing. No English baron's daughter would have gone out as she had. Or, if there were English girls like herself, she'd like to meet them.

She'd gladly come along for this London adventure for the sheer diversion of it, but she hadn't really expected to be accepted into polite society. Mother's divorced status and her own questionable legitimacy made it unlikely. Why Lady Fiona had invited them, she wasn't quite certain, but somehow it involved the reunion of her parents the night before. Though legally, they were not married. Might they decide to wed again?

She wasn't at all certain she wanted to marry. When Mother died—many years in the future, she hoped—she would inherit the use of Macbeth castle, and when father died, she would be the Baroness of Calder. The title was insignificant, and the castle and land didn't offer the sort of income that would entice a man looking for a well-dowered wife, but they would do for an independent spinster.

The wind flapped the cloak around her, stirring up scents: good wool, horse, and something that smelled both expensive and manly. Malcolm used a scented soap when he shaved. She knew, because she'd asked him about it, and he'd told her young ladies didn't discuss such things with men.

The memory made her smile again. She was certain Captain Lord Rudgwick, if she asked him about his soap, would not be so stodgy. He seemed the jolly sort. 'Twas a pity young single men and young single ladies could not truly be friends, as he was likely to be a good sort of mate. And, if they were friends, perhaps he might allow her to exercise his very fine horse.

They turned down a mostly dark street lined with white terraced homes. The large, generous edifices crowded together shoulder to shoulder, some shimmering white in the light from their neighbor's windows.

As they fell in behind their escort, Lucy ogled his mount. The mare was exquisite, a golden chestnut with a fair mane, as well-formed as the man riding her.

Cavalry officers kept more than one horse at the ready. She wondered what others he had in his stable and whether or not he might allow her to ride them. His oldest, most rackety hack would be a far cry better than the fellow carrying her and Mother tonight.

He pulled up in front of a door that looked like all the others on the street, except that this one had two lamps burning brightly in front, as if the occupants expected guests. Dismounting, he handed his reins to the soldier who'd followed behind them, and came around to assist them.

"We've arrived," he said. "May I lift you down, ma'am?"

With an unnecessary *oof* from Mother, he set her gently onto the ground. She'd pulled the warm mantle along with her, and cold air rushed Lucie, the rain pelting her already soggy coats.

She looked down to see him dusting his gloved hands and looking up at her. In the freezing wet shadows, she couldn't read his face, but she was certain he was silently laughing at her.

She swung her leg over and hopped down on her own, turning to face him, dusting her own hands.

He was not so much taller than herself, not as tall as Father or Malcolm, and with a leaner frame.

"This fellow is from the Rose and Crown," she said.

"A livery horse. I thought as much."

"Needs must," she said.

"The rain seems to be falling more briskly." 'Twas Mother's genteel way of chiding Lucie to stop dawdling.

"Right then." Captain Lord Rudgwick hurried the other soldier over and handed him the reins to her plodder. He tucked Mother's hand over his arm and led them both up the steps to the covered portico.

He hadn't offered Lucie his arm. But of course, she was perfectly capable of managing the steps in her sturdy boots. Mother, on the other hand, was still very much the lady, even in her wrinkled clothing and disheveled headpiece with its limp feathers.

At the door, he lifted the locker and let it drop. When nothing happened, he fished around in his coat and produced a key. "The staff are probably below stairs. I wasn't expected tonight."

"Have ye been on duty since Monday?" Mother asked.

The riots had started on Monday afternoon, Lucie knew that from the newspapers.

"Yes, more or less."

"How invigorating," Lucie said. Men had all the fun.

The key turned and he ushered them in. An oil lamp burned dimly, illuminating the stark black and white tiles of the expansive hall and the carpeted lower steps and ornate balustrade of a staircase. The scent of fresh wood, paint, and plaster spoke to the newness of the construction.

He removed his plumed shako, lifted his wet cape from Mother and tossed both aside, just as a man wearing a work smock over his shirtsleeves and waistcoat appeared from the back corridor. To be interrupted at some domestic task this late at night, the captain's servant must be a conscientious sort.

"My lord," he said, bowing. "I do beg your pardon. We were not—"

"Expecting me, yes. I have brought along two refugees from the rioting. Have fires made in the parlor and in my mother's bedchamber, send a tray to the parlor—something warm and substantial, whatever you have on hand, and tell Mrs. Lutton I want to see her there immediately."

She felt strangely grateful he hadn't revealed her sex. Oh, that would come about soon enough, but he'd kept her secret so far.

He led them to a door at the side of the hall and ushered them through. The room's chill assaulted her and she shivered. This parlor hadn't been used in quite some time.

After inviting them to be seated, he found the tinderbox and began lighting candles—good beeswax, she noted, another comforting scent. The candlelight shimmered in his thick brown hair.

He was a remarkably handsome fellow. Perhaps she should go and help him.

Mother, being Mother, and knowing her only too well, snatched her hand and tugged her to a pair of chairs.

"I'm too wet to sit, Mother."

"Don't be silly." Captain Lord Rudgwick waved a hand toward the front window. "My mother keeps shawls under that window seat, if you'd like to have a look."

A draft wafted in, bringing with it a footman carrying a scuttle filled with coal. The man hurriedly set about making a fire. While he did that, Lucie fetched a knitted wrap and draped it over her mother's shoulders. In her lowcut evening gown, Mama was likely freezing, even with the heavy shawl she'd wisely donned for the carriage ride and hadn't managed to lose. She was also still clad in her half boots. Her party slippers must still be in the carriage.

Gentlemen had so much more of comfort in their trousers and coats.

After what seemed like forever the fire finally caught, flames licking the air, warmth seeping into the room and making the candle flames dance. Captain Lord Rudgwick had lit the space bright as a ballroom—not that she'd been in a London ballroom, but she'd heard stories of candle-filled chandeliers dripping wax on the dancers.

She sighed. Chances were, she'd never attend a ball. Not after this night's work.

She would never agree to call it foolish though. She'd helped to save Mother. Mother's escapade had been the foolish one, an uncharacteristic act for her usually careful mother. They must have a talk about this before the evening was out.

The footman stood and wiped his hands, and the butler and an older woman entered carrying trays.

The woman curtsied to her employer. "You wanted to see me, my lord?"

He dismissed the butler and footman and closed the door on them. "My lady," he said, with a courtly bow to Mother, "this is my housekeeper, Mrs. Lutton. She'll see you and Miss Macbeth provided with dry clothing. Something of my mother's or sister's ought to do, Mrs. Lutton."

***

Greer felt the heat rising in her cheeks. The housekeeper's shocked appraisal of Lucie, Lucie's look of defiant pleasure, and Lord Rudgwick's barely concealed amusement brought her to her feet.

"That won't be necessary, I assure ye. Once we warm up by the fire and the rain stops, we'll leave. If one of your servants would but fetch a hack for us then, we'll make our way home."

"I insist," his lordship said. "I've promised Major Lord Macbeth, and you must allow me to help you."

She opened her mouth to correct the captain and quickly closed it when he caught her eye. Being no more than a minor Scots baron, Finnley wasn't properly called lord anything. Rudgwick was gilding the lily to ease their path with his servants.

"In any case, your husband will join you here as soon as he may. Mrs. Lutton, the ladies have had a very difficult evening, all through no fault of their own." He leveled that amused gaze on Lucie, and Greer winced. "Mrs. Lutton is not a gossip, are you Mrs. Lutton? It's one of the reasons my mother, who is quite strict about these sorts of things, hired you."

The light touch of Rudgwick's threat was clear. Perhaps a season for Lucie would not be entirely out of the question, though it would not be in the company of Rudgwick's mother and sister. It was also clear that Rudgwick's circle was far higher than her own.

"I know that you'll extend the ladies every courtesy."

The housekeeper's head bobbed up and down, her shock dissipating. She left them to go ready the bedchamber and have suitable clothing waiting, promising to return for them.

"Will you pour, my lady?" he asked. "As for you, miss," he told Lucie, "it behooves me to tell you that the rules of etiquette require a gentleman to remove his hat."

Lucie's gaze narrowed, but her lips twitched, and whether she would bite off his head or laugh was uncertain. Whatever avenue she pursued she couldn't humiliate herself any more than she'd already done.

"For heaven's sake," Greer said. "Just remove that awful cap."

With a shake of her head, Lucie tore off the cap, and her red hair defied whatever restraints she'd imposed on it, tumbling about her shoulders and down to her waist.

Rudgwick's eyes lit and his mouth dropped open.

Greer's pulse pounded. 'Twas true, Lucie had shocked the officer, but the spark in his eyes spoke of a carnal interest, a man's interest. Lucie was no diamond of the first water, but she was an attractive girl, and her red hair was her crowning glory, a color that some gentlemen believed signaled a passionate nature.

Dear heavens. Lucie had never played the wanton, and wasn't doing so now. Her flaming hoyden had no idea she was casting a lure.

Rudgwick laughed, breaking the spell, his eyes filling with humor again. "Well you are certainly the Major's daughter."

"That I am," Lucie said.

"Your cup, my lord," Greer said, handing him the delicate porcelain. It was altogether too feminine a cup for the large masculine hand. "I take it your mother and sister are from home?"

"In the country still," he said. "They'll be coming for Easter."

Easter was two weeks away.

"Does your sister ride?" Lucie asked.

"In the country, yes. In town, I fear, mother keeps her quite busy with shopping, and social events, and whatnot."

He drained his teacup altogether more quickly than was polite and stood. "Regrettably, I must take my leave. I've promised to go to your husband's aid. Do not hesitate to ask the servants if there is anything you require."

Banquo had played her false this night, luring her into a trap. Another one might be waiting for Finnley. When Rudgwick bowed over Greer's hand, she grasped his between her own. "Sir." Her vision blurred. "Major Macbeth..." She shook her head. "I thank ye for helping him. I know all of this must seem very odd to ye. Know that we are grateful."

"We cannot thank ye enough," Lucie said, coming to stand next to her. "Will ye look after my father? Since I am not permitted the honor."

He chuckled. "Yes, Miss Macbeth. I'll try to be just as valiant as you were tonight defending your mother."

When he left, Greer went to the tray, while Lucie paced to the window. The servants had laid out a generous helping of meats, cheese and bread. "Come and eat," Greer said. "'Twill be a long night, and we don't want to seem ungrateful."

"He's gone out a back way." Lucie tramped back, her footsteps in the heavy boots muffled by the Axminster carpet. "I should like to have met his sister." She sighed, filling a plate, and lifting her gaze with a grimace. "I suppose I've ruined things. Did ye see his mount? I should like to have had a chance—"

"Lucie." She took her daughter's hand. "Look around ye."

Lucie blinked.

"'Twas never likely for us to be taken into the bosom of people this high. Lord Rudgwick is a braw man it's true, dashing, and well-bred, and clearly wealthy. But, yes, should your...adventure tonight become known, his mother won't welcome ye as a friend to her daughter." She squeezed her hand and went on. She must show no mercy. They both must face facts. "But she never would have anyway, considering your parentage."

Lucie shrugged and nodded. "Yes mother. I have always understood that."

Greer squeezed her eyes closed on sudden tears and felt Lucie's hand covering hers.

"Was Father very angry with ye?"

"I fear so." She wiped her cheek with the back of her frcc hand.

"And with me, as well?"

She thought about that moment when he'd realized Lucie was there with them. He'd come close to swooning again. Was that because of the Sight? Had he seen the danger coming beforehand? And if so, why hadn't he warned her?

Anger flared in her, but she remembered Lady Fiona's words: He doesn't trust himself. Perhaps Lady Fiona had the right of it. Perhaps Finnley had been trying to shield her from his fears, even as she was trying to help him and Malcolm.

"Mother," Lucie said, "was father angry with me?"

Greer rubbed at her forehead. "I don't think so, at least, not at the moment he realized who ye were. Perhaps once the shock wears off, he'll decide to address the issue with ye. He won't abandon his daughter though. Of that I'm certain."

Lucie's hand tightened around hers. "He must take us as a matched set, Mother, or not at all." Her gaze narrowed, her mouth quirking. "Especially after last night."

Greer spluttered trying to craft a reply when the housekeeper mercifully appeared to fetch them away.

They followed her up the stairs into a bedchamber. A low fire burned in the grate, too freshly set to have dispersed the room's chill. Golden brocade festooned the high tester bed and the windows. and covered the couch stretching across the foot of the bed. Two elegant wing chairs sat near the fire. 'Twas clear that Lord Rudgwick thought well of his mother.

The young maid who moved out of the shadows gave Lucie a startled look and then raised her eyebrows at the housekeeper.

"This is Tess," the housekeeper said, stiffly. "She's laid out nightgowns—"

"No," Greer said. "I do thank ye, but we are certainly not staying the night."

'Twas not just the room that was chilled, but also the demeanor of the housekeeper and maid. Lord Rudgwick had been more than kind, but he was no longer present to issue more threats to his servants. "We'll not do more than warm ourselves by the fire." Much as she hated the notion of Lucie arriving at Lady Fiona's dressed as a boy, the thought of accepting another lady's gown from the hands of puffed-up servants touched her pride.

"There's no need for us to borrow any of Lady Rudgwick or Miss Rudgwick's gowns. We'll be set for the short journey home, once we've warmed ourselves."

The housekeeper took in a long breath, her lips pressing primly. With her master departed, she didn't hide her emotions well, and Greer sensed her distaste. "I see. Tess will assist you with anything you need."

The door closed softly on her, and they both moved to stand near the hearth.

"Should you like to dry your clothing, there are two of Lady Emily's robes," the maid said, pointing to the bed.

"Lady Emily?" Lucie asked.

"His lordship's sister."

"Ah," Lucie said, "So she is not a Miss Rudgwick."

"No. She is Lady Emily Howton."

"My father, Major Macbeth, served with Captain Lord Rudgwick in the Peninsula," Lucie said, "but we're not one bit acquainted with him, nor did we have time for a proper introduction tonight. Is he an earl then?"

Tess looked her astonishment; at the question itself or the brazenness of it being asked, Greer wasn't sure.

"Don't ye know, lass, me father, mother and I, we all hail from Scotland," Lucie spoke the words with a sly grin and a heavy Scots accent.

Tess's eyes narrowed. "Yes. He is an earl."

"And where is his family seat?" Lucie asked.

"Let us not interrogate the servants, daughter," Greer said.

Lucie chuckled. "Do Lady Rudgwick and Lady Emily reside here in London often?" Lucie asked. "Perhaps we could pay them a call. It must be lively when they're in town. Is there a ballroom? 'Tis certainly a grand house for a ball."

Tess blinked at the question, frowned—perhaps over the notion of Lucie paying a call, and then pursed her lips. "Her ladyship hosted a ball in January." Her gaze narrowed on Lucie. "A grand ball to celebrate Lord Rudgwick's betrothal to a duke's granddaughter."

Lucie blinked and quickly managed a saucy grin. "'Tis as ye said, Mother." She laughed, and only Greer would know it was forced.

Lucie would never be cowed. She had been, however, thunderstruck by that snippet of news, and the manner in which it had been delivered.

And why shouldn't she be? Lucie had seen the flash of interest in the Captain's eye, and on her part, it had not been unwelcome, and not on account of his stable of horses, at least not entirely.

Her daughter had grown up, and the thought shook her. Lucie had just experienced the power of a man's attraction, a man who interested her. In the space of a short encounter, she had, perhaps, fallen a wee bit in love. The news of his engagement had smacked her and brought her back to her senses.

It was a small bit of suffering, but one that hurt a mother's heart.

'Twould be silly of Lucie to imagine herself matched with Rudgwick and his horses, and good for her to come back to earth. Instant attraction didn't always lead to true love.

And yet...the moment her eyes had met Finnley's...

What was she to do about him? More than likely he'd throw her over again, once he learned that she'd agreed to meet Banquo.

"Mother," Lucie said, yanking her out of her dark thoughts.

Lucie had squashed whatever disappointment she'd felt and appeared perfectly composed. "In the time it takes one of Captain Lord Rudgwick's servants to fetch a hackney, I believe I'll be quite dry enough not to catch my death on the way home."

Greer bit her lip. Finnley had made them promise to stay with Lord Rudgwick, but he was gone. 'Twas not far to Chelsea, and surely Banquo had been caught by now.

"Mother?" Lucy asked.

Trouble flashed in those amber eyes. Her lass was not so composed after all.

Greer nodded. "Yes. Despite Lord Rudgwick's generous words, our presence here is an imposition. If we may have some hairpins, Tess?" She stripped off her gloves and glanced around the room, looking for a chair that might withstand their damp clothing.

There was nothing. All the chairs were wrapped in sparkling brocade. "Lucie, stand here by the fire and I'll tidy your hair."

Frowning and silent, the maid fetched a comb and a box of hairpins from the adjoining room and hovered nearby.

"That will be all, Tess," Greer said. "Please ask the butler to have one of the men arrange a hackney for us. When I've finished here, we'll return to the hall and await its arrival." The girl hesitated a moment, casting a quick gaze around the room as if memorizing the contents, and then left, leaving the door ajar.

Lucie stood very quietly while Greer combed out knots and began plaiting the thick red tresses.

"I wonder if his sister is as haughty, ungracious, and high in the instep as his parlor maid," Lucie said loudly, casting a grin toward the open door. "I wonder if he'll ask us how we were treated."

"He won't," Greer said, relieved that Lucie was taking the cut in stride. "Most men leave managing the staff to their ladies. He won't think twice about it."

"I see now what's what, Mother. Captain Lord Rudgwick is very jolly, but I could never be friends with him."

"Or his horses."

"Yes." She laughed. "Do ye suppose his betrothal is a love match?"

"That is not our concern."

"Of course, it isn't. Nor will it ever be. I'm only assessing Captain Lord Rudgwick's character."

Greer rolled the plait, pinned it high on the back of Lucie's head, and turned her around, holding her by her shoulders. "And?" she asked.

"I do hope he has enough honor to not play Father false. If his engagement is a love match...well, I saw the spark in his eye. Had ye not been there to chaperone...I must speculate that his character may not be the best." She frowned. "But on the other hand, if it's not a love match, he has still pledged himself to one lady, and should not be looking with interest on the daughter of a fellow officer."

Her lips pressed together and she sighed. "What a pity. Such a handsome fellow, with such a grand horse. Do not worry, Mother. I'm not tempted to sin, nor is my heart broken. And yours won't be broken either. We'll leave word for Father to find us at Lady Fiona's."

CHAPTER FIFTEEN

At Lady Camden's, a footman cast a gaze over Finnley's red coat and sent for the butler, who called the hostess for a discreet inquiry.

Banquo had not appeared for the night's entertainment. In fact, the lady lamented, many of her guests had sent their regrets. She was eager for a report on the riots, and so, he shared what he knew, and left as quickly as possible.

He joined Hyde, who'd waited outside with the horses.

"Not there?" Hyde asked.

"No, dammit. I asked her where he lodged, and she claimed not to know."

"I know where he lives," Hyde said.

"Ye told me this evening ye couldn't discover his direction."

"I've since learned it. As ye predicted, Major, his lodgings are near Covent Garden."

Near Banquo's favorite bawdy house.

They rode off together, spurring their horse through the crowds and onto Piccadilly. Most of the rioters had moved into Mayfair, and they could still hear occasional shouting.

Lost in the maze of streets, they asked a passerby for directions, and then stopped a flower- seller, and a street musician.

"'Twas over a pawn shop, they said."

"Whoever gave ye this information," Finnley said. "They were having ye on."

Hyde grimaced. "'Twas one of Lady Fiona's servants."

"What?"

Hyde screwed up his lip again and clamped it shut.

A white-hot sense of foreboding rose in him. "Tell me, dammit."

"The lady had a man carry a note to Banquo, and then he sent one back."

"What lady?"

"Your...er...your lady."

He rode on, his hands numb, his heart in his belly. At the next corner, they turned down an alley and saw the shop.

A short while later, they were headed back to Whitehall.

Ready to do murder, he'd barged into the first-floor rooms, finding a man and his woman at dinner. They directed him up a flight of stairs to a set of rooms and an unlocked door. Except for a few furnishings, the landlord's probably, the man living there had cleared out his things.

He'd made one more stop at the bawdy house, daring to interrupt Banquo's favorite courtesan while she was entertaining.

Fuming, his heart in his throat from swallowing so much anger, they proceeded to

Horse Guards, and were directed to a cell where the two prisoners waited.

He left Hyde to see to the horses and entered the warren of offices. Rudgwick rose from a bench.

"No luck?" he asked.

"No. He never appeared at the rout, and he's scarpered from his lodging. Are the ladies—"

"Safely tucked away. My servants will see to them."

"I thank ye, Rudgwick. I hate imposing. I hope they didn't cause any trouble."

Rudgwick laughed. "I have a mother and younger sister. I know ladies are not the meek, compliant creatures we expect them to be. That is a delusion of the grandest proportions."

He mumbled his agreement, grateful for Rudgwick's unexpected understanding. "Where are the prisoners?" he asked.

"Separated, and under guard." He pointed to a door. "Sir Thomas is in with that one."

"Abernathy?"

Rudgwick nodded. "He asked for you to be shown in as soon as you arrived. Shall we?"

Lamps lit the small room, giving him a clear view of the occupants. Abernathy, nattily dressed as ever, nodded a greeting. A bigger man, in plain coats and trousers, stood nearby, hands crossed over his chest, a bemused look on his scarred face.

The prisoner was seated, hands bound, as were his ankles. Upon Finnley's entry, he sneered defiantly, revealing chipped yellow teeth. His broad width and the swell of his belly proclaimed a man more well-fed than many of the rioters. His nose had been, on one occasion or another, broken and badly mended. Not recently though—

not in the previous night's altercation, nor tonight's.

"Meet Harold Smith," Abernathy said.

The prisoner tipped his head and spat on the floor. The plainly clothed guard smacked the back of his head.

"'Ere now," the prisoner shouted.

"Who hired ye, Smith?" Finnley asked.

The man snickered. "She's a fine one, that lady of yours. A real looker. Got me a handful of—"

Crack. Finnley's quick fist landed squarely upon the prisoner's jaw evoking a strangled laugh.

Smith moved his jaw side to side. "Meeting up with Banquo, wasn't she?"

Anger churned in Finnley's stomach, eating away his insides and firing his muscles. In one easy move he could snap the man's neck. The haze of ire climbed to his head, clouding his mind, obscuring all but a vision of Greer being tugged from a carriage.

A different carriage. His eyes snapped open, and his chest constricted.

"Where is Banquo now?" Abernathy's calm demeanor brought him back to the present, asking the question he couldn't find the air for.

"Hah." Another round of spittle was launched. Finnley was forced to jump back for the sake of his boots.

The guard smacked the man's head again.

Abernathy nodded. "Very well," he said. "I'll send in another man to continue the questioning. Come, gentlemen."

Rudgwick and Finnley followed Abernathy from the room, and another man, dressed in plain coats, entered.

His nerves on a thin edge, Finnley looked back with longing. He owed the man a thrashing, not for his own sake but for Greer's.

"He won't help us find Banquo," Abernathy said. "We don't have time to beat it out of him, if it's even possible to do so. Come with me."

They entered another room where the other prisoner lolled in a chair, unbound. He was whippet thin, yet Finnley recalled his strength. Hyde had barely managed to beat him off Greer.

Abernathy's man, seated across the table from the prisoner, looked up and jerked his head toward the new arrivals. "Tell them," he said.

The man rubbed at a spot of blood on his upper lip. "It weren't personal," the prisoner said. "Harry said he had work for a nob. Needed two steady hands."

"Go on," said the interrogator.

"He was to pay me a whole guinea."

"Who?"

"Never learned his name."

"Tell us what he looked like."

"Never dealt with him. Only talked to Harry."

Finnley glanced at Abernathy. He'd settled into a chair and crossed his legs. His man asking the questions seemed equally at ease.

Meanwhile, his own temper was rising. While they were asking gentle questions, Banquo was slipping the noose.

"Never got that guinea," the prisoner said.

Finnley's hands fisted. He cleared his throat. "Grant me a boon. A few moments alone with the prisoner."

Abernathy screwed up his mouth in a frown, nodded, and stood. The other man shoved back his chair and got to his feet.

"'Ere now," the prisoner said, sitting up with a wince. Perspiration beaded his forehead, and his right arm dangled as if it had been broken or pulled out of the socket.

"Go on," Abernathy said.

"It weren't personal for me. Not for Harry nor...nor the other fellow neither. We was to rough up the big Scotsman." He nodded toward Finnley. "Him."

Finnley pressed his palms to the tabletop and leaned in. "To rough me up, or to kill me?"

Mottled spots of red appeared on the bristled cheeks. "I'm no killer. Can't speak for Harry."

"And tonight?" Rudgwick asked, his tone casual. "What were your plans for the lady in the carriage?"

"My wife," Finnley said.

The thin man's Adam's apple bobbed up and down in dry gulps. "We were to take her. Had a carriage waiting."

"Take her where?" Finnley asked.

The scabbed lips pressed together in a last grasp at defiance. Finnley lunged for the dangling arm and tugged, ignoring the yelps of pain.

"Chelsea."

His heart leapt into his throat and he swallowed hard, maintaining his grip. "Where in Chelsea?"

"An inn there. The Rose and Crown. We was to pick up the woman, keep her quiet like, and wait for the girl."

The girl. He was after Lucie as well.

The need to be off on his horse raced through Finnley's veins. "I'll head for Chelsea." There was nothing he wanted more than a chance at the man who'd threatened his life and Greer's.

"Hold up a moment." Abernathy led him and Rudgwick out and spoke a few words with one of his men before turning back to them. "The ladies are safe?"

"In the care of my servants," Rudgwick said.

"Let us take a moment to think." Abernathy ushered them into another room. Moments later, a servant entered with a steaming pot and three cups. He left, and Abernathy poured cups and handed them around, then went to the door and spoke to someone.

"I've sent a man over to check on them and keep watch. Banquo may have had someone follow you there."

Perspiration broke out on his forehead. Of course. Banquo probably had someone watching on Arlington Street, perhaps had even been there himself. He paced to the door. Blast it. He'd wasted far too much time chatting with the hostess at the rout and looking for Banquo's rooms.

His instincts about Banquo had proven correct. The man was a deceiving piece of shite.

And...Abernathy knew more about Banquo than he'd admitted to. "Ye know something more, Sir Thomas." Finnley said. "What do ye know that ye haven't told me?"

Abernathy's lips pressed together and he nodded. "Banquo made many trips to the Peninsula, supposedly overseeing military supplies. He was in Madrid. And when the army moved on to Burgos... Questions arose about what the French knew and how they knew it. Nothing proven of course."

The siege of Burgos had been a dispiriting failure.

"Last autumn Banquo paid a visit to Tuscany," Abernathy said. "Though no one could track him to Elba, well...we suspect he's made contact with Bonaparte."

"He's that much of a traitor?" Rudgwick asked.

"It's uncertain."

Finnley paced to the door again. "Why didn't ye haul him in for questioning?"

"With regard to Bonaparte, this is new information," Abernathy said. "Tonight, however, the personal motive you attribute to his actions, Macbeth, is more to the point. Your wife and daughter are residing at Lord Menteith's aunt's in Chelsea, are they not? Lord Menteith as well?"

"Yes. But, respectfully, Abernathy, we've talked enough. I need to be on my way."

"Grant me a moment longer, a moment to think this through. Banquo has been unsuccessful in kidnapping your wife and daughter—damn clever of the girl to slip away from home. Probably under the nose of one of his men as well as Menteith's. She has your courage, Macbeth. I've sent men to Menteith's aunt's home as well, though I'm assuming Lord Menteith and his aunt's servants might hold off Banquo's men."

"Banquo won't find Menteith there, or his aunt. They are both away from home for the night."

Abernathy's chin came up a notch. "Where has Menteith gone?"

"That I don't know. He wrote that he had business to see to, and my impression was that he expected to be away for several days."

Abernathy pursed his lips and stared off at the corner. Perhaps he was another man having visions. Or...

A shiver passed through him. Might Banquo have done away with Malcolm?

"I must go," he said.

"He's luring you, Major." Rudgwick frowned. "I'll go with you and bring some of my men."

A patrol of mounted men might encircle the inn. Perhaps they could trap Banquo on the premises.

"I fear your men are still needed to keep order in Mayfair," Abernathy said. "And I doubt, he'll be waiting at the inn, not if he knows his men have been compromised. We should wait for my men to report."

"I can't wait," Finnley said. "I'll go now, and return later to see if ye have news."

Rudgwick set down his cup. "Mayfair is quieter tonight, and my men can handle whatever trouble arises. Besides, a traitor is a more important quarry than starving laborers. I'll accompany you."

They walked down the corridor together. "First let me fetch you to my house and we'll check on your ladies. If you plan to ring a peal over their heads, I'd ask that you wait until you've taken them home."

"Aye," Finnley said, almost unable to speak, the full force of the night's events overwhelming him. Lucie had put herself in terrible danger. And Greer...she'd betrayed him again. Perhaps.

His women did not behave as they ought. They didn't trust him.

And why should they? Trust had to be earned. When he saw them, he'd sweep them up and make sure they were safe. That was his most sacred duty, one he'd neglected for too many years, and they could damn well allow it.

Outside, Hyde brought the horses around and the three of them headed west, but they hadn't gone past the park before a liveried rider approached at a reckless gallop. Rudgwick hailed the man, who drew up and came nearer, relief flooding his face. "My lord," he huffed, short of breath. "They've been taken."

"Taken?" Rudgwick, rounded on the man, for the first time this evening, rattled.

The servant blanched. "The ladies insisted on leaving. Refused to stay. Said they would walk if need be. They asked for a hack, but given your orders, the butler thought it best to rouse the coachman and have him deliver them. They were taken not long after leaving."

"How long ago?"

"Not thirty minutes."

"Description of the men?"

Finnley didn't wait for the groom's answer. He knew who the kidnapper was. He spurred his horse toward Knightsbridge, the others following.

***

Too tense to relax against the padded squab, Greer clutched the seat edge and peered out the window of Lord Rudgwick's coach. Elegant and new, it was also well-sprung, and smelled of wood polish and a subtle lady's perfume. She doubted it was used much by Rudgwick, yet his servants had kept it well-maintained.

"A plain hack would have done just as well," Lucie grumbled. "Or I might have ridden the livery horse Father's man Hyde got for me."

"With me sitting behind ye trying not to slip off?" They were both in waspish moods. Like mother, like daughter. "'Twill be a short journey," Greer said, hoping to sooth her own nerves as well as Lucie's.

Lucy scoffed. "Even with the need to wake the coachman and grooms, it took them an inordinate amount of time to bring Captain Lord Rudgwick's fine carriage around."

That had been purposeful. Their request to leave had engendered a conflict below stairs. The housekeeper and butler had exchanged heated words, audible from the entry hall. One would guess that the butler was none too happy with Lady Rudgwick's choice of a housekeeper. Especially not this night. He'd apparently received orders to keep Lucie and herself safe at all costs, and his tongue had delivered a thorough lashing to the housekeeper and the maid, Tess, for making his task more difficult. She and Lucie had heard it all.

'Twas an astounding occurrence, and Greer, mistress of her own home, poor as it was, had minced no words in telling Rudgwick's servants so when they left.

"Do ye suppose Father found Banquo?" Lucie asked.

"I don't know." She took in a breath, suddenly certain. "No. Banquo is too crafty for that."

She'd fallen into Banquo's trap once this night, just as he'd known she would. And now...

Her heart pounded fiercely with a sudden urge to order the coachman to turn back to Lord Rudgwick's.

Easing in another breath that quietened this sudden panic, she reached for Lucie's hand. "I'll be happy to arrive at Lady Fiona's and lock the doors up tight. In truth, I'll be happy to go home to Scotland." Except that she'd wish to have Finnley come with her, and heaven only knew if he would trust her again.

"As would I." Lucie sighed, "but first, I must attend at least one ball or assembly, Mother. Ye must give me that. And, we must puzzle out what is afoot with Malcolm and Banquo and Father."

Her heart went out to her rebellious daughter. "Agreed. We'll not go scurrying off to the Highlands just yet." A movement outside caught her eye and her heart leapt into her throat as the coach slowed.

"Lucie, your dirk."

Lucie fetched the weapon from her boot as the coach rolled to a stop, and men began shouting. The door flapped open.

And for the second time that night, she kicked at a man reaching in for her.

A gust of wind flew through as the opposite door opened, and Lucie shouted.

While Greer kicked and flailed, she heard Lucie's grunts and a yowl of pain, and then Lucie's blade flashed at Greer's attacker. He fell back, but so did Lucie, and then the devil appeared at her daughter's coach door.

CHAPTER SIXTEEN

"Banquo." Lucie growled, struggling. She lashed out with her blade.

He parried the strike and grabbed hold of her wrist, dodging her kicks, bending her hand back. She grunted and fought on, her mouth twisting, until she shrieked and the blade fell. Still grasping her, he brought back his fist.

Greer threw herself in between. The blow glanced off her cheek, pain pulsing around her eye and into her temple.

"Damn ye to hell, Banquo," Lucie shouted.

He brought his hand back to strike again, but Greer blocked him. "No." She tasted blood where her lip had split. "Enough."

A younger man, a lad really, climbed into the carriage on Greer's side, his eyes widening. "What—"

"Tie her up." Banquo shoved Greer toward the lad and tossed a length of rope.

"She's bleeding," the lad said.

"Do what I say." He yanked Lucie's arms behind her.

Lucie's cap slipped and her braid fell over her shoulder.

The boy's mouth dropped open. "You're a girl." He blinked. "What are you doing, sir?"

"Tie her hands and take her out."

The lad flinched, but pulled Greer's hands together in her lap.

"In the back, you dolt," Banquo growled.

The lad's mouth hardened as he forced her hands behind her. She took a good look over her shoulder. Brown hair spiked up, straight and unruly, one cowlick rising from a low hairline just like Banquo's.

"Master Banquo," she whispered, "assaulting ladies is a serious offense. Even for one as young as yourself."

He jerked the rope tighter.

"Ow. Ye're hurting me."

The rope slackened, and she eased her palms farther apart. "There's no need to bind us," Greer said. "We are kin. Lucie is your cousin."

"She attacked him with a knife."

"In self-defense. Ought we not to be able to defend ourselves when brigands invade our carriage and assault us?"

He tied off the rope and wrestled her out. They'd been stopped on a quiet stretch of road near one of the large market gardens, and no one else was about. Rudgwick's coachman and groom lay face down in the dirt, the man she'd kicked holding a cudgel over them.

Two stout men taken down so easily—'twas another mark against Lord Rudgwick's servants.

"Are ye men injured?" she called.

The coachman grunted. The groom glanced up at her, wild-eyed.

She shook her head in a warning, and glanced back to where Banquo was hustling Lucie to another coach. There ought to be a fourth man somewhere, but perhaps Lucie had disposed of him.

"Let these men go, Banquo," she called. "They're not your quarry. They're completely innocent."

"Shut up, Greer. Bring her over here."

The lad tugged her arm. She dug in her heels. "Ye must release these men. They've done ye no harm."

"Bring her now."

"Would ye be a party to murder?" she whispered.

"She's right, sir," the lad said.

"Dammit," Banquo roared. "Do as you're told."

The lad stiffened, his fear as palpable as that of the groom on the ground.

Lucie chose that moment to twist in Banquo's arms, and he smacked her.

Dear God. Banquo had gone mad. She must have a care.

She swallowed a rising bile. "Banquo," she called, "ye're a sensible man. Abducting a baron's daughter is one thing, but needlessly killing the servants of the powerful and influential Earl of Rudgwick, an officer in the Horse Guards, will bring the full force of his men and the government upon ye. They'll spare no cost whatsoever to hunt ye down. Good heavens, ye'll hang. All of these men serving ye will hang. Your son who ye're implicating in the crime, will hang. Your other son will be hunted down, and perhaps he'll hang as well or be transported. Your line will be either extinct, or forever banned. There'll never be a Banquo holding the title of Earl of Menteith."

Next to her, the boy stiffened, and Lucie looked up in shock.

Greer sucked in a breath and went on. "Be sensible. For the sake of your sons and your name. There's no need to harm the coachman and groom. Let them go. 'Twill work to your plan. They'll cause Macbeth to come to ye, and ye may do what ye wish with him. Perhaps Lord Menteith will be drawn in as well," she added for good measure.

Banquo's lips twisted into a smile. "An excellent point, Greer." He signaled his man, who bent and struck each man on the head.

Dear Lord, those had been heavy blows.

Banquo's minion hopped up to join a fourth man in the driver's seat of the second coach.

Greer allowed the boy to nudge her closer to where Lucie stood frowning fiercely at a spot on the ground. "Your father will come," she whispered.

Lucie glanced up, her gaze stormy, her mouth firm, and nodded.

Her daughter was strong. If Lucie could get free, help would come quicker. Meanwhile, they must stall for time.

"Let Lucie go as well, Banquo. Ye have no quarrel with her. She has no title to grant ye."

"Oh?" he said. "Will she not be a baroness when her father departs the earth?"

Lucie scoffed. "Why ye—"

"Ye're overplaying your hand, Banquo," Greer said. "Let Lucie go."

"Get in." He shoved her, none too gently.

"Don't shove my mother," Lucie cried. Banquo's hand shot out, but she ducked in time. "Where are ye taking us?" She dodged another swing.

The lad shoved in between them, a blow landing on him, startling both father and son.

"Damn it, Father," he said, rubbing his jaw. "Where are ye taking us?"

Banquo gritted his teeth and leveled a glare at his son. "Scotland."

Lucie flashed her a look of horror.

"Scotland," the lad cried. "Whatever for?"

"I'm securing your future," he said, and picking up a struggling Lucie, pitched her into the carriage.

Greer was tossed in after, and the boy settled next to her across from Lucie and Banquo.

They must hope that the coachman and groom hadn't been knocked unconscious and that they would be able to raise the alarm. They must also hope that Finnley would come soon. Whatever was to happen, they should certainly turn the boy to their side.

The faint glow of the coach light cast shadows inside. She caught Lucie's golden gaze and held it. *We'll escape this. Somehow.*

Lucie dipped her head once. Greer let out a breath and began working her ropes loose under the cover of her shawl, which somehow, still clung around her.

"And where is Menteith coming from, Greer?" Banquo asked.

There'd been a coyness to that question. She had a sense that he knew where Malcolm had gone.

She shifted on the hard bench. The hired coach was considerably less padded than Lady Fiona's or Lord Rudgwick's. "Why do ye ask, Banquo, when ye already know?"

He chuckled softly. Next to him, Lucie stirred.

"Ye've killed Malcolm," Lucie said, her voice tight, "else ye wouldn't be laughing."

"No, Lucie. Not yet."

"Ye're mad," she said, her face fixed in a mulish look.

His gaze narrowed on her.

"Lucie," Greer cautioned, leveling another long look at her daughter, praying she could see enough of her face to heed the warning. Prodding the serpent at such close quarters wasn't wise.

Lucie's head and shoulders sagged, her gaze fixed on the small stretch of carriage floor.

"Will ye tell us then, why ye sent Malcolm that letter questioning his claim to Menteith?" Greer asked. "Surely it's not that old witch's prophecy?"

"You know about that, Greer?"

He hadn't denied being the letter-writer.

"Of course," she said, infusing the words with false bravado.

Lucie still studied the floor, but Greer knew she was listening, as was the lad at her side.

"Macbeth would be Earl, and then your son." She scoffed. "But Macbeth lost the lawsuit two decades ago. Duncan produced a healthy, hale son, who's still young enough to marry and father a brood. So much for the witch's skill at divining the future."

"Malcolm is a by-blow."

Her pulse quickened. So that was his threat. He'd uncovered some stain on Malcolm's parentage. And the document Malcolm had held in his hand the night before... Lady Fiona knew about this. She'd gone to Brighton to visit a friend, and it had something to do with Malcolm.

But Malcolm... Malcolm had surely gone elsewhere. She felt certain he hadn't joined Lady Fiona for an overnight stay in Brighton.

"If that's the case, then there is no need to murder him."

"Murder? Such a violent imagination you have, Greer. Though his death would be more expedient than a long legal battle."

"If he is in fact illegitimate, I don't believe he would fight over the title." She glanced at the lad next to her. "Malcolm, at least, is a young man with a sense of honor."

Banquo laughed outright. "I am banking on it. He's away finding the evidence himself. And what of my other cousin, Finnley Macbeth? What's to be done with him?"

"Surely ye can find some evidence that he is also illegitimate? I believe Finnley wouldn't contest the matter. He's heartily sick of the fight over Menteith."

"Ah." He chuckled. "So, you and Finnley are on intimate terms again?"

"We are." Anger rose in her. "If Malcolm truly should not be the heir, he'll happily let the title pass him as well. In fact, to ensure the witch's prophecy comes true exactly as stated, he and Finnley can see to it that the title passes over ye as well and goes to your son."

A long silence ensued while the coach slowed and came to a stop. The smell of the river had been growing and now filled the small space completely. Lucie could swim, and so could she, and, if need be, they would—if they could get out of these ropes, if they could survive the cold of the March water. And the uncleanliness—good heavens. At least, this far upstream the water wasn't quite as foul.

"'Tis not wise for you to threaten me, Greer," Banquo said.

"Ye believe I was threatening ye? No. Not at all. I'm but thinking of this lad here to whom the witch promised the title. Or was it perhaps your second son promised Menteith? Is he to be the favored one?"

She heard the lad's sharp intake of breath. Banquo scoffed but said nothing.

She turned to the boy. "Some titles come through great acts of heroism and honor, Master Banquo. More usually, they are passed along through death. Ye know that, I suppose. Know also that I've no wish for either of your deaths."

It was only half a lie. The son ought not to die for the sins of his father.

The carriage rolled to a stop. Lucie sat up and Greer took the meaning of the long look her daughter sent her. Lucie wanted to attempt an escape.

She gave a small shake of her head. First they must get out of these bindings.

The door opened and Banquo shoved Lucie into the arms of a new henchman and climbed out behind her.

Greer glanced back over her shoulder at the lad's grim face. He was as much a prisoner as she and Lucie. "Your cousin, Finnley Macbeth, when he comes, will help you," she whispered with as much confidence as she could muster. "And so will I. Please help us. Your father has gone mad. There's no honor in this night's work."

He gripped her elbow and fetched her down from the carriage. They'd stopped at the end of a street downstream of the Botanical Gardens, near the ruins of a building recently torn down. There were no homes or industrial buildings here, and there was no embankment. On a night such as this, few boats or barges traveled the river, but in the dark, she could see the glimmer of a hull bobbing near the shoreline.

"Let's go," Banquo growled, tugging at Lucie.

The boy nudged her and they stumbled single file downstream and crossed a plank onto a small darkly painted yacht anchored there.

***

Finnley, Rudgwick, and Hyde arrived at the townhouse in Knightsbridge just as the coach was circling around to the mews.

"Milord." A groom called and came running. "We just brought them inside."

His heart quickened. He tossed the reins to Hyde and hurried after the man, Rudgwick close behind. They found the cook tending to two wounded men in the kitchen, with a few other servants gathered around, some of them in their nightclothes. The wounded men shot to their feet when they spotted their master.

"Where are the ladies?" Finnley asked.

Shocked eyes turned on him.

Rudgwick moved up next to him. "This is Major Macbeth." His tone was sharp enough to cut stone. "It was his wife and daughter you were supposed to be safeguarding. What happened?"

"Knocked me out, they did," the younger of the two men said.

"Aye. But a man roused us both. Said he was going after them."

"He said he was sent by Sir Thomas Abernathy," an older man, well-spoken and fully dressed in dark coats and a poorly-tied neckcloth—the butler most likely—moved closer, the other servants giving way. "He arrived after the ladies left, and demanded to know which way they'd gone."

"How many men attacked the carriage?" Finnley asked.

"There was four," the older of the wounded men said. "A...er, gentleman, and a tall lad, naught more than a boy, but gentlemanly like. The other two, I'd swear they come from the stews."

"That boy's heart weren't in it," the younger one said. "Wished I'd had the carriage gun for the others."

Finnley's hands fisted. Two men expected to protect the passengers they were carrying had easily been overcome by three men and a boy whose heart wasn't in it.

And why the devil had Greer and Lucie left Rudgwick's home? He'd told them to stay there. They'd promised to do so.

"Coach they was driving was hired. Horses too," the bigger man, probably the coachman, said. "Don't know from where."

He glanced at Rudgwick. Stony-faced and silent, he wasn't one for theatrics, yet his anger was palpable.

And his servants felt it as well. "He was going to have his man do us in. The lady talked him out of it. Said they'd hang and his son would hang too and would never be Earl of something or other. Can't remember what."

Greer. "Was the lady hurt?" Finnley asked.

"Bleedin' at the lip."

Finnley stepped closer, fists clinched. The cook stepped away and the man blanched.

"And the other lady?"

His Adam's apple moved with a nervous swallow. "He was rough with the lady in trousers too."

Finnley cursed and headed for the door.

"You had your orders," Rudgwick said, addressing the servants. "Why did you send them off?"

Finnley turned to see the butler's face grow paler. "The ladies...wouldn't stay." He glanced over his shoulder where a middle-aged woman hovered in her night robe, the younger woman next to her shrinking back. "They took offense."

Offense. Finnley swore silently. Pride had driven Greer off, the damn stubborn woman.

And why? Because he'd shamed her, so many years ago. Like the rest of this night, the blame could be laid at his door.

"Who attended them?" Rudgwick asked.

"Mrs. Lutton and the new maid, Tess."

Rudgwick looked past the butler. "You two, pack your bags, and be gone by morning." He turned to the head groomsman who hovered nearby. "The Major and I will retrace the coach's route. If Abernathy's man returns before we do, send word. In fact, send word if any news at all arrives." He looked at the two wounded men. "You two will not go anywhere. You're to stay here until I send a man for you. You'll be needed to give evidence."

They walked out together and reached Hyde and the waiting horses.

"We'll find them, Major, and I'll make this up to your wife and your daughter," Rudgwick said, "If I have to host another bloody ball myself."

"Bugger that," Finnley said, spurring his horse.

Banquo had been rough with Greer and Lucie? He was a dead man.

They reached the spot on the road where the coach had been stopped and, seeing no evidence left behind, they made their way to Lady Fiona's. Abernathy's men there had seen nothing and prepared to join them in the search. As they turned into the lane, a man approached on a horse and hailed them.

Finnley recognized him as another Home Office man. "Where are they?" he asked.

"I tracked them to a yacht. On a quiet stretch of the river. Three men on deck. I didn't see the ladies board. But the carriage was nearby, a man up top holding the horses. Got close enough to spot a plume on the seat, like one from a lady's headpiece. Another man came back across the plank and drove the coach away."

"Dammit," Finnley said. "They might have sailed by now."

"Sails were still furled. No light below deck."

"He's returning the carriage?" Rudgwick said. "Damned strange for a kidnapper."

"Ye two," Finnley called the men stationed at Lady Fiona's, "hie to the Rose and Crown, and if that's his destination hold him for me. And ye," he said to the man who'd tracked the coach, "show us that yacht."

When they reached the river, the vessel was gone.

CHAPTER SEVENTEEN

Banquo's son and a sailor with foul breath and worse body odor, hustled them down to the sloop's small cabin and left. As soon as the cabin door closed. Lucie drew her legs up on the bench seat and began squirming. "I'll get us free, Mother."

The cabin was dark, but dim light trickled in through a series of portholes.

"I have play in this rope." Greer fumbled with her bindings. "We'll go through that large porthole." Heavy footsteps set the ship rocking. "They're preparing to sail."

"Get free and then ye can cut me loose."

"But ye lost your dagger." Greer hooked a thumb over the rope, easing it down, scraping her skin raw. Thankfully, she'd left her gloves at Rudgwick's.

Lucie grunted and writhed, scrunching her shoulders and bringing her hands under her bottom. "I have a second one in my other boot."

Hope rose in her, and she almost chuckled. "Of course, ye do."

"Is that truly Banquo's son?"

"Yes," she said.

"Is Banquo really taking us to Scotland?"

Not in this sloop. He must have a larger ship waiting, with more men aboard. "I don't know."

"Does he mean to kill us?"

Greer eased in a breath. "We're more valuable alive."

Dear God. Especially Lucie, with her vibrant hair, and still a virgin. She'd bring a steep price in the slave markets of Tripoli. "We must put our mind to escaping as quickly as possible."

"If he's using us to draw Father, he'll stop somewhere nearby."

"Yes. We must turn the lad. I've told him we'll help him. 'Tis better to have him on our side." The rope scraped over her knuckles, and she pulled it off, shaking the numbness out of her hands. "I'm free. Which boot?"

Lucie had managed to move her hands under her knees, but the heavy boots made the rest of the journey difficult.

"My left."

Still trailing rope from one wrist, she fetched the blade and began sawing.

"Ye may help the lad, Mother. I plan to cosh him."

Greer breached one strand. "Let's try to reason with him first. He's afraid. I don't think he truly knows his father."

Another rope frayed and broke.

"And if he betrays us?"

Greer broke through the last binding. "There. Then we will cosh him."

"And I'll toss his body into the river." Lucie shook out her hands.

"No one will be tossed into the river. If ye cosh the heir and his body is never found, 'twill be years of waiting for the next man in line for the title."

Lucie chuckled. "We must have the body."

"Aye. Now hold still. Let's get the rest of these ropes off."

Finnley, Rudgwick, and Hyde were halfway to the Rose and Crown when another rider hailed them, one of the men who'd been guarding Lady Fiona's.

"We've got your man, Major Macbeth" he said, "and he was carrying this."

Finnley accepted a note. It was too blasted dark to see more than a square of folded white paper, and the rain was starting up again.

"Come this way Major. We've lit the coach lights."

They'd caught up to the coach on a quiet residential street lined with terraced homes. Macbeth threw his reins to Hyde and climbed in. The villain sat bound and tied, the other guard next to him.

Finnley opened the unsealed note and read.

Meet at the Lambeth Timber Yards at dawn. Come alone.

He shot a hand across the small space and clutched the man's throat. "How many on the boat?"

The villain's eyes popped with defiance. Finnley squeezed harder.

"Three." He choked out the word, and Finnley eased his grip.

"Plus the ladies?"

The man nodded.

"What sort of craft?"

The door on the other side opened and Rudgwick peered in.

"It's a pink," the man growled.

"What the devil is a pink?" Finnley asked.

"A small craft," Rudgwick said, "Shallow draught. Where is he taking the ladies?"

The craven mouth closed and stayed firmly shut. Finnley tightened his grip.

"Scotland," the villain wheezed.

Rudgwick's eyes met his and he frowned.

"Why Scotland?" Finnley asked, though he could make a good guess at the answer.

"The young one is to marry his boy."

The words confirming his fears sent a chill through him. His mind went back to the discussion in Lady Fiona's drawing room. Banquo had touched Lucie's hand.

"I didn't know. Just drive the man and his boy in the carriage, he told me."

"Which is why you were going to to kill my coachman and groom?" Rudgwick asked.

"Describe the boat," Finnley said. He needed to move, and quickly.

The man clamped his chapped lips together again.

"My servants are giving evidence against you," Rudgwick said. "I'll make sure they show up to testify. It might go easier for you if you help this man find his wife and daughter."

The villain's throat moved under Finnley's grip, and his eyes flared.

Finnley squeezed again. "'Tis a personal matter, ye see."

When he started to blubber the name and description of the boat, Finnley released him and sat back.

"Where's the other man who was with ye?"

"Dropped him. Had a horse waiting. He went off with another message."

"Get those details out of him," Finnley told the guard, "whatever way ye must."

Outside on the dark street, he conferred with Rudgwick and Hyde.

"Lambeth," Rudgwick mused. "Surely not."

"'Tis a trap. His men will be waiting for me crossing the nearest bridge."

"He'll assume you'll take that rickety Battersea Bridge. Pity that Vauxhall's not yet complete."

"How many men does he have?" Hyde asked.

Finnley wiped rain from his cheek. "How big a crew?" Banquo had been full of surprises. "A boat named Amie," he mused, thinking over the details the thug in the coach had provided. "Small. Plainly outfitted. No gilding, no striped awnings."

"A smuggler's ship," Hyde said. "Named after his wife or lady, mebbe?"

"Amie sounds French," Rudgwick said. "Perhaps he is spying for them."

"Highland ties to the French go back centuries," Finnley said. He ought to have poked about more into Banquo's marriage.

"Right," Rudgwick said. "I'll ride back and gather some men. We'll join up with you on this side of the bridge and go across together."

It would take too long and likely unnerve Banquo. "Ye've done enough, Rudgwick. Hyde," he said, "If ye're willing to fight some more, the two of us will go after them in a skiff. Do ye still have the pistol?"

"Reckon the powder might be wet. Good as a club, though. I've got one of those as well."

He swiped a hand through his wet hair. Hyde was probably right. The pistols might be useless.

"I've my blade as well, Major."

"As do I. Let's go find a boat."

"Naval maneuvers," Rudgwick mused. "Spent my boyhood on the sea. Almost joined the navy, but my father wouldn't hear of it. Come. We'll send word to Abernathy and secure a skiff at Cheyne Walk."

***

While Lucie shook the last of the coils from her wrists, Greer worked the rusty latch on the largest window. "If I can get this open, I believe we can squeeze through it. 'Twill be cold in the water, but we just need to reach the riverbank."

"Ye'll need to shed the shawl and we'll cut off your train. And let's get that last bit of rope hanging from your wrist."

Footsteps creaked down the ladder to the tiny cabin.

"Drat," Lucie said. She picked up the blade and sat down.

Greer put a finger to her lips and plopped down across from her. "Hands in back," she whispered.

The door opened and the lad appeared, crouching through the doorway, a cudgel in one hand and a lantern in the other.

"Oh, it's Banquo's sprout," Lucie said. "Come to beat us with that club, have ye?"

He cast her a dark look. "You've changed sides. You were not to move."

"My mother was cold," Lucie said. "Where are we really going?"

He frowned and said nothing. Greer would wager a year's rents the lad was annoyed about being kept in the dark by his own father.

"What is your name, lad?" Greer asked.

He gave her another, long look.

"He must certainly be a Giles, Mother," Lucie said, "after his father."

"I'm Fleance," he said. "My brother is Giles."

"I'm Greer Douglas. You may call me Greer as we are kin. And this is my daughter, Miss Lucie Macbeth."

"We are cousins," Lucie said. "Distant ones, though. And I won't marry ye, in case ye were wondering."

His mouth dropped open.

To a lad of his age, a forced marriage was perhaps a threat more frightening than death.

"That is the plan, then, is it?" Greer asked, gentling her tone. In truth it was better than Lucie being sold into a Musselman's harem. "Your father is kidnapping Lucie to force a marriage between ye? So ye'll inherit the barony as well as the Menteith title?"

"N-no." His mouth contorted. "I won't marry a girl who swans about in trousers."

"Ugh," Lucie said. "Nor will I marry Banquo's spawn. Nor him either."

"Him?" The boy blinked. "M-my father?"

"Yes." She shuddered dramatically. "Mother will explain. For now, I'm very hungry. Is there anything to eat on this boat?"

"We've raised the sails and shoved off. You'll toss up your accounts if you eat."

They needed this boy, and he needed them. How to go about turning him?

Greer cleared her throat. "I was just telling Lucie more about the witch's prophecy."

After a long pause, the boy said "Witches are so much twaddle."

"Have ye met our cousin, Malcolm Comyn?" Lucie asked. "The Earl of Menteith."

"No."

"I was to marry Malcolm. Or so everyone thought. Not Mother. She's never pushed me one way or the other. But our other cousins—my mother's not yours—thought a marriage between Malcolm and me would settle things nicely. Fortunately, Malcolm agrees with me that it's a dreadful idea. Mother, is Malcolm really a bastard?"

Illegitimate, not bastard. She bit back the scold, not wanting to distract the lad who was firmly hooked. Either the witch or the threat of marriage had captured his full attention.

"I don't know, Lucie."

"I'm a bastard, as well, Fleance," Lucie said.

"No ye are not," Greer declared.

Lucy tossed back her head as best she could with her hands behind her, yet her shoulders and elbows moved too freely. Young Fleance didn't notice. He stepped closer, drawn to the story.

"My parents weren't married when I was born," Lucie explained.

"Your father and I were married when ye were conceived, and thus ye're legitimate which is why ye bear your father's name. Do close the door, Fleance. Ye're letting in a fierce draft."

He hesitated, and looked back, then closed the door, propping himself against it. The light from the lantern caught dark smudges under his eyes. The lad was exhausted, and likely just as cold and soaked as themselves. Probably hungry as well, for weren't boys his age always hungry? He was, she decided, younger than she'd previously thought, but tall for his age.

"Have ye just turned fourteen?" Greer probed.

"I'm fifteen," he said, defiantly.

"A boy may marry in Scotland at fourteen," Lucie said. "I'm almost twenty. Far too old for a child like yourself."

His eyes flashed anger at the prick to his manhood. He was already as tall as his father, and he'd someday be a handsomer man than the elder Banquo. The dim light picked up shimmers of red in his unruly brown hair, a lighter shade than Banquo's dark mane. His eyes might be hazel, not the murky blue of his father's, though it was difficult to discern.

"Shall I tell ye the story?" she asked.

"Yes, please, Mother." Lucie's shoulders shifted, as though she were releasing a kink and not poised to strike with her knife.

Greer leveled a questioning look at the boy. They must hurry this along before they reached the docks where a ship surely was waiting.

He nodded tersely and set the lantern onto a small shelf.

The boat hit a swell. Greer clutched the free end of the rope still attached to her wrist and squeezed her eyes against a sudden rise of bile.

She took in deep breaths until the current and her stomach had eased and she was able to speak. "Once upon a time, when Finnley Macbeth, Duncan Comyn, and Giles Banquo were out running the Highlands as lads they came upon a hidden away bothy in the woods."

She rushed the story through quick embellishments about the moor, the white-haired woman and her bubbling cauldron.

Above on the narrow deck, Banquo's men toiled quietly. Did he have a ship waiting at the London docks or might it be at the Nore?

They must escape as soon as possible. All three of them.

"And so, Cousin," Lucie said, after Greer had finished the tale, "Ye're to be Earl of Menteith." She took in a breath. "I do wish ye wouldn't kill Malcolm though."

"I'm not killing anyone." The lad spoke so fiercely Greer knew he was not part of his father's plan.

"Good," Lucie said. "And do not kill my father either."

A thump sounded against the hull.

"We've hit something," Lucie said. "Are we docking?"

The boy's knees bumped theirs as he peered out first one side and then the other.

"We're in the middle of the river," he said.

Lucie joined him, just as a shouted oath sounded above.

Fleance turned and faced the dagger in Lucie's hand.

"Ye'll help us," Greer said, rising and prying the cudgel from him. "And we'll help ye, in return."

"Cousin," Lucie said. "Your father is mad."

He swiped a hand through his hair, knocking his cap askew, looking even younger.

Gruff voices murmured outside. He lunged for the window, slid back the latch and peered out. Greer went to another. A waterman's skiff had pulled alongside and was launching a boarding party—two men in uniform coats, one red and one a dark shade that might be blue, plus the third man who was plainly clad.

"Do we need to bind ye, Fleance?" Lucie asked.

"No," the boy said, his back turned to them. "I don't want to be here either."

Greer eased the blade from Lucie and handed her the cudgel. "Lucie will guard ye, Fleance. Or she will cosh ye," she bluffed. "Your choice."

She tossed off her shawl, clutched the knife in one hand, and her skirts in the other and hurried out.

Above decks, a fierce but small battle was raging, three against three from what she could make out. She recognized Finnley's man Hyde battling the foul-smelling sailor who'd forced her below decks, while a soldier in uniform—dear God, it was Rudgwick, battled one of the men who'd taken them from the carriage.

At the bow of the boat, two men struggled.

Her heart rose into her throat. Banquo had Finnley cornered against the railing, his dagger raised over him while Finnley struggled to turn the blade away from his heart.

She dodged around Hyde, and skirted the Captain's fight. The train of her dress caught on a rope peg, and she ripped it away, tearing the delicate cloth, gathering the length of rope still knotted around her wrist, holding her breath whilst edging nearer.

Finnley's neckcloth bore a dark stain, and his arm trembled with the effort of holding the blade away from his throat.

"Banquo," she shrieked. Startled, he turned, Finnley rolled away, and the blade caught his sleeve.

Banquo charged her.

She snapped the rope at his face, narrowly missing. Before she could try again, he shot out a hand, and gripped it.

She slashed at his arm and the rope fell. With a bellow, he lunged again and she scrabbled back, her bottom hitting the railing. Heart pounding, she slid sideways, Banquo advancing on her.

Of a sudden, Banquo flew back, Finnley's arm crushing his neck. Both men crashed backward into the bulwark.

Finnley had found a blade, and the two men battled on, smashing and parrying, equally matched only because Finnley's thrashing by Banquo's thugs had taken a toll on him.

As the men fought, Greer danced around them seeking a chance to strike without hitting the wrong man.

Behind her the scuffling had turned to grunts and oaths but she couldn't turn away.

"Father."

Lucie was here?

Or...was that Fleance? Had he betrayed them? Was Lucie all right? She turned, and in that moment, was yanked back and felt the cold press of steel at her neck.

CHAPTER EIGHTEEN

Greer. Finnley's heart leapt into his throat.

"Drop your weapon." Banquo edged along the side of the ship, dragging Greer along with him. They slid under a rope, and Finnley kept pace, inch by inch.

"Father." The voice came from near the cabin door and it wasn't Lucie's. A young man—a lad really—stepped into view, Lucie following close behind.

"What are you doing, Father?" the lad asked, his voice filled with equal parts anger and horror.

A dim light leaked from the ship's shuttered lantern. The boy stepped closer.

"This is for you, Fleance," Banquo said, breathless. "Greer, Greer, so much loveliness. You ought to have been mine. He always was a bully, he and Duncan. Ach, I do believe you'd go back to this beast who cast you away." A spasm went through the man. "You were supposed to die at Burgos," he shouted. "You were supposed to die. But you always had luck, and Duncan always had money."

Burgos? The blast that came from nowhere and blew him back from the battle? "That business at Burgos was your doing?" Finnley asked.

"Never trust the French to do what they're paid to do."

Finnley took a step and Banquo jerked Greer back.

"Let her go," Finnley said. "Let her live. It's me ye want. It's only me blocking your way to the title."

Banquo laughed. "You'll never marry another but Greer, else you would have done so by now. And I can't have you breeding a son with her now, can I? Or... you've already been at her, you rutting... You ought to have died at Burgos. You can't have Greer."

Greer gasped and Finnley spotted a trickle of blood on her neck.

"No, Father. Don't harm the lady. Please. Don't harm her."

"Step over here, Fleance."

Lucie moved closer. "Let her go, Banquo, let her go, and then I'll marry your spawn here."

"I don't want to marry you," the boy cried.

Banquo's face hardened more, his knife hand trembling.

Finnley lifted his foot, but Greer caught his eye, and gave her head a little shake.

"Not even to save my mother?" Lucie shouted.

"You're mad," the lad shouted back. "You're as mad as him." He flung out an arm. "Stop this, Father."

"Fleance," Banquo roared. Distracted, he pointed the knife at the boy. Greer jerked to the side, and swung a hand at her captor.

Banquo bellowed. The blade fell from his hand. While Greer scrabbled away, he looked down at his belly and clutched a hand to it.

What happened next was the stuff of nightmares. The scene flashed before Finnley, mere seconds that dragged along slowly, painfully, like the horror of one of his visions.

Snatching a handful of Greer's skirts, Banquo hopped the bulwark, pulling her over with him.

Finnley's feet moved as through a bog, carrying him to the rail. Greer hung from the side, the skiff tied and bobbing below her. Banquo had one leg in the small craft, the other dragging the water, whilst he dodged Greer's kicks and yanked on her. A rope cinched her wrist and a loop of it had caught on a belaying pin. She hung by the line, while a mad man pulled on her, and another tangle of skirt trailed in the water.

"I've got ye," Finnley roared. He snatched at the tangled rope and pulled. Below, Banquo grunted and swore, and the sound of cloth ripping vied with the whip of the wind through the sails.

Banquo scrambled his other leg into the skiff and grabbed both Greer's legs. With a sharp yank and a scream, the rope came loose from the pin, slicing the skin on Finnley's hands. Greer rocketed into the water, pulling Banquo with her, and they both went under.

Heart racing, he tore off his coat and plunged in after them. The icy water cut like the sharpest of blades. His head came up, and he called her name.

Fierce splashing, and oaths, and the sound of a struggle sent him spinning, while the wind whipped with more rain, and the sloop with the skiff still tied up to it drifted away downstream.

"Greer," he called again.

Her scream was like a wild Highland war cry, echoed by another bellow of pain.

Struggling with the current and the cold, and the damn weight of his boots, he swam to the sound of her voice and found her thrashing about, trying to stay afloat.

He saw then: Banquo writhed in the water, clutching the rope still attached to her wrist, sinking and pulling her down with him.

Lungs burning, Finnley reached her and yanked her backward against him, kicking with all of his might. Banquo lost the grip on the rope, but he snatched at her skirts.

She screamed and chopped at the water fiercely.

With another howl, Banquo let go and sank into the darkness.

"Kick, Greer," he said, huffing and kicking as hard as he could himself.

They'd make it, to the boat, to the bank, wherever. He wouldn't lose her, he couldn't.

Downstream, the ship rocked in the water, sails dropping, figures rushing around on the deck. Closer than the riverbank. He changed course and kicked more.

As they drew closer, Rudgwick extended an oar. Muscles burning, Finnley grabbed it, clinging with one hand, his other arm wrapping Greer close. Rudgwick and Lucie reached over the railing.

"Take her," he said, moving Greer nearer. She reached both hands up.

One hand was frozen around her dagger.

"Father," the boy cried. "Where's my father?"

The wind had picked up again, churning the water, and releasing a fresh downpour of rain. Rudgwick pried the knife from Greer's frigid hand

and passed it to Lucie, then hauled Greer out of the water, settling her onto the deck.

Finnley reached for their hands and scrambled over the rail. He knelt, taking in big gulps of air and crawled to Greer where she lay puddled and shivering.

"*Mo chridh*," he murmured, taking her into his arms.

"Get her below, Major," Rudgwick said. "You, boy, help with these sails."

"Where is my father?"

Greer got to her knees. "W-we sh-should l-look f-for h-him." She chattered the words out, trembling fiercely.

"Get her below, Major," Rudgwick said. "Else she'll freeze and so will you."

"Go, Father," Lucie said. "Your arm's bleeding and ye're wet." She rounded on the boy. "I told ye your father was mad. Now we don't even have a body."

The sloop tilted in a fierce blast of wind. "We'd best do something quickly or we'll all be in the river," Rudgwick said. "Hyde, watch those prisoners. You boy, can go and join the prisoners or you can help me with the sails. If you spot your villainous father, speak up."

Finnley helped Greer to her feet. "D-don't hurt the b-boy," she called.

"Get Mother below," Lucie said. "Fleance, ye'll stay and help. Hyde, help with the sails. I'll guard these two shites. Do ye know how to sail this, Captain Lord Rudgwick?"

Rudgwick's answering chuckle carried on the wind, as Finnley and Greer struggled together down the few stairs into the cabin, her torn skirts tripping her like winding sheets. How close she'd come to death made his heart ache.

He sat her down, feeling his way around the cabin for a blanket and then stripping off her soaking gown and bundling her.

"I'd wish for some spirits to clean that wound to your neck," he said.

"'Tis a mere prick," she said. "But ye were cut. How bad is your wound?"

The shock of the cold water was wearing off, yet he knew from past battles this wasn't a deep cut. "'Tis a mere scratch."

"If I had the lantern... Surely there are bandages—"

"It will keep." He dropped a kiss on her forehead. "We'll tend to it once we find shelter and a warm fire."

"Where are we going?"

"Wherever Rudgwick takes us."

"Will Banquo get away?" she whispered.

Banquo wouldn't likely survive the river, not if he was injured. He'd cut the man and landed a few punches. Greer's poke to his belly was probably not deep. "Did ye stab him again in the water, Greer?"

"Yes. Yes, I think so." She took in a breath. "We don't have a body. We'll never know whether he'll c-come b-back t-to h-haunt us."

He threw off his waistcoat and joined her under the blanket. "We've been haunted too long, haven't we, *mo chridh*? If he comes back, we'll deal with him. I'll not let him separate us again. I'll not live without you any longer."

Friday, 10, March 1815

It was two hours past the gray sunrise before Finnley's and Greer's wounds—all thankfully minor—had been thoroughly tended to and both of them had bathed away the stench of the river in blissfully steaming water hauled up by Lady Fiona's servants, along with the large hip bath.

Greer had wanted Finnley to bathe first, his wounds being worse, but the stubborn man fought her on it, finally proposing a compromise that served both their interests. He settled into the tub first and she joined him there, letting him scrub her from head to toe.

Rudgwick had proved himself a skilled yachtsman, delivering them back to Cheyne Walk where they were met by a cohort of his soldiers. The Captain had settled up with the waterman and ordered troops to scour both sides of the river for Banquo and to alert the authorities that a body might wash up. For Fleance's sake, she prayed that they'd learn Banquo's fate.

After depositing them upon Lady Fiona's startled butler and briefly questioning Banquo's son, Rudgwick had left, saying that he must report to his commander. What sort of leave-taking he'd had with Lucie, Greer hadn't been able to observe, but Lucie had stayed with the boy while Rudgwick questioned him, and then she'd led Fleance to Malcolm's vacant bedchamber and assigned a footman to tend to him.

Now Greer and Finnley sat alone in the breakfast room, drinking strong coffee and waiting for the kitchen to catch up with their early hours.

"I should like ye to meet Fleance in the light of day," she said.

"The future Lord Menteith? Hmmph. I'd like to blister his arse for being part of his father's crimes."

He poured another cup, his face haggard. He was bone weary, like herself. Like Rudgwick, who had promised to return later this morning. None of them would sleep any time soon.

Thankfully, she'd looked in on Lucie before coming downstairs and found her asleep. Fleance's footman, seated outside his bedchamber, had let her peek in on him. He lay in his bed, eyes closed, though she wondered whether he could truly sleep, given the circumstances. The poor lad had arrived in London only the day before. Banquo had summoned him from his school in Norwich and sent one of his minions to meet him at the coaching inn. His first night in London had been a disaster.

"Rudgwick ought to have carted the boy off to Bow Street last night," Finnley said.

"Come, Finnley. He's a victim in all of this as well. I don't want Rudgwick or anyone in the government harming him."

She poured herself another cup of coffee, thinking about the Captain, his valor, and the obvious spark between him and her daughter. "He won't marry Lucie," she mused.

"Lucie will certainly never marry that scoundrel's son."

"Of course not. But ye mistake me. I was thinking out loud. Not of Fleance; I meant Rudgwick."

He blinked and his eyes narrowed. "Greer. What the devil happened last night? 'Twas foolish of ye to leave."

So now they came to it. "We are both very tired. Shall we argue now or wait until we are rested?"

"Give me the bare bones of it and I won't utter a word."

"I believe I told ye. I went to meet Banquo to question him—"

"No." He waved a hand at her. "I meant leave Rudgwick's. Why did ye not stay there as ye were supposed to do?"

She let out a breath. "He's very charming, your friend, Rudgwick. And quite handsome. And I discovered last night that your daughter, for all she's a hoyden, is not immune to a handsome man's charm. However, Rudgwick is also engaged to be married." She pinched her nose and looked down it at him. "Lord Rudgwick is to be married to the granddaughter of a duke," she said in lofty tones.

She reached for her cup, shaking her head. "His servants behaved shabbily relating that tidbit to the young lady wearing trousers."

Finnley rubbed at his wounded arm, frowning.

"And then, when we ordered a carriage, there was a row, quite a noisy one, below stairs between the housekeeper and the butler. A house run by a bachelor—'twill no doubt be more orderly when the duke's granddaughter takes up residence."

Finnley's lips turned up at the corners, his eyes twinkling. "Ach, well. He sacked the housekeeper and maid last night."

"Oh." Moisture momentarily clouded her vision and she blinked it away.

Perhaps the Captain did feel some regard for Lucie. "I do like a man of action," she said.

"As long as that action is not directed at my daughter."

A throat cleared and she looked up. "Fleance," she cried. "Come." She hurried to the door and escorted him to the table. "Finnley, meet Fleance Banquo. Fleance, this is your cousin, Major Finnley Macbeth, Baron of Calder."

CHAPTER NINETEEN

The boy was a tall skinny sprout who must favor his mother, Finnley decided, as he looked very little like Giles Banquo. His face was pinched white, his eyes red and rheumy. At some point in the night he'd shed tears.

And, God's teeth, the boy was terrified.

"How old are ye, lad?" Finnley asked.

"Fifteen, sir."

He pointed to a chair. "Sit. Greer, will ye find someone to see where our breakfast is?" She busied herself pouring coffee for the boy, who sniffed the cup, blinking.

"Do you prefer tea?" Greer asked.

Before the lad could answer, Finnley slid him the sugar and made a shooing motion to Greer, who finally took the hint and left.

"'Tis coffee. 'Twill perk up your spirits. I've no news on your father yet. Captain Rudgwick will send word, or report here himself. Add milk also."

He watched the boy stir and take a tentative taste, and then a deeper draught.

"There's a high chance your father drowned in the river. If that's the case, his body will wash up or be fished out sooner or later. But with every passing day that it doesn't, I'd wager that he made his way to the shore and crabbed his way out, and is coming back to plague us again. I won't hold his offenses against ye," he said. "Unless it's deserved."

Fleance's chin shot up. "I never threatened your lady or your daughter. I didn't know—"

Finnley raised a staying hand. "I believe ye."

"I never coveted the title. I didn't know anything... only that Father was somewhere in the line of inheritance for a title, but so far down it would never come to him. I thought..."

His Adam's apple moved on his scrawny neck.

"What did ye think, lad?"

"I thought he wanted to take me into his business. That I could be done with that miserable school."

"Ye didn't like your school?"

"My brother is still there. I thought father would take us both. We are there all the time now since my grand-mère died."

An ache stirred near his heart. But he reminded himself, the lad was Banquo's son. He might have inherited his father's skill at playing a man's sympathies.

"What is your father's business?" he asked.

"He's a trader. He has a ship. Not just that sloop, but a proper ship, a lugger."

"I see." Banquo might be a legitimate trader— but more likely he was a free trader.

And likely a traitor to England as well, or at least a man whose loyalty was to only himself.

"I know his trade wasn't always legal, but he's my father." The boy chewed his lip a moment.

"Not that he'd told me that. I heard my grandparents whispering about it when they thought I couldn't understand."

"Whispering in Gaelic?" he asked.

He blinked and shook his head. "My mother wasn't Scottish. She was French. They were émigrés. They were from the Vendee."

"Your mother is not living?"

"No one is living, except my bro-other." His voice broke on the last word and fortunately Greer arrived at that moment with a footman and maid, all of them carrying trays.

Her lip was swollen, a bruise colored one cheekbone, and fatigue smudged shadows under her eyes, but still her beauty made his heart dance. She was the finest of women, and yet not too finely bred that she couldn't carry a tray with fresh coffee.

And Greer's instincts were calling her to protect Fleance. In the Highlands, he'd be considered a man. Hell, in most of London and the country as well. Yet he seemed very much a lad, and a lost lad at that. "We'll send for your brother." Finnley laughed. "Though I don't know where I'll put ye. I'm living in bachelor rooms now. I don't have a home."

Greer refilled cups. "Ye have a home, Finnley."

His heart swelled as he exchanged a long look with the woman who'd been there, in his heart all these many years.

"We've a castle, ye see, Fleance," she said.

Finnley accepted a plate from the footman. "Is it still a drafty and leaky pile?"

"We've mended the roof." She reached for Fleance's hand and patted it. "Ye and your brother may live there with us but ye must pledge ye won't cosh Macbeth in the hopes of claiming Malcolm Comyn's title."

"No, ma'am,'" the boy said. "I mean, y-yes ma'am, I promise."

And just like that, he'd acquired two sons, though he knew it might not be so easy. There would no doubt be guardians and trustees to be dealt with.

And of course, there was Banquo, who might still be very much alive and after that bloody title.

Lucie entered then, looking sleepy and cross. He rose and went to her, taking her by the shoulders and studying her. She'd donned a white dress sprigged throughout with flowers as bright as her hair.

Lucie bore a bruise just like her mother's. If Banquo wasn't already dead, he might have to kill him, Fleance or no Fleance.

He swallowed his anger, reminding himself to be grateful. "I'm heartened to see ye properly outfitted."

Her frown deepened.

"Ye'll have a permanent scowl, love. I'm not angry." He sighed. "Well, not exactly. Not at yourself." He drew her into a tight embrace and leaned close to her ear. "Had ye been killed though on my account I'd have never been able to live with myself."

Lucie froze. "I'm sorry, Father," she whispered. "Not about helping Mother. I'm not sorry about that. But I didn't intend to be kidnapped."

He held her close uncertain what to say.

"Father, ye may give me a birching later, but for now, may I eat?"

"A birching?" He stepped back, still holding her shoulders. "Would that keep ye out of trews?"

She pursed her mouth and lifted one shoulder.

It was all he could do not to laugh, so grateful was he to see her spirit still strong. "We'll have a talk later," he said, forcing a frown. "Come." He seated her, and brought her a plate of eggs from the sideboard.

He was seating himself when they heard a commotion in the front hall, followed by voices.

The lad looked up, the play of emotion in his face part hope, part dread.

"I'll investigate." Finnley pushed back his chair, but before he could stand, Lady Fiona walked through the breakfast room door, followed closely by Rudgwick.

A short while later, he and Rudgwick were on the road again, heading toward Whitehall and Abernathy's office.

There'd been no news of Banquo, but his lugger had been discovered and stopped before reaching the Nore. He hadn't been aboard, and that news had given everyone pause. Had his ship failed to wait for him? Or had they received word to meet him elsewhere in Essex or Kent?

Still, Abernathy's summons had taken priority over everything. Rudgwick, who had returned to his own lodgings for fresh clothing and an hour's rest had decided to fetch Finnley himself.

He'd been the perfect gentleman with Greer, Lucie, and Lady Fiona. That lady's fatigue had lifted when she saw the injuries to Greer and Lucie and met Banquo's boy.

Beyond conveying the news about Banquo's ship and Abernathy's summons, Rudgwick had no time to linger. They'd left Greer and Lucie to explain the previous night's events to Lady Fiona.

As the traffic of market wagons increased, they slowed to a walk. "How fared your men last night with the rioters?" Finnley asked.

"It was lighter, and better contained. No injuries last night."

A man and a woman had died two nights before. Violence begat violence, and didn't he know that.

The street widened and they squeezed past carts and had nary a chance to speak again until they arrived. Inside, the offices were bustling. They were left to cool their heels in the anteroom before Abernathy finally called them in.

The starch had gone out of Abernathy's neckcloth, and Finnley would wager he wore the same coats as the night before.

"Macbeth, Rudgwick, thank you for coming. Both of you, please sit. Harrowing business for you last night, what I've heard of it. Are your ladies safe, Macbeth?"

"Yes."

Abernathy tapped the desk distractedly, his gaze faraway.

The room suddenly darkened, clouds passing over outside, lamps dimming.

Finnley gripped the arms of his chair and tried to breathe, tried to bring himself back into his body. For the first time in days, the new vision stirred again...fire, explosions, rain and suffocating mud. Men screaming, horses plunging. Shouting.

A vision of Hell.

"Macbeth." Abernathy's voice came from far away. "Are you well?"

He managed a nod, gulping in air, trying to get hold of his senses. Praise be to God, he hadn't passed out. "Aye, Sir Thomas."

"Good. As it happens, I'll need you immediately. No time for a visit home. You as well, Rudgwick." He grimaced. "Rothschild has passed on a message he received through his contacts."

"Rothschild the banker?" Rudgwick asked.

The nightmare of the vision still had all his nerves tingling, and Abernathy's uncharacteristic tension worsened them. He focused on the man's bald pate, listening.

"Yes. Quite a communication network he has. Pigeons, smugglers, and international bankers. Always gets the news first." He tapped the desk. "In any case, Bonaparte left Elba the end of last month with a contingent of guards and Polish hussars. Landed in Frejus and is gathering the remnants of his old army to him. He's advancing toward Paris. May be there by now."

Finnley's breath tightened. War. Bloody battle and more bloody battle. Fields drenched in rain and mud and blood.

"I'm at your service," Rudgwick said.

The younger man's calm resolve brought him back to his senses.

"As am I," Finnley said, his mind clearing.

Banquo would have to wait. Scotland would have to wait. And Greer...dear Greer. They must wed again, and the sooner the better.

***

After an early dinner, Lady Fiona insisted they all retire—all of them having had little sleep the night before and little rest in their attempts to nap that afternoon.

Greer couldn't protest. She was anxious for time alone with Finnley. He'd returned home in the afternoon in a pensive mood. Likewise, Lady Fiona had been somber and closed-mouthed about her visit to Brighton.

The news from there would keep until the morrow. Finnley's worries were more concerning.

Lucie and Fleance went off to bed discussing Waverley and its author. The new-found cousins would probably be huddled together near the fire in one of their bedchambers reading.

She didn't care. Where Fleance was concerned, she trusted Lucie's strong will and mostly good sense. And Fleance, though not a known quantity just yet, seemed a serious sort of young man, thoroughly overwhelmed by his circumstances, and youthfully naïve. She sensed that he appreciated Lucie's friendship—the friendship of an older girl being a novelty for a boy who'd spent much of his life away at school.

Greer, Finnley, and Lady Fiona proceeded up the stairs together.

"I know you are greatly fatigued," Lady Fiona said, "but I would speak with the both of you about Malcolm. I'm terribly worried about the lad."

Finnley exchanged a glance with Greer and made a courtly bow. "We are at your service, my lady."

Relief flashed on the older lady's face, and Greer's heart flooded with love. In the years of their separation, he'd become a true gentleman, one who cared about relieving a lady's pain. That of a young lad as well, even a lad who, by all the traditions of Scottish feuding, he was entitled to hate.

They followed Lady Fiona into her private parlor and seated themselves on her sofa. The lady poured them whisky, and took the wing chair opposite them.

"Malcolm," she began, "has gone off in search of his mother."

Greer caught her breath, and the lady raised her hand.

"'I fear 'tis true—Duncan's wife was not his mother." She sighed. "Poor lad. None of it his doing, and he's a worthy son to his father."

"Go on, my lady," Finnley said tiredly.

"I traveled to Brighton to speak to an old friend, a lady who escaped from France at the start of the Terror. The émigré community kept fairly close ties, and I hoped she would know the fate of the woman who birthed Malcolm. I asked him to wait for my news, but he wouldn't. He wanted to visit my friend himself, but... she's advanced in years. Not entirely sensible all the time."

Lady Fiona plucked at her skirt and took a sip of her whisky. Greer's hand found Finnley's and gripped it.

"His mother was French, the wife of a Comte. She was Duncan's mistress for a time. Duncan's wife couldn't bear him a child. When the Comtesse, Malcolm's mother, fell pregnant, they concocted a scheme. Duncan took two houses at Matlock Bath and stayed there for several months. The Comtesse left the child with him, and they passed him off as his lady's." She sighed heavily. "Do not think badly of Duncan. It's common enough for a man to... to care for more than one woman. I suppose, he might have been thinking, none too soundly, about the prophecy."

Greer squeezed Finnley's hand.

"When the Vendee rebellion erupted shortly after Malcolm's birth, the Comtesse left England. She came from a family of title and wealth, and she wanted to fight with the Royalists."

"What happened to her?" Greer asked.

"She was guillotined. The Comte had remained in England. It was several years before he was able to confirm her death."

"Poor Malcolm," she said.

"What evidence does Banquo have?" Finnley asked.

"An old declaration sworn by a housekeeper in Matlock Bath. It arrived by post on Tuesday morning. Malcolm spent that day searching for records. How Banquo obtained that document... Do you suppose he's dead? I fear for that son of his." She shook her head. "I fear for Malcolm as well."

"The lad said they were French," Finnley mused.

"Fleance?" Greer asked.

"His mother's parents were French, from the Vendee, he told me."

Greer shared a look with him.

"Lady Fiona, do ye know where Malcolm was going?" Greer asked.

"Devon. That was the last place the Comte was known to reside. But I believe, as I have been getting to know Malcolm, I believe he is like a dog with a bone. He will follow this through to the end. Mayhap even all the way to France if he won't accept that his mother is dead."

She felt Finnley stiffen, and when she looked at him, his face had gone pale in the shimmering light of the Argand lamp.

"I have news as well," he said. "It will be in the newspaper tomorrow. Bonaparte has escaped Elba. He's gathering an army and advancing on Paris."

Fear shot through Greer, fear for Malcolm and for Finnley. He would fight again. He would have to fight again.

"Dear God." Lady Fiona rubbed at her temples. "I'll write letters. I have some resources. We'll find Malcolm before he sails for France."

Greer watched the emotions play over Finnley's face. There was more he wasn't telling her.

"I'll help in any way I am able," he said, rising, and drawing Greer to her feet.

They exchanged their goodnights and he led her off. By unspoken agreement—their hostess's as well—they would share the same bedchamber. Lady Fiona would not object, or had not, thankfully.

Greer held her peace until the bedchamber door closed, and then she rounded on him. "Tell me," she said.

CHAPTER TWENTY

He took in a deep breath, swallowed, and his mouth firmed. "I'm to help assemble the Highlanders and head for Flanders."

The air stilled around her, time stopping. He was leaving. He was going back to war. She might lose him again.

She clutched his hands. "I will follow the drum. We'll not be parted again, not as long as the both of us are breathing. We'll bring Lucie. Fleance and young Giles as well. Ye'll not travel alone."

He opened his mouth to object and she went up on her toes and kissed him, grasping his neck, pulling him close in an open-mouthed kiss, staking her claim to him.

***

Finnley held on for dear life, deepening the kiss, dueling tongue upon tongue with more passion than two nights before, more passion than in their youth. He worked the fastening of her gown, while she tore at his neck cloth and coats.

He wanted her, only her, here and now, and if she wanted to come, he'd take her anywhere, in a tent, in borrowed rooms, wherever she'd have him.

"My dearest love," he said in a frenzy, stripping coats and trousers, her gown and her corset, shoes and stockings and garters. "My dearest love," as he tossed her upon the bed, and "Greer" as he plunged into her.

He pleasured her, quickly and furiously, and they both collapsed back, almost senseless.

"Finnley," she said, "my love. My dear husband."

Cold fear tickled his hands and his feet, crept up his legs, skirting his heart, so filled with heat, filling his head with stark visions.

Death. Death. Death all around.

He clutched her to him and held on, his breath coming in tight bursts.

"Greer," he groaned. "Oh, my dear."

Malcolm stood before him, bloodied, eyes wide in shock. An unhorsed cuirassier rose behind him.

Finnley gripped his saber. Raised it.

"Finnley."

'Twas heaven, not hell. 'Twas the voice of an angel calling him home. "Yes," he cried, and "Malcolm, behind ye."

"Finnley, come back."

The shrill panic and hands shaking him roused him. He opened his eyes.

"Greer?" Tears flooded his eyes. Coursed down his cheeks. "Greer?"

He looked around him. He was naked, in a bed, Greer lying atop him, a look of fear in her eyes.

No. Not fear. She had no reason to fear him.

He rolled her beside him his tears mingling with the kisses he dropped on her. "Greer, my love," he whispered, over and over choking back tears, until he finally fell back.

Her fingers stroked his cheeks and raked through the hair falling across his forehead, soothing, consoling, loving. He didn't deserve her compassion. He didn't deserve her.

"Tell me," she said. "I'll not leave ye. Only tell me. I love ye."

He gritted his teeth. "A bloody man doesna weep."

"I don't believe that."

"Not a Highlander."

"Hmm," she said, nestling closer, tickling the hair on his chest. "Ye're having a vision."

He huffed out a breath. "Battle. A great battle."

"Malcolm is there."

"Yes."

She sat up. "And ye'll save him."

"I've not seen that far. And I know not whether any of it is true."

"Have they ever been true?"

He thought of her carriage ride the night before. "Aye."

"I will be there. Not on the battlefield. And...I will pray for your safety. I will make Lucie pray also, and these two boys of Banquo's." She stretched next to him propping her head on her hand. "Ye must go."

It wasn't a question. Fresh tears welled. His Greer knew him too well.

"Aye."

"We must take whatever time God gives us." Her fingers floated over his chest and down.

He clamped a hand over hers. "Greer, will ye marry me again?"

"I pledge my troth to ye tonight," she said. "There. The English may not think that legal, but

God scoffs at the notion that our sacred bond was ever broken."

"Aye." He rolled toward her. "And I am yours, again and forever."

Brussels
Late June, 1815

"There, now, Hyde. Do not tell me ye're not happy to feel a cool breeze on your face."

"Whatever ye say, Miss Lucie."

Hyde tripped on a broken brick and she gripped his elbow, steadying him. "Are ye bosky?" she teased, keeping her tone light, though seeing Hyde's weakness in the brightness of the garden she wanted to howl. His actual wounds lay hidden under his garments, and she'd not been able to persuade him to let her have a look at them.

But now he laughed, cheering her with his good-nature, and allowing her to settle him onto a bench near an arbor flooded with climbing pink roses.

Hyde had gone into battle with her father and Malcolm, and had been separated during the worst of the fighting. When the shooting stopped, and their men couldn't be found, she, and Mama, and Malcolm's lady, Marielle, had ridden for hours, searching the battlefield. They'd found Father and Malcolm, but not Hyde.

After combing the makeshift hospitals, she'd finally discovered the lowly infantryman on a cot in a stifling garret room of this villa. After assuring Hyde that her father lived, she'd found him a dressing gown and ushered him downstairs for some fresh air and sunshine.

At this early morning hour, the garden was mostly empty, but wounded men were stumbling down, accompanied by servants and orderlies, and in some cases, women—wives, sweethearts or sisters, most likely.

She was none of those to Hyde, but he was family nonetheless.

"Ye're leaving this place today," she said.

"Is that so, Miss Lucie?" His smile was unexpectedly wan.

She stripped off a glove and set the back of her hand to his forehead, making him wince. "Ye're hot, but not feverish. My father needs ye. He's alive, yet he was gravely wounded. While ye're lying about here, my mother is tending to him. Your presence will go a long way toward healing him. He's been fashing about, wondering what became of that mouthy Hyde."

Hyde laughed out loud.

Two men, both in the blue coats of cavalry officers, entered the garden and took the bench next to theirs. One was not one of the wounded, but likely a friend of the other whose head bore a bandage. The men settled into conversation.

Her own head swam with the memory of another dragoon. Captain Lord Rudgwick had arrived in Flanders after them, having been delayed by family matters, he'd told Father. Most of the time he was off drilling his men in the countryside, but she'd seen him from time to time at the routs and parties she was allowed to attend. On those occasions, they were always in company—she'd made sure of it, and after one of Lady Conyngham's balls, she'd avoided him even more. He'd teased her into a waltz there, teased her about wishing to see her again in trews, whilst his hand had burned through the silk of her new gown, and his steady gaze had made her insides puddle.

She'd not seen him again until the Duchess of Richmond's grand ball, which she'd only attended because Father's men opened the event with a display of Highland dancing. While dressing, they'd heard the distant booming of cannons, and all knew the battle was looming. Rudgwick hadn't attended, neither had Malcolm, and Father wished to leave early. Not wanting to intrude upon Mother's last night with Father, Lucie had arranged to stay on at the ball with the Ord family, who promised to convey her home.

She'd walked out though to wish Father farewell—for who knew if he would be gone in the night—and whilst she was waving the carriage off, Rudgwick appeared out of nowhere and, spotting her, had tugged her around the corner of the building. Mud-spattered, he said he'd just delivered a dispatch and he wished her farewell.

And then he kissed her. The memory of that kiss, that went on and on and promised so much that could not be, sent her head spinning.

She'd been ever so relieved to find his name on the injured list. Likely, his powerful patron, his fiancée's grandfather, had ferried him directly home to England, because she hadn't found him in any of the hospitals she'd visited. Not that she'd been looking, not really.

In any case, he was the duke's granddaughter's worry. He must be nothing to her.

She looked up to find Hyde watching her. "No more of this malingering," she said. "Ye'll pack up your kit. I'll send the carriage back for ye before noon."

The conversation at the next bench went quiet, and Lucie glanced their way. They were studying her and Hyde with puzzled expressions.

Ought she to ask about Rudgwick? No. She mustn't.

She found Hyde giving her another long look.

"What?" she asked him.

He struggled to his feet, faced the two dragoons and saluted. "Begging your pardons, sirs," he said, "but do ye know anything about Captain Lord Rudgwick? He was a particular friend of my officer, Major Macbeth."

"Colonel Macbeth," Lucie said. Heat flooded her cheeks as the men turned their gaze from Hyde to her, sparks lighting their eyes, no doubt the fault of this miniscule bonnet revealing so much of her cursed hair. "Colonel Macbeth is my father. 'Tis true, he'll want to know."

"Why, Rudgwick is here," the wounded dragoon said. "Don't know what bed. That is, he's probably still here. I haven't heard that he's succumbed to his wounds."

Her heart quickened. "What were his wounds?" she asked.

The man screwed up his mouth. "I've been in no state to know details."

"Wait here, Hyde. Don't move from this bench."

"Aye, miss."

She heard the injured man's friend call after her offering his escort, but she ignored him.

If Rudgwick was alive, Father would want to know. He'd want to see him.

But he was nothing to her, nothing at all.

***

"Stop fussing, Mother." Major Lord Rudgwick's remaining hand swiped at a fly that had been plaguing him the last hour.

"It's dreadfully hot in this ungodly swamp." Lady Rudgwick ruffled her handkerchief back and forth over his head, stirring annoyance instead of cool air. "Are you sure you won't get up and step down to the garden?"

He shook his head. The spot of laudanum was wearing off, irritation and pain rising in turns, the large west facing window letting in hot sunlight but not a bit of westerly breeze. Still, the improvised hospital, a converted home in a wealthy section of the city, was likely luxurious by comparison to other field hospitals, providing quality beds for mostly quality wounded like himself.

He squeezed his eyes shut on the images, fighting them as fiercely as he'd fought the French, remembering. There were no differences of class and rank in death. Men from the rookeries had died side by side with their betters.

Yet he was alive. Why was he still alive?

He swallowed the bile that sometimes came from the numbing, wishing for more laudanum, never mind that it sometimes made him puke.

He'd done his duty, an officer, and an earl, and one of God's chosen ones who'd lived.

A damp cloth touched his brow. She was trying to comfort him, and he ought to be grateful. And he was, dammit.

He mumbled his thanks. Having placated his fiancée's interfering grandfather for him, and seen to his sister's rushed spring wedding, Mother had traveled to join him in Brussels, arriving the day of the Duchess's ball, relieved to find civilization in a city reeling with soldiers, and arms, and all the paraphernalia of war.

There was quite a bit less of all of those now. Including arms.

He chuckled to himself, wishing ever so much for another drop of the poppy.

"My darling boy," she said, and he heard the quiver in her voice.

He opened his eyes. "I do thank you for coming, Mother."

The doctor had been after him to rise from his bed, but he'd just rather not. Mother looked at him, concern clouding her gaze.

Her concern wasn't a matter of the title going to a cousin if he died. She'd always be cared for. Father had made sure of that, and his cousin was a decent fellow.

He knew she truly cared for him, her only son, and he was blessed for it. Not all men could say that.

She gave him a quivery smile, her eyes shining. "Well, look who is here. Fair greetings to ye."

The knock came after the fair greetings. He lifted his head unable to focus at first. Bright ginger hair and a yellow gown and...

He struggled up on his elbow. Was he dreaming again? "Lucie? Lucie Macbeth?"

"'Tis I." She laughed. "In the flesh and dressed quite properly as a lady ought to be."

She dropped a curtsy to Mother who sat, jaw dropped, looking with astonishment at the flaming haired girl in the doorway.

"Do come in," he said. "Your father—"

"Is wounded," she said, approaching the bed, "but will recover. My cousin, Malcolm, Lord Menteith, came through mostly unscathed, thanks to Father. Hyde survived as well. He's here in the very same house. I've just walked him around the garden and escorted him back to his third-floor garret to pack. Now that I've found him, I'm making arrangements to bring him home with us. Every Scots officer needs a stout man like Hyde. 'Twill be a happy surprise for Father." She bit her lip and frowned. "Must I introduce myself, Captain Lord Rudgwick?"

He laughed out loud, and his mother sent him a startled look, one that she then turned on Lucie.

"I'm Major Lord Rudgwick now, haven't you heard? Mother, may I introduce Lucie Macbeth, Maid of Calder, daughter and heir of a Scottish baron, Major Macbeth—"

"Colonel now," she said.

He dipped his head. "Well done him. Lucie...er...Miss Macbeth, please meet my mother, Lady Rudgwick.

Lucie curtsied again and he held his breath until she took the chair he'd pointed to. He must keep her talking. He didn't want her to leave.

"Is your mother well?" he asked.

"Yes, indeed, now that Father has come through without mortal wounds."

"How did you and my son become acquainted?" Lady Rudgwick asked.

Lucie blinked, for once speechless and searching for words. He laughed out loud again. Damn, but she cheered him.

"Mother, Macbeth required my assistance when Lucie and her mother had an unfortunate adventure. Bye the bye, did you ever discover what happened to Banquo?"

She pressed her lips together, choosing her words. "He survived the river and... died later."

There was a story there she didn't wish to tell, not now.

"But," she went on, "not before giving over his boys to Father's and Malcolm's...er...Lord Menteith's care. And mother insists they live with us, so I now have two younger brothers. They're both here in Brussels, plaguing me daily." She smiled.

Lucky boys. "You adore them," he said.

Her smile widened. "I do. But never tell them I said so."

She shifted in her chair, as though she would stand.

"Are you going home to Scotland after this?" he asked. "Or will you return to dip your toes in London society?"

"Happily, I will have another chance at London. Lady Fiona begs us to return for a visit when Father is well enough to travel. And though it won't be the proper season, still I'm looking forward to seeing more of the city. If invitations are scarce, at least I might visit the museums and Vauxhall, and perhaps even attend the theater. I would dearly love to see a London play."

"Would you, Lucie? Well, then, I shall escort you to one myself."

Mother sent him another astonished look. After the tiniest of pauses, Lucie laughed, and it sounded false.

"No, ye will not," she said, standing. "My lady. Your son is no doubt being given laudanum and he's not thinking clearly. He knows—he may tell ye the details later—that I am from a disreputable Scots family, and I know and accept that your family are much above us. It is perhaps, not the thing to say so directly, but I do prefer candor. And now, I must be off. I have a wedding to prepare for."

He didn't want her to leave. She'd brought in a fresh breeze and she would take it out with her.

"Whose wedding?" he asked.

"My cousin's. Malcolm went off and found the most delightful bride. I adore her as well." She took in a breath and frowned down at his arm, or rather what was left of it, bound up in a white bandage under the sleeve of his nightshirt. "Major Lord Rudgwick, ye're as pale as a wraith, but I've seen for myself that ye're alive. Ye must, if the doctor allows it and ye're strong enough, ye must take a turn in the garden. There are orderlies here who will help ye. Ye must see that ye get well, for I know that my father will be anxious to call on ye as soon as he's able."

He sat up fully. "Where is the wedding?"

It was madness, but he wanted to be there.

She sent him a quizzical look. "Malcolm has arranged for a priest—his bride is Catholic, ye know—to come to our home so that Father might be present. And now, I truly must be off. I have errands to see to before I send the carriage back for Hyde." She curtsied again, graceful and sure of herself, and then vanished.

He fell back remembering: Lucy in trousers, slinging her crop at the men assaulting her mother; Lucie ripping off her cap in his parlor; Lucie pulling her father out of the river, and then ordering Hyde and the boy to help with the sails. Their waltz. Their kiss.

A brave girl. A woman. And beautiful. He had to see her again. Today. This afternoon.

"Mother," he said, "is there a servant who can help me dress?"

254 · ALINA K. FIELD

"You mean to get up?" she asked.

"Yes." He pushed himself up on his arm. "Fetch someone please. And my clothing."

"But—"

"And have someone find out where Major...Colonel Macbeth is quartering. Or...perhaps I'll tag along with Hyde. You may come along as well, Mother. I'm attending that wedding."

"But we haven't been invited. And I don't even know the bride and groom."

He laughed. "Nor do I, Mother. Nor do I."

***

Finnley gripped the banister, a sturdy footman at his side ready to steady him if need be as he made his way down the long flight of stairs.

The elegant villa had been his home for several weeks, and Malcolm, having resurfaced from his disappearance in March with a lady and Banquo's other lad in tow, had joined him here before the battle.

A fortunate thing, since Malcolm was paying the lease on their quarters. He'd been quite generous, believing that the Menteith funds rightly belonged to Finnley, along with the title.

Greer smiled up at him from the bottom of the stairs. She'd had a new gown made for the occasion in a pure shade of blue that brought out the color in her eyes. He'd not be here now, walking and smiling back at her, had it not been for her.

On the day after the battle, having received no news of either him or Malcolm, she'd gathered Lucie and Malcolm's stalwart lady and searched the battlefield. They'd not been able to find Hyde's whereabouts though. Not yet.

He stepped down the final stair, and the footman handed him off to Greer, like a bride being transferred to her new husband. The thought made him laugh. He took her into his arms and planted a kiss on her forehead.

"Come," Greer said. "I'm told that Father Luc has arrived. Malcolm and Marielle are waiting, the boys are here, and Lucie has arranged a surprise for ye." She linked arms with him. "Ye may feel free to lean on me."

"May I? I'd like to do more than lean, my love."

"I'm sure that ye'll be strong enough to carry me across the threshold of Castle Menteith when we take up residence there."

Malcolm had asked Finnley to manage the earldom, while he and his lady made an extended visit to France to see to her business, as well as his own.

When they entered the parlor, Hyde grinned from his place next to Lucie, and then limped over to salute and shake hands.

Finnley's gaze shifted to a lean young man in blue regimentals, his arm in a sling, seated next to a handsome older woman. Their eyes met and the soldier eased himself up from the chair, the older woman rising as well.

"Rudgwick," he cried and went to him, clapping the younger man on his shoulder. "How good it is to see ye, my friend."

"And you." Rudgwick blushed accepting a kiss on the cheek from Greer, and then introduced his mother, who winced at the sight of Finnley's scabbed head and blinked away tears. The cuirassier who'd attacked Malcolm had tried to take off Finnley's head. Good thing he was a thick-headed Scotsman.

Greer reached for Rudgwick's hand, and 'twas then Finnley saw that the slinged right arm was short, the cuff turned over and pinned.

Greer seemed not to have noticed. "I cannot tell ye, Lord Rudgwick, how happy we are to see ye and to share this joyful day with ye. It is such a happy surprise that ye're here. Ye're both most welcome."

"Thank you," Lady Rudgwick said. "I feared we might be intruding."

"Never," Finnley said. "In fact, this villa has empty bedchambers. If ye're in need of new quarters, ye must avail yourself of them."

Greer smiled. "I can make the arrangements this afternoon and ye may send for your things today. Ye have only to ask."

Malcolm and his lady, Marielle, came to stand with them. A handsome woman with blonde hair and merry blue eyes, by way of greeting she kissed Greer and himself on both cheeks.

"Have ye met Menteith and his lady, the Comtesse de Fontenay?" Finnley asked.

"We have indeed," Rudgwick said. "They've made us most welcome."

Father Luc approached, clutching his prayer book. "Will we begin, then?" he asked, a twinkle in his eye.

The priest donned his stole, and Malcolm and his lady, Finnley and Greer stood before him. Rudgwick, refusing to resume his seat, escorted his mother and joined Lucie, Hyde, and the boys.

Malcolm and his bride said their vows and kissed. Before the others might congratulate them, however, the priest turned to Finnley and Greer.

"Dearly beloved," Father Luc said, "we have one more wedding to perform today. You must know in the eyes of God we are merely renewing vows. Whom the Lord joins, let no man put asunder."

"Aye," Finnley said. "But we would have the people we love witness our promises today."

He and Greer repeated the vows they'd made over twenty years earlier, and then accepted congratulations and wishes for happiness. Father Luc handed Malcolm and Marielle the document proving their marriage. "You are sure you do not want a certificate?" Father Luc asked them.

"No."

"It will be necessary should God bless you with a child, will it not?" the priest asked.

Malcolm pointed at Lucie. "There is one of my heirs," he said, and then turned toward the boys, "and there are the others."

Should he and Greer be blessed with another child, they'd see to the child's future. For certain, he, Malcolm, Marielle and Greer had agreed: they'd never engage in a wasteful dispute over the Menteith title. Lucie would inherit the barony when he died. Fleance would be Lord Menteith someday.

After the wedding breakfast, Lady Rudgwick sought him out. "Was your offer of hospitality sincere?" she asked.

"In the Highlands, hospitality is sacred."

"It seems I've heard of feuds where the visitors slew the host or vice versa." The twinkle in her eyes told him where Rudgwick had got his charm.

He laughed. "Aye, mayhap it's so. However, my offer was sincere, and I know that neither your son nor I are in any position to slay the other. We've had more than our share of battle."

"Yes." She sighed. "Your daughter came to visit today. Quite by chance, or so it seemed."

Ah. Lucie had overstepped the social bounds again. "She is the light of my life," he said.

"Quite. I...I was not criticizing. I owe her my thanks. She pulled Rudgwick straight out of the valley he'd fallen into. I'd been trying to get him out of bed for days. And look at him."

Rudgwick, looking tired but happy, was engaged in conversation with Fleance and Giles.

"I should like him to lodge here, Colonel Macbeth. But I must add...he is engaged to be married."

"So I have heard. But his heart is not engaged?"

She sighed. "There are contracts."

"And ye worry that he has feelings for Lucie."

She pressed her lips together and blinked. "He undoubtedly has feelings for Lucie."

"Yes," he said. "Greer noticed that the night they first met. And do ye know what Lucie said when she later learned that your son was engaged? She questioned his character."

Her eyes widened and her face fell into a frown.

"She saw his interest and when she learned he had already promised himself to another woman, she decided he was just another man likely to be unfaithful."

He would leave off telling her that Lucie had been smitten by Rudgwick. He'd watched them dancing together.

"Do not mistake me, my lady. Your son is the finest of men, a man's man, and a hero. But he is a man, and if his heart is not engaged with his betrothed..." He sighed. Lady Rudgwick would know how society marriages worked. "We'll be returning to England soon. In the short time we're here, I don't think Lucie would welcome his attentions. She's not an easy sort of girl. To win her heart...well, it will take more than what he has to offer, knowing, as she does, that he is promised elsewhere." Sooner or later, Rudgwick would take a mistress, but he felt certain it wouldn't be his girl. In fact, he'd intervene if he must to prevent that.

She sighed. "He lost his right hand."

"Aye." He reached for the hand she was twisting and patted it. "But that is not what I mean when I say he has little to offer her. His hand and heart are not enough. 'Twas his wholehearted future I was thinking of. Still, ye're both most welcome here. We'll see that ye're comfortable. And... if ye're to be here a while longer, why not send for the lad's fiancée? We have the bedchambers and ye can chaperone them."

She nodded, watching her son. "You've given me much to think about."

Greer smiled and approached from the other side of the room.

"The world has turned upside down, Colonel." Lady Rudgwick stood. "No, do not get up. I thank you for your gallantry in battle and your offer of hospitality, and I wish you and your lady much happiness."

She greeted Greer and then left to rejoin the others.

Greer took the seat she'd vacated. "Poor woman," she said. "Poor Rudgwick. Poor Lucie."

He squeezed her hand, hope coursing through him. The visions had stopped. The pain was a blessed reminder that he was alive, that the dark day of battle was past. "The world has turned upside down, Lady Rudgwick said, and she is right. Rudgwick and Lucie will find their way, whatever that might be. And we are right again, my love."

"We are."

"I fear I can't give ye a proper wedding night."

She smiled fondly and placed a hand to his unblemished cheek. "We shall see about that."

Hope surged through him, hope and faith and strength. And love. Most of all love.

The End

If you enjoyed this story please consider telling other readers by leaving a review at the bookseller of your choice, or at Goodreads.com or Bookbub.com.

A Note from the Author

The real Macbeth lived and ruled in a bloody time when kings seized power by force. In Celtic governance, the passing of leadership from one king to the next was called tanistry. Titles weren't automatically passed from father to son. Rather, the heir was chosen from kinsmen related through the male line.

It sounds like a recipe for conflict, and we see that in what we know of the real Macbeth's history.

As I planned this story, cherry-picking through the known details of the real Macbeth, I took heart in the knowledge that William Shakespeare did the same thing. The Bard presented his Scottish play in 1611 with one audience member in mind: King James I.

Macbeth, the last Celtic king of Scotland, was displaced by Duncan's son, who allied with the English. Ever after, the Celts would not be able to shake off the English yoke, culminating in the reign of James who ruled first in Scotland as James VI and then, upon the death of Elizabeth I in 1603, united both crowns and ruled England as James I.

The witches were a nice touch conjured by Shakespeare, perhaps to ingratiate himself further with James. The late 16th century was an era of witch hunts and persecutions in Scotland. Shakespeare would have known of his new king's obsession with witchcraft, and James's 1597 book, *Daemonology.*

Early on, I decided to make Macbeth a baron, and was disappointed to discover that Scottish barons are not part of the peerage and are not addressed as "Lord" and "Lady". (This topic is covered in fascinating detail in a Wikimedia article.)

I hope you've enjoyed this retelling of the story of Macbeth. Transporting the characters to this turbulent week in Regency England involved a great deal of research. Any historical errors are mine alone.

Many thanks go to editor Tessa Shapcott for catching my many Americanisms. I also wish to thank author Regina Jeffers for organizing the Tragic Characters in Literature project, and as ever, I'm grateful to my husband for his support and encouragement.

To find out more about *Fated Hearts* and my other books, visit my website, https://alinakfield.com, and sign up for my monthly newsletter.

All the best,

Alina K. Field

p.s. How could I forget?! If you're wondering how Malcolm met his lady, look for his story in *The Comtesse of Midnight*, part of the *Storm & Shelter* anthology due out in April 2021.

**Other books in the
Tragic Characters in Classic Literature
Project**

The Monster Within, The Monster Without
by Lindsay Downs (Frankenstein)

I Shot the Sheriff
by Regina Jeffers (Robin Hood and the Sheriff of
Nottingham)

The Colonel's Spinster
by Audrey Harrison (Pride and Prejudice)

The Redemption of Heathcliff
by Alanna Lucas (Wuthering Heights)

The Company She Keeps
by Nancy Lawrence (Madame Bovary)

Captain Stanwick's Bride
by Regina Jeffers (The Courtship of Miles
Standish)

Glorious Obsession
by Louisa Cornell (Orpheus and Eurydice)

Books by Alina K. Field
Sons of the Spy Lord Series

Marrying Mr. Gibson

Previously titled *The Bastard's Iberian Bride*

Paulette Heardwyn rushes to visit her dying guardian,
set on learning the truth about her father. But the only man
with answers takes his secrets to the grave, leaving her
penniless—unless she marries his illegitimate son

The Viscount's Seduction

Lady Sirena Hollister has lost everything, even her fey
abilities. But when the fairies hand her a chance at a London
Season, her schemes for revenge stir up an unknown enemy,
and spark danger of a different sort, in the person of a
handsome Viscount.

The Rogue's Last Scandal

Falling—literally—into the arms of the *ton*'s most
outrageous rogue seems a risky path of escape, but Maria
Graciela Kingsley y Romero has no other choice. Only
England's greatest spy lord can help her, and he is not to be
found—so his son will have to do!

The Counterfeit Lady

Vowing she'll never submit to an arranged marriage, an
earl's daughter bolts for the seaside cottage that will
someday be hers. But she finds her quiet refuge occupied by
the last man she ever wants to see—an American artist,
who's also a thief. And, quite possibly one of her father's
spies.

Avenging the Earl's Lady

The long war is over, but honor requires vanquishing one
last enemy, and the Earl of Shaldon has no time for romance. But when the lady he longs for interferes in his plot,
and his enemy strikes at her, nothing else matters but
avenging his lady.

Novellas and Holiday Stories

The Marquess and the Midwife
A Christmas Novella
Finalist, 2016 National Reader's Choice Award

Uncovering a lie drives a new marquess back from a self-imposed exile at Christmas to find the only woman he's ever loved. Finding her turns out to be easy, uncovering her stunning secrets, a bit harder. But winning her back will be the greatest challenge of all.

A Leap Into Love
A Sweet Regence Romance Novella, a sequel to
The Marquess and the Midwife

Can a gentleman be too charming?
The ladies of Upper Upton think so.
When the single ladies of the village conspire to teach their charmer a lesson that might bankrupt him, the town's loveliest young widow—who's sworn off marriage forever— steps up to warn him.

Liliana's Letter
Finalist, 2015 National Reader's Choice Award

The Matchmaker Meets the Matchbreaker

Liliana Ashford's future as a professional chaperone depends on her wealthy charge's successful marriage, but her own close encounter with a scoundrel years ago makes her determined to save the girl from the same kind of rogue.

The Ghost of Depford Hall
A short, sweet Halloween story, a sequel to
Liliana's Letter

It's her mother's last All Hallows' Eve.
When family, friends, and tenants gather, goblins, ghouls, and ghosts are banned from this All Hallows' Eve party.
Only, no one told the Ghost of Depford Hall!

Courted by the Earl
Previously titled *Bella's Band*
A 2015 RONE Award Finalist

Saddled with his brother's title and debts, nothing about this new life makes the Earl of Hackwell want to stay—until he meets a lady with a secret that can change everything.

Rosalyn's Ring
2014 Book Buyer's Best Winner, Novella Category

Done with grieving her losses, a late nobleman's daughter has fallen into a tidy spinster's life in London. But when one snowy Christmas Eve, a young woman needs rescue, she seizes the chance to do good—and to recover a family heirloom that ought to be hers.

Haunting Miss Fenwick

Thrilled to finally have a permanent home, a Squire's daughter won't let a supernatural creature scare her away. While hunting the ghost she doesn't believe in, she stumbles upon a mysterious flesh and blood man who might be the key to all of her problems.

The Duke She Despised

Hiding her true identity, a young vicar's widow takes a position as housekeeper in a remote Scottish castle at Christmas for a new duke who years ago sabotaged her chance for happiness. She quickly falls for the duke's charming but not very competent factor, not knowing that he's hiding something also—he's the duke she despised!

Convincing the Countess
In the *Mistletoe & Mayhem Regency Holiday Romance Anthology*

When a business-minded aristocrat encounters a fetching widow he knew years earlier as the bride of a ne'er-do-well earl, temptation steers him along a track that may derail all his plans. Can he convince her to set a course for her future that includes him?

The Comtesse of Midnight
In the *Storm & Shelter Bluestocking Belles and Friends Anthology*
Coming April 2021

A Scottish Earl on a quest for the elusive Comtesse de Fontenay, rescues a French lady smuggler during a devastating
storm, taking shelter with her. As the stormy night drags on,
he suspects she knows the lady he's seeking, the lady who
holds the secret to his identity. When she admits she herself
is the Comtesse de Fontenay, just not the one he's seeking,
she dashes all his hopes—and promises him new ones.

*Find out more at
https://AlinaKField.com
and sign up for my monthly emails
for news about upcoming books and
sales.*

www.ingramcontent.com/pod-product-compliance
Lightning Source LLC
Chambersburg PA
CBHW071131170626
46809CB00002B/571